GAME OF WITCHES

WITCHES OF NEW YORK

BOOK 2

KIM RICHARDSON

KR PUBLISHING

Game of Witches, Witches of New York, Book Two
Copyright © 2022 by Kim Richardson
Cover designer: Karen Dimmick/ArcaneCovers.com
All rights reserved, including the right of reproduction
in whole or in any form.

www.kimrichardsonbooks.com

GAME OF WITCHES

WITCHES OF NEW YORK

BOOK 2

KIM RICHARDSON

KR PUBLISHING

CHAPTER 1

I hadn't seen or heard from Valen since we'd removed the curse from Jimmy and put him back in his human body. That was five days ago. Maybe the giant was avoiding me. Perhaps he regretted the kiss he'd planted on me. Just thinking about the kiss sent a flash of heat through my nether regions. But it didn't stop me from doing a little research on my own.

I spent days browsing every Google link, trying to decipher myth from reality, because sometimes fairy tales hid a bit of truth. I didn't want to overlook anything. We'd all heard the stories and seen the movies about vampires and werewolves, and they were as real as you and me. So why not giants?

Still, I couldn't find much on giants. I'd discovered from human mythology that giants were described as stupid and violent monsters, sometimes said to eat humans. That totally wasn't like Valen at all.

Yes, he was violent. I'd seen it with my own eyes. But that was because he had protected me and the others from demons who wanted to eat our faces. He'd described himself to me as a protector, a watcher. So the stuff on the internet was a bust, despite my best efforts.

I'd even searched the Merlins' mainframe database and was seriously disappointed when I found nothing. Only when I'd called the Gray Council and spoken to one of their secretaries to ask for permission to look at their archives here in New York City did I find anything of real value.

"Can you point me in the direction of giants? I'd like to see everything you've got on them," I'd told a frowning old man, who'd gone bald many years ago, as he sat at the archives' front desk.

"*Giants?*" he'd repeated, like I was a simpleton.

"That's what I said. *Giants,*" I repeated, louder than was necessary.

"Why? Giants have been extinct for hundreds of years. I'm afraid someone is leading you on a ghost hunt."

He was wrong, but at least he knew they were real. "So, where to?"

Even though the old bookkeeper thought I was mental, in the end, he took me to a restricted section and handed me a single, thin tome.

"Here," he said. "It's the only material we have on giants. Written by Theodore Paine himself, head of the White witch court at the time."

I'd never heard of Theodore Paine, but the tome dated back three hundred years. It seemed to be a journal of sorts, depicting his own experience with a giant called Otar.

From his entries, I'd learned both parents didn't need to be giants in order to produce a giant offspring. Interesting. Female giants were often barren, most suffering stillbirths and miscarriages if they did become pregnant. I'd learned these facts because, apparently, the Gray Council had taken to trying and breeding an army of giants to protect them. However, according to the entries, that hadn't gone all that well, and many babies had died.

And like us, giants had demon blood. They were descendants of a demon called Gigas, described as big as a house, though the giants were considerably smaller.

Unmatched in their strength, giants also possessed healing abilities. I believed that after the direct contact with Valen's skin while riding on his shoulder had healed my wounds. This just validated that.

I couldn't find anything about a giant's glamour or other abilities, but I'd experienced them as well, so there was that.

After my discovery in the archives, I decided to take a more hands-on approach to my research.

I decided to stalk Valen.

Yup. I was a total stalker. For the last three nights in a row, I'd waited on the roof of the Twilight Hotel around midnight. All three nights, I'd caught glimpses of Valen taking his clothes off in the alley between his restaurant and the hotel. Then, with a flash of light, he transformed into his magnificent giant self—all naked, all glorious, and all very *big*.

I wanted to see what he did without having me tag along, like that night when I sat on his shoulder. At first, it was easy enough to follow him. I blended in with the Manhattan crowds, the human population oblivious that they had a giant strolling among them, and protecting them, as I followed him through the streets.

But when Valen leaped and soared to the rooftop of some building, I couldn't follow. If I could fly, I would have, but I didn't have a flying broom or magical levitation spells. I wasn't that kind of witch. Some magical aspects were just out of reach for a Starlight witch.

My body fluttered with warmth at the memory of the kiss we'd shared a few days ago. It had only been a kiss, but you'd think by how my body was reacting, we'd done the assault-with-a-friendly-weapon more than once.

"Earth to Leana?"

"Hmmm?" I turned and found Jade standing next to me in the hotel lobby, her blonde hair done up like a beehive. Pink, plastic earrings hung from her ears, grazing her denim jacket. She didn't have her roller blades on today. Instead, she'd opted for a pair of black-and-white Converse sneakers.

Right above her, secured over the lobby's front

entrance, a sign read CASINO WEEK AT THE TWILIGHT HOTEL.

After the dealings with the Rifts and the demons, guests avoided the Twilight Hotel like the plague. Word had spread of the deaths, and although we'd handled the issue, the hotel was only filled to a quarter capacity, if I were being generous. It felt like less than that.

Basil had the idea of hosting a casino event to get more guests to stay at the hotel and, in turn, keep his job. The lobby and conference rooms were trans-formed into game rooms with blackjack, baccarat, roulette, poker tables, and way more slot machines than were necessary.

I spotted Errol in an expensive blue three-piece suit, his pale skin practically translucent. He was adjusting an A-frame floor sign next to the front counter that read CASINO CHIP EXCHANGE—NO REFUNDS! He caught me staring and sent a disdainful look in my direction. With his sharp features and jerky movements, he really did look like a lizard, now that I knew his shifter animal.

Today was the first day of Casino Week, and so far, only three guests were sitting at a blackjack table in the lobby. Two females were nestled next to Julian, who caught me looking and flashed me a you-know-I'm-getting-laid-tonight kind of grin. The other was an elderly witch male, who kept hitting his cane at one of the slot machines. Guess he couldn't magic his winnings.

Errol dragged another A-frame floor sign across

the lobby and settled it at the entrance. This one read NO MAGIC USE ALLOWED ON THE GAMES. CHEATERS WILL BE CURSED AND REMOVED.

In fact, a group of very powerful witches and wizards had come this morning to put special wards and spells to keep magical practitioners from cheating. They could try, but they'd end up with a nasty case of hives or warts—their call.

Sounded acceptable to me, if only we had more guests.

"You're totally gone," said Jade, pulling my attention back to her and seeing her smile. "I'd love to know what you're thinking about. Is it dirty? I bet it's dirty. It is. Isn't it?"

Yup. Yup. Yup. "No. Just… thinking about boring stuff."

Jade snorted. "Sure. I bet you're thinking about a certain *giant*," she added with a whisper.

Damn her perception. "He might have circled around my thoughts."

The five of us, including Jimmy, had sworn not to tell anyone about Valen being a giant. The guy hadn't shared his true nature with anyone apart from the hotel owners and Basil, and he had only revealed himself to us to save our asses. We decided to respect that and keep his secret to ourselves.

"Where is he, by the way?"

"Who?"

Jade rolled her eyes. "Valen. You know, the not-so-grumpy-anymore-since-he's-met-you   restaurant owner?"

I shrugged. "No idea. I haven't seen him in a while." Total lie. I'd seen him last night.

The way Jade was staring at me told me she didn't buy a single word coming out of my mouth. "Well, I think you've changed him."

My pulse gave a tug. "How so?"

Jade attempted to brush a strand of hair, but when she touched the side of her hair, the entire section moved like a single entity, like it was superglued. "He's not so grumpy anymore. Haven't you noticed? He's not smiling or doing anything that crazy, but he's… nicer. A lot nicer. And I think that's because of you."

I made a face. "No, it isn't. I barely know the guy. Why would I have any effect on him?" But her words had my pulse racing, and heat pooled around my middle.

"Because you do," said Jade. "He's different now. You've had a real effect on him. I can tell."

"What can you tell?" asked a female voice.

We spun to see Elsa joining us. Her mess of curly red hair brushed against her deep-orange blouse. As she walked forward, green garden clogs peeked from under a long, navy skirt.

"That Valen is into Leana," answered Jade with a grin.

"I could have told you that," replied the older witch, smiling, her blue eyes lined with crow's feet. "He lusts over her."

Heat rushed to my face. "I don't think so. Besides, I don't think he's over his wife's death. Not that he should be. I mean, if I loved someone deeply, and they were taken away from me too soon by a horrible disease, I probably wouldn't be over them either." No. It just made me like him even more.

Elsa smacked my arm harder than necessary. "Don't talk like that. No one deserves to be alone. I'm sure his wife wouldn't want him to be lonely. You can love again, you know. Have more than one love in your life."

"Says the witch who keeps the locks of her dead husband close to her neck," said Jade, eyeing the vintage locket hanging from Elsa's neck.

Elsa stiffened and grabbed her pendant. "That's different. I choose to be alone. Cedric was my one and only true love, and I know in my heart I will never love again. And I'm okay with that. I have no regrets. I'm perfectly content. I feel lucky to have had a great love. Not everyone can say that. And I don't need another."

"You're really lucky," I told her, meaning every word.

Elsa wrapped her hands around her locket. "I know. I'm one of the lucky ones."

I didn't need a great love, or a man, to feel happy, but having experienced a great love the way Elsa had did sound amazing. Not everyone was so lucky, though. I'd married a man who'd tried to kill me in a back alley just because I'd broken his penis. That was my luck.

I hadn't seen or heard from Martin since, and I

was hoping he'd gotten the message from Valen—the I'll-pound-your-head-in-if-you-come-near-her-again message.

I'd seen something dark in Martin's eyes that day —blurry, but I'd seen it. Maybe it was more of a feeling, an instinct, that told me he wouldn't let it go.

A tiny man with a tuft of white hair and a matching white beard stepped into my line of sight. His dark suit fit him perfectly, and his typical pale skin was blotched in red.

Basil, the hotel manager, marched over, his eyes wide under his glasses. "What are you doing? You're supposed to be greeting the guests, not chitchatting with your friends."

He pushed his round glasses up his nose, his fingers trembling lightly. The scent of pine needles and earth hit me, along with a familiar prick of energy.

His magic was in full mode, like it was leaking out of him. That happened when witches were upset or in a battle. The guy was stressed.

"You told me to be in the lobby at one p.m., and here I am," I told the small witch. "I'd greet the guests if there *were* actual guests. What else do you want?"

"The hotel is paying you," said Basil, eyeing the main entrance door behind me. "You are an employee, and your job requirement is to welcome the guests—oh! Here they come now!"

I turned to see a middle-aged couple, dressed in

expensive-looking clothes and wearing identical looks of disdain, walk through the front doors, their eyes traveling over the game tables.

Basil grabbed me by the arm with strength that surprised me, given his size, and hauled me with him.

"Hello, hello! Welcome, welcome!" said Basil, his voice high as he addressed the new guests. "Welcome to Casino Week, where games are your heart's desire. We have everything you could wish for. We have themed game rooms, dice, blackjack, roulette tables, and slot machines."

The couple stared at Basil like they thought he was insane. He did sound a little mad, if not a whole lot desperate.

When their eyes flicked over the lobby with concerned brows, Basil blurted, "This is Leana, the hotel's Merlin." He pushed me forward as I gave them an awkward smile. "She singled-handily defeated the demon that had taken residence in the hotel."

I noticed how he said "demon," like there had only been the one.

"She's the Starlight witch everyone's talking about. Say hello, Leana."

"Hello, Leana," I said, feeling like a pet Labrador retriever.

The couple seemed to visibly relax at this bit of news, though I wasn't sure I appreciated him parading me around in hopes of having the guests unwind and stay. Especially the part where he disclosed my magical attributes. Not good.

"Let me get you settled in." Basil ushered the new couple to the front desk to an awaiting, disgusted Errol.

"Do you feel dirty?" asked Jade as she joined me.

"No, why?"

"To be used like that?" she added with a smirk. "He's whoring you around to the guests. You do know that. Right?"

"Leave her alone," said Elsa as she stood with her hands on her hips, watching Basil with a frown. Guess she didn't like it either.

"Oh, there's Jimmy." Jade gestured to the conference room, now a game room, where Jimmy came strolling out. A dark suit wrapped his lean frame. His light hair was shorter than it had been, telling me he'd gotten a haircut. He smiled at the guests, his back straight, as he walked with a nice confident gait.

"He seems to be enjoying his new post," I said. "Assistant manager suits him. He knows the hotel better than Basil, so he's perfect for the job." The post had opened after the late assistant manager, Raymond, had been killed... or rather fell into a Rift and then was most probably killed by the hundreds of demons waiting on the other side. Jimmy hadn't wasted a single second and had asked for the job, which Basil had happily given him.

After the curse was removed, Jimmy took one of the vacant apartments previously belonging to one of the families, who did not return to the thirteenth floor after the demon attacks. With his own place and a new job, our Jimmy looked complete.

"He looks very happy," said Elsa. "But I do miss the toy dog. He was so cute."

I laughed. "He was, but don't tell him that."

"He looks great. Doesn't he?" said Jade with a strange, dreamy expression on her face, like she was staring at Jon Bon Jovi.

"He does." I nodded. "And it looks like he's coming our way."

Jimmy's face beamed as he took us all in. "Ladies," he said, and Jade's face flamed a bright red.

It looked like Jade was developing a crush. I bit the inside of my cheek to keep from laughing. "Assistant manager," I teased, bowing my head.

Jimmy laughed as he tapped his flashing name tag. "Has a good ring to it."

"It does. It's the perfect job for you." Basil couldn't have found a more eager and perfect assistant. "You looking for someone?"

Jimmy nodded. "Yeah. You, actually. This just came in." He handed me a small white envelope.

I took it. "Who's it from?"

"The Gray Council," he answered as my eyes found the inscription on the front.

The Gray Council? I'd never received a letter from them before. Why would they send me a letter when they could reach me by phone? I wasn't sure how I felt about that.

Elsa crossed her arms over her chest. "I'll never understand why they can't contact people through email like everyone else. They're still in the Stone Age. I wonder what they want?"

"Maybe you're going to get a promotion!" said Jade, excitement in her voice. "Or maybe that's a big bonus check. You can finally get that car you wanted."

I shook my head. "No. The hotel pays me. Not the council." I tore open the envelope, hating my shaking hands, and took a breath as I read the letter.

Dear Leana Fairchild,
This letter confirms that we will be investigating a matter that concerns you. A complaint has been made about your conduct. We can change or add to these concerns in light of our investigation. We take all complaints seriously and will investigate thoroughly and fairly. After the investigation, a decision will be made as to whether further action (including disciplinary action) is needed.
You must cooperate with our investigations and answer any queries. We will set up a time to meet with you and give you a full opportunity to provide your account of events.
Yours sincerely,
Clive Vespertine
Gray Council

"What's it say?" asked Jade. "You look pale, like you're about to throw up."

I stuffed the letter back inside the envelope. "There's going to be an investigation. Someone has launched a complaint about me. And I bet I know who."

"Who?" Jimmy was watching me with a frown.

"The only person I pissed off lately whose ass sits on the White witch council," I told them, my heart pounding as anger swept through me.

"Adele?" Elsa's face twisted in horror. "You think so? You think she would do that?"

I nodded. "I do. This is her. For the Gray Council to open an investigation for someone means that someone must have some power and leverage. Merlins are always bad-mouthing each other, comes with the job, but we don't seek to ruin others. And we keep our problems within the Merlin group. We don't go crying to the Gray Council. Ever."

I knew Adele didn't like me and was pissed that, with the help of my friends, we'd managed to save the hotel and expose her psychotic plans. This was her payback.

"Okay, so what?" asked Jimmy. "You didn't do anything wrong. We can attest to that to the investigator. We know what happened."

"It's easy to twist the truth," I told them. "She could have told them I put everyone's lives in danger when I refused to help her force people out of the hotel when I knew there were demons. She could make it seem like I was responsible for some of the deaths. Like maybe I should have come forward sooner. She can make it look horrible."

Elsa was shaking her head. "So, what does that mean?"

I let out a breath. "It means, if I'm found guilty of whatever trumped-up charges, or if they think I've done something wrong, then… then… I'll lose my license and my job. I'll lose everything."

CHAPTER 2

After spending the rest of the day forcing myself to smile as I welcomed guests, which was just another handful, I was back inside my apartment. My anger was making me on edge, and I wanted to punch something, preferably Adele's face. Still, the way Errol kept throwing me snotty glances and correcting me as I explained the game table settings, I'd settle for his ugly face.

I was irritable, and Basil finally told me to leave around 7:00 p.m. "Go have a rest. You look like you need a break. But I expect you back here tonight. Tonight, more guests will come. You'll see. It'll be just like the old days. We'll have to turn away guests!"

He was so happy at the thought I didn't have the heart to tell him I doubted it. Casino Week was a great idea. I just didn't think the paranormal community would easily forget what had happened here. A lot of ugly rumors were circulating, one in particular that demons were still in the hotel, and management had lied to keep their jobs and the hotel open. And well, it seemed it was keeping guests away.

I paced my apartment, clenching and unclenching my fingers as a deep dread filled my gut. If I lost my Merlin's license, I'd lose my position here. I liked it here. I liked the people. They felt like family, and I didn't want to lose them.

If Adele wanted me sacked, she was pulling all her cards to make it happen. Sure, she could have my Merlin's license, but that didn't mean I couldn't find work as a witch for hire. I could be a private paranormal investigator, a rogue agent, or just a plain witch for hire.

There were other ways to make a living. She wouldn't get rid of me that easily, and I wasn't going to sit back and let her ruin my reputation either.

The letter hadn't said when they would send an investigator, just that there would be one. That being said, I was pretty sure they would send someone local—someone who'd done this before with loads of experience.

Valen knew a lot of people in the paranormal community. I was willing to bet he knew who they would send as an investigator.

I yanked out my phone and decided to text him at the phone number Basil had given me. Yeah, okay, I'd told him it was for work stuff, so he had grudgingly given it to me.

Me: *Hi it's Leana. Do you know any investigators who work for the Gray Council?*

I stared at the text, feeling both nervous and

stupid. Then I changed my mind and erased it. It would be better if we spoke. I could show him the letter. Plus, then he wouldn't know I'd gotten his phone number.

Using that as an excuse—because we all know I'd use any excuse to talk to the giant again and see how he'd react to seeing me—I grabbed a jacket, looped my shoulder bag over my neck, and left my apartment. After a short elevator ride, I found myself back in the lobby, which was practically deserted.

"Leana! Want to join us?" Julian sat at the same blackjack table he'd been at since this afternoon. The only difference was he was surrounded by four females, all trying to get his special attention. Everyone was different, in terms of age and weight. The only thing they had in common was how they were all glaring at me. Clearly, they didn't want any more competition.

I laughed. "Maybe later, *darling*." I winked at the females. Their collective anger made me all giddy inside.

I spotted Elsa and Jade bickering at one of the slot machines. I hoped they didn't spend too much money on these things.

I thought about going over there but then changed my mind and made for the front doors.

"Leana! Where are you going?" shouted Basil, marching toward me, as red-faced as this morning. If he didn't calm down, he was going to give himself a heart attack. "You need to be here!"

"I need to step out for a bit. Be right back. Promise." I pushed the doors open and hit the sidewalk. The doors closing behind me cut off whatever Basil was shouting after me.

I had no idea why he was yelling. The guy had told me to take a break. This was me taking a break.

I walked over to the building next door, Valen's restaurant, my heart thrashing the whole time, like I'd jogged here. I was nervous. Why was I nervous?

The AFTER DARK sign was illuminated in soft red lights as I walked under it. The restaurant door banged behind me as I went in. The familiar smells of cooked food were welcoming. My friends and I had eaten here twice since the whole demon episode with Raymond, but Valen wasn't around either time. Or at least, that's what the hostess had told us. Whether that was true or not, I didn't know. But she was annoyingly loyal to the giant. He could have been in his office.

The interior housed modern dark-gray seats and tables in an open-concept room, with twelve-foot ceilings and exposed beams and pipes. Floor-to-ceiling windows at the front let in the last of the evening light.

The lighting was dim. Most of the tables were occupied by paranormals enjoying their dinner. None of them glanced up as I strolled through. They were all preoccupied with their meals, and I didn't blame them. The food here was incredible.

"Eating alone?"

I looked up to the sound of the voice and saw the same irritating hostess standing behind her podium. She had long, flowing brown hair, a perfectly tight body under her white blouse, and I was guessing a black skirt behind the counter. She was pretty, cold-pretty, if that was even a thing. But if you looked closely enough, her skin had a subtle rippled effect, and I swear for a second, I saw gills. Maybe she was a mermaid.

Valen had told me her name, and of course, I'd forgotten it the moment it left his lips.

"No. I'm actually looking for Valen."

If she told me he wasn't here, again, I would deep-fry her and serve her bits to the guests at the hotel.

Her face went from blank to her lips curling at the corners. "He's busy at the moment," she said, tapping her long fingers with blue fingernails on the counter.

Okay, cue in the anger now. "It's important."

The hostess gave me a mocking smile. "Of course, it is. It's always important with you. Isn't it? Always more important than anyone else."

"That's because it is." That's it. I was going to smack that grin off her face.

The hostess laughed, actually laughed. "He's over there." She pointed to the left, to a spot across the restaurant.

I cast my gaze to where she gestured, and my heart sank, heat rushing to my face like I'd poured hot coffee over it.

Valen *was* here. I hadn't spotted him when I came in. Trouble was, he wasn't alone.

A beautiful blonde sat across from him with her hand over his. The way they were both leaning across the table to get closer to each other told me this was a very intimate encounter. They were so close they could probably kiss at that distance.

Worse was that he was… smiling. Valen was *smiling*—a pretty rare emotion for him. I could count how many times I'd seen him smile. Okay, maybe not. But it was few and far between.

I'd never seen this woman before. Maybe she was his girlfriend? Was he dating her? Was she the reason he'd pulled back from our kiss? Well, if he had a girlfriend, he had no business kissing me at all. Jimmy had said that Valen had *many* girlfriends. He was a fool if he thought I was okay being in his harem.

The hostess leaned over the counter, her expression giddy at what she saw on my face. "Told you he was busy. But by all means… go see him. I'm sure he won't mind you *disturbing* him right now."

I stiffened, and a flame of anger hardened my insides. Without another word, I turned on the spot and headed back out of the restaurant. The laughter from the hostess only added more heat to my face, like I had a mega sunburn.

I knew I was acting like an immature fool. He wasn't mine, and we were by no means a couple. He could date or sleep with whoever he wanted. And now I'd basically told the world how I felt about him with my reaction. *Nice one, Leana.*

That hostess would have a real laugh at my expense. She already had.

I was humiliated, and I felt let down. I'd been an idiot to think Valen and I had shared something special. Apparently, it was all in my head.

With my heart pounding, I pulled open the door and marched out. I hit the street, turned right at the first block, and kept going, my legs pumping with a charge of adrenaline. My pace was fast, and I kept it without slowing down. Cars and cabs honked as I crossed the street, but I barely noticed.

While I walked, I kept replaying that kiss over and over again. I wasn't perfect, and sometimes I wasn't as strong as I thought, my emotions taking over my mind. I hated when that happened. It meant I couldn't think straight. That my feelings got in the way of making decisions.

I needed to be rational. I needed to think with my head and not my heart. Because this was how people got hurt. I knew if I wanted to keep my job and live in the Twilight Hotel, I needed to push away these feelings and learn to live with the giant since he was so near and had such a close connection with the hotel.

And I knew I could never share a kiss with Valen ever again.

I let out a long breath as I reeled in all those conflicting emotions. It wasn't the end of the world. So, the guy had many women in his life. I wasn't about to let it break me down into a thousand sad pieces. It would take a hell of a lot more to break me. All this meant was Valen and I weren't meant to be. It was that simple.

And with that thought in my head, I walked straighter, feeling better that I had chatted with myself. Of course, chatting with oneself happened a lot over forty.

The moon was a solid, glowing white disk in the inky sky. The lengthening shadows began to trigger streetlights as the town's skyline cast deep, cold shadows over me. Even surrounded by tall buildings, I still felt it was darker than it should be.

I slowed to a stop, realizing I had walked off, not caring where I was going. And looking around now, I was somewhere behind the hotel on one of the small side streets, more like an alley. Still, it shouldn't be this dark.

Dark windows stared back at me from the neighboring buildings. The streets were quieter than usual for a Friday night as darkness rushed in, filling the spaces not lit by the streetlights.

That's right. It was Friday night. I should have been having fun, not walking off my emotions.

"I should be playing at the game tables with the girls," I muttered.

I spun around and smiled at the thought of enjoying a nice glass of wine and laughing at Elsa as she lost more money at the slot machine.

Small pools of water from last night's rain cast silvery hues from the moonlight. I walked faster, wrinkling my nose at the sudden stench of garbage. I'd been so focused before that I hadn't even noticed it, which seemed nearly impossible given how potent it was. The stench was a mix of dirty feet, smoke, and rot, like the bins hadn't been picked up in weeks.

Holding my breath, I kept going. My eyes flicked to the large metal garbage bin next to one of the buildings.

And then I halted.

There, sticking out from a pile of black garbage bags, at the base of the bin, was a leg.

No, *two* legs.

"What the hell?"

I stepped forward, still holding my breath, and clasped my hand over my mouth.

There wasn't just one pair of legs. There were three. Three bodies, judging by the degree of decomposition. I yanked out my phone and switched on the flashlight.

I could make out the first body as a male. The others were piled under him, and I wasn't about to touch them without gloves—no need to be putting my DNA on that.

Judging by the waxy, gray color of his skin, the blue on the tips of his fingers, and the pale lips, the body was still in the "fresh stage" and hadn't begun the second stage of decomposition, which put his death around the six-to-twelve-hour mark, if I had to guess.

But the fact that I'd just discovered three dead

bodies wasn't the reason I nearly dropped my phone or felt the sudden spike of dread in my gut.

It was the long canines peering from the lips of the dead male.

"Holy shit. You're paranormals."

CHAPTER 3

"What do you think happened to them?" Jade had a cloth over her mouth as she leaned over the three cadavers. "God, they stink." She pulled out a small perfume sample mini bottle and sprayed the air above the dead in great big arcs. She was contaminating the scene, but I didn't see the point in stopping her. It was too late now.

I shook my head, a dark feeling creeping into my gut. "No idea. And why are they here? Like someone just dumped them next to a human garbage bin."

"Because whoever dumped them was hoping for the human police to find them," answered Elsa, her fingers fumbling with her locket, something I now realized she did when she was nervous and stressed.

Julian was leaning over the bodies, next to Jade, with his mouth open. I knew he was breathing through it to avoid the stench, but that seemed worse to me. "This poor bastard's a vampire. Are they all paranormals? I can't see the faces of the two others.

They could have thrown the vamp in with a couple of dead humans and hoped no one would notice his fangs. It's possible they didn't know he was a vamp."

I was surprised he'd ditched his lady friends to come and help when I called Jade. It meant a lot.

"Let's find out." I looked at Elsa. "Did you bring me some gloves like I asked?"

"Here." Elsa drew yellow kitchen gloves from her soft cloth bag. At my reaction, she said, "I'm not a healer. I don't have latex gloves at my disposal. It's all I could find on such short notice."

"It's fine. Thank you." I pulled on the kitchen gloves, grabbed the dead vamp's leg, and began dragging him off the others. "Damn. He's a heavy sonofabitch." I'd barely pulled him halfway when I felt resistance, like he was tangled with the others.

"Let me help." Julian joined me, grabbing the other leg with a pair of blue latex gloves, which appeared out of nowhere. He easily hauled the dead vamp to a spot on the pavement.

Seeing as he was a lot stronger than me, I let Julian pull the other two bodies next to the bin until he'd lined them up, side by side, on the pavement. The streetlight illuminated enough of their faces to see that one of the dead was female. The other two were males.

"Are they all vampires, you think?" asked Jade, the cloth still over her mouth.

I'd gotten used to the smell now. What did that say about me? "Let's see." I knelt next to the female and gently lifted her top lip. "She's got sharp canines.

Yeah. Wait a second. Something's here." I grabbed my phone from my pocket and flashed the flashlight over the dead female. "Look. She's got a hairy neck."

"That's something I never want to hear again," said Julian, looking mortified.

I rolled my eyes. "Well, she does." I grabbed the female's hand. "It's more like fur. She's got furry hands too. And I'm pretty sure she's got some seriously woolly toes."

"Urgh." Julian shook his body like he'd just felt some cold shiver running over him.

"She's not a vampire." Elsa's clogs appeared at my side as she leaned over me. "She's a werewolf or some kind of shifter. Vampires don't like hair on their bodies." She caught my eye and added, "So, I've been told."

"What about the other guy?" asked Jade. "Is he a werewolf too?"

I crabbed-walked over to the next one and checked his teeth. "Canines. No signs of fur on him. Vampire." I leaned back on my heels. "So, one werewolf and two vampires. Killed and then tossed here like garbage? That doesn't make a lot of sense."

I was glad the alley was nearly completely covered in darkness. I wouldn't want some wandering human to happen upon us because that would be bad. We didn't need the human police involved here. This was clearly a paranormal issue.

Elsa took a breath and let it out. "It means whoever did this didn't give two hoots about these people." I had to agree with her on that.

"What do you think killed them?" asked Jade.

I let out a sigh. "I can't see any blood. Let's see if I can find signs of a struggle or something." I moved to the closest dead vampire and checked his neck and arms. When I lifted his shirt to check for wounds, I saw a smooth chest—a decomposing one, mind you, but so far, no cuts, bruises, nothing that would give us an idea of how he died.

"Maybe she was boning both dudes, and they got in a fight," said Julian. "Jealousy is an ugly thing. Plays with the mind."

"Okay. Say that's true. So one of the vampires kills the other vampire for stealing his girl, and then kills the girl and offs himself? That doesn't sound like a vampire. And there'd be blood. Lots and lots of blood."

"She's right," agreed Elsa. "Vampires are brutal. When they fight, it's usually to the very violent end. I'm not seeing any signs of violence here."

Jade lifted the cloth from her face. "What about poison? That could be it if there's no sign of violence. I bet they were poisoned."

I looked at Julian. "You're the poison expert. What do you think?"

Julian knelt next to me and shone his phone's flashlight over the corpse's lips. Then he carefully opened their eyes one by one. When he was done, he stood up. "It's not poison."

"How can you tell?" I asked.

He pointed with his free hand. "See their lips? If it was poison, they'd have sores around the mouth.

And their pupils are normal. They would be enlarged and red. They're not. And there's usually a lingering smell when poisoned."

I frowned. "You mean this isn't smelly enough for you?"

The male witch shook his head. "No, what I mean is that each poison gives off a certain smell. If they were poisoned, I'd be able to smell it and tell you which poison was used."

"I'm not sure how I feel about that," I told him with a smile. Yet, part of me was impressed. I knew next to nothing about poisons. Julian clearly was a master of his craft.

Elsa wrapped her arms around herself. "How dreadful. Their families must be worried sick."

Something occurred to me. "They've been dead for a while… how come we didn't hear of anyone missing?" The paranormal community was small and tight. We took care of our own. If some were missing, we should have heard something. Even Valen. He would have known and would have been looking for them.

"I'll check their IDs." I checked the vampire closest to me first, feeling bad that I had to go through his pockets, but I didn't have a choice. "Nothing. No wallet." Weird. Then I checked the last two. Again, nothing. "Okay, this is even weirder. No wallets on any of them. How are we supposed to identify them without their wallets?" And then it hit me. "Because we're not supposed to."

"I don't like the sound of that," said Elsa. "Sounds premeditated."

"Yeah, it does," I said. "Whoever did this, I'm willing to bet they're hoping they'd be found by the human police and marked off as John and Jane Does. Problem solved." Pretty psychotic.

"Maybe they were robbed?" Jade's worried face was cast in shadow. "It's New York City. A lot of people get mugged here. Maybe they were killed and robbed by humans."

"But that's just it," I told her. "They weren't. There're no wounds on the bodies. Humans couldn't have done this. Not to mention that paranormals can easily get rid of a few human muggers. We'd be staring at dead humans, if that were the case. Not dead vampires and a shifter."

The longer I thought about why or who had killed these paranormals, the worse I felt. The fact that we had found no evidence of how they died left a dark feeling wrapped around my chest.

"I don't think they were killed here," I said, knowing it was true. "It would explain the lack of evidence and blood and why they were dumped. They were killed somewhere else."

"So, who did this, then? And why?" Elsa's eyes were round, the whites showing from her eyes in the dark.

"Good question." I looked over my friends' worried faces, sharing their sentiments exactly. "My guess is paranormals. Not humans. But as to why? That's the million-dollar question."

"How did you find them?" Julian was staring at me, and from this angle, shadows covered half his face. "I mean, this is, like, nowhere near the hotel. What were you doing out here?"

My face flushed at the memory of seeing Valen smiling at the pretty blonde, and I was glad for the cloak of darkness. That way, they wouldn't see the redness on my face. I pushed back to my feet, my thighs burning in protest. I needed to do more yoga and stretches. "I went for a walk." I wasn't about to tell my friends about my humiliating episode at Valen's restaurant. Sometimes it was better to keep the humiliation to oneself.

"Here?" Jade turned around on the spot, a frightened expression on her face. "In this creepy alley? With mountains of garbage? At night with places for rapists and muggers to hide?"

My lips parted at the seriousness on her face. "I just went for a walk. Wasn't really paying attention to where I was going." No, because my head was full of Valen.

"Well..." Elsa sighed. "It's good you found them. At least one of us did. Maybe with the help of the courts, we can identify these poor people. They deserve better."

"I agree." I felt sick to my stomach at how callous the scene was. "Let me call Basil. We need the cleanup crew here. He can contact the paranormal courts. See if anyone's gone missing."

Elsa shook her head. "But this is far from the

hotel's borders. You sure this isn't maybe Valen's territory?"

"Yeah, call Valen," agreed Julian. "He's the right giant for this job. He might know something."

More heat rushed to my face. "He's busy," I said, my voice rougher than I would have liked. "I went to see him before." I swallowed. "He's not available. So… Basil, it is."

Guilt fluttered through me at lying to my friends, but I just couldn't handle Valen right now. I needed some more time to process what I'd seen. Like a few days. More like a few months.

I pressed Basil's number. After four rings, it went straight to voicemail. "Basil, it's Leana. We found bodies in an alley. Call me back." I ended the call and texted him a 9-1-1. Hopefully, the witch would get the message.

"I doubt he's going to answer," said Jade. "He's really busy with his"—she made finger quotes —"Casino Week."

I shrugged. "He barely has any guests."

"Don't tell him that," laughed Julian.

"Why don't you want to call Valen?" Elsa pressed her hands to her hips, the light of the moon high-lighting her red hair. "Did something happen?"

I belted out a fake laugh that came off way too strong. "I didn't say I didn't *want* to call him. I said he was busy."

Elsa pressed her lips into a thin line, searching my face. "I don't believe you."

I cocked a brow. "What makes you say that?" I was a terrible liar.

"Yeah, you're acting weird," said Jade, narrowing her eyes. "Oh, my God! You slept with him!"

"What? No." If I could have melted into the pavement, I would have.

"Yes! You slept with him, and he's not calling you back!" Jade continued and clapped her hands, like she'd just won big at one of the slot machines. "That's why you went to see him just now. You wanted to confront him."

I shook my head. "I wanted to ask him about the letter I got from the Gray Council. I didn't sleep with him." Who was I kidding? I did want to sleep with him. *Had* wanted. Not anymore.

Jade made a face, clearly sticking to her story. "Yeah, right."

A snort came from Julian, and when I looked at Elsa, she had an I-don't-believe-you smirk on her lips.

"I'll prove it," I told them, feeling nervous all of a sudden as I swiped the screen on my phone. His name was on my list of contacts. Weird. I'd put him as my number one contact and never even remembered doing it. "I'll call him right now."

I didn't want to, but it wasn't like she was giving me a choice. Besides, maybe it was better that Valen got involved. Perhaps he could shed some light on these bodies too. The giant was still a mystery. Who knew what other abilities he had? Maybe he'd know how these paranormals were killed. From the looks of it, the werewolf and two vampires had been in their prime—strong, capable, and healthy.

A werewolf and two vampires, I repeated in my head.

A werewolf and two vampires!

"Hang on." I stuffed my phone back in my pocket, my heart hammering hard.

"Told you," said a smiling Jade. "Sex, sex, sex."

Ignoring her, I stepped forward and leaned over the bodies. "Something's off about them."

"What do you mean?" Elsa joined me. "Like what? Other than they're dead, and we can't seem to figure out how they got that way."

I shook my head. "Not that." I knelt again, knowing in my gut that I was onto something. "They're not giving off any energies."

"What? Are you sure?" Elsa threw her palms over the bodies like she was searching for heat waves. I felt a tug of her magic, like a change in air pressure, and then it was gone. She lowered her hands. "I'm not getting anything either. But maybe that's just because they're dead."

"No, Leana's right." Julian stared at the body with a confused frown. "We should be able to sense something. Even dead paranormals still have an energy pulse. It'd be faint, but I'd sense it. And I'm not sensing anything."

"Me neither," said Jade after a moment of silence.

I rubbed my eyes. "Could be… could be a curse or something to hide their true nature," I said, thinking of Valen. "Let me see if I can dig deeper. See if anyone put a glamour on them."

I took a deep breath and called to that well of magic, the foundation of power from the stars high above me. My hair and clothes lifted as I felt the thrumming of power from the stars. The air hissed with energy, crackling against my skin and tingling like cold pricks.

I yanked on the stars' magical elements and merged them with my own. A sphere of brilliant white hovered over my hand like a miniature star.

Then I blew on my palm.

The globe climbed in the air, and then with a pop, it burst into thousands of tiny stars of light. The miniature stars fired forward, leaving a trail of bright light in their wake like pixie dust, before settling over the three bodies.

I was as connected to my starlight as they were to me. I felt what they felt. And at the moment, all I felt was a whole lot of nothing.

No cold pulses of vampire energy, no prickly tingles from the power of werewolves.

Nothing.

I gave a final tug on my starlight and let them go. Then, with a soft plop, they vanished.

"Nothing," I said. "No glamour and no para-normal vibes."

Jade began to rub her arms. "I don't like this. Nope. Not at all. What do you think it means?"

"I don't know what these are," I said. "But they're not paranormals. It's almost as though… it's almost as though they're human?" I knew that couldn't be, but it still needed to be said.

Julian made a sound in his throat. "But that's impossible. Clearly, they're not. I mean, look at them. Even the biggest idiot can see that they're not human."

"I know, but that's the feeling I got." Staring at the bodies, and seeing with my eyes that they were indeed paranormal, but they didn't *feel* it, was starting to freak me out. "They're paranormals, but they're not paranormals. This is crazy."

"But…" Elsa shared a look with Jade. "If they're not paranormals, what are they?"

"Good question." That was an excellent question. Because if they weren't, I had no idea what they were.

And they were dead.

CHAPTER 4

Basil's cleanup crew—a group of two men and one child—showed up about ten minutes after he'd called me back. Well, the young one looked about fourteen, and in my book, that was a child.

They were dressed in black suits without the sunglasses this time but equipped with medical briefcases. We all stood in silence and watched as the cleanup crew took a few pictures and cataloged the crime scene. But when the kid took out a vial from his briefcase, I couldn't hold it anymore.

"You're a kid?" I said to the youngest of the cleanup crew gang.

The kid, boy, teen, glared at me with brown eyes and a fatty face filled with zits. "I'm not a kid."

I raised a brow. "You've got a kid's voice. Do your parents know what you're doing?"

The teen straightened. "I graduated years before everyone else. I'm one of the best. Better than you old geezers. And now, you're in my way."

I raised my hands in surrender and stepped back. "Go for it."

"Boy genius who likes to pick up dead bodies as his career of choice," said Julian. "Think about that."

Yup, that was creepy. The teen dumped the contents of the vial over the bodies. A sudden prickling of energy rippled over my skin, and then the three corpses rose from the ground, hovering in the air. After the same kid sprinkled some white powder, the bodies disappeared, just as I'd seen happen before, and the cleanup crew left. Three white, misty tethers followed the teen boy, like the bodies were floating behind him.

It took all but about ten minutes, and then it seemed as though the bodies had never been there. But not before I'd taken as many pictures as I could. My memory wasn't as sharp as it had been in my twenties, so every bit of saved information would help.

After leaving Elsa, Jade, and Julian in the lobby at the game tables, I went back to my apartment to start up a file on the two dead vampires and the werewolf. I had kept Eddie, the last Merlin's, laptop and used my dining table as my designated workplace. Call it morbid, but why waste a good computer when I was in the market for one? Besides, we were both Merlins, so that kind of made it mine in a way. Not really, but that's what I told myself.

Eddie, being the highly organized and thorough Merlin he was, had blank files already prepared as templates. So, with a glass of red wine, I began to fill them out with as much detail as possible while they were still fresh in my mind.

I logged on to the Merlin central mainframe, wondering if I'd even be allowed since I was under investigation. But as soon as I typed in my login and password, I was in.

I searched the database for any missing persons and found nothing recent. A witch by the name of Karrin Weber had been missing since 1993, but she was never found, and the case was still open. Other than that, I found nothing. It was possible these paranormals hadn't been missing long enough to alert their loved ones of their disappearance. I'd keep an eye on that.

Next, I searched the database's list of all known paranormals, creatures and all, for a clue as to why I wasn't sensing their energies. But after an hour of exploring all the files, I came up with nothing. According to the database, all paranormals gave off a thrum of energy.

Except for the ones I'd found.

The sound of the floorboards creaking under the carpet pulled me around.

Valen crossed the short hallway in my apartment and came forward.

My heart did a funny bungee jump at the sight of him. The dim light in my apartment only accentuated his rugged good looks—his square jaw, straight nose, and dark, wavy hair brushing his broad shoulders that I wanted to run my hands through.

He wore a brown leather jacket over a black shirt

and a pair of dark jeans that fit his slim waist and were snug against his muscular thighs. My eyes rolled over his ridiculously powerful and broad chest, and I wondered what it would feel like to have his hot skin under my palms.

Heat blossomed over me, and I hated that my body reacted this way at seeing him. My hormones were out of control. Maybe I needed meds?

We stared at each other for a moment. My insides felt like they were being rearranged in my belly and swirling up into my throat with an added uncomfortable silence accented by the ticking of the refrigerator.

"Don't you knock?" My voice came out rough. Apparently, I was not over seeing him with that pretty blonde. I really shouldn't be. We weren't a couple or really anything apart from being friends.

Valen's eyes narrowed at my tone. "The door was open."

I pulled my eyes away from him and stared at my screen. "Still, should have knocked. I'm kinda in the middle of something."

"The something being the bodies you found?" He came up right behind me, looking down at my laptop. "You kept Eddie's laptop."

"I did. I didn't think it was right to toss it. It's practically new." I let my head fall back to see his face. "Can I help you with something?" I hated how impersonal my voice was. It was betraying me, betraying what I was feeling for him. I didn't know why I was feeling like this. I was acting like a jealous twenty-year-old girlfriend, which I wasn't. I was a grown-ass woman, and I needed to start acting like it.

Valen leaned back and crossed his arms over his ample chest. "You found bodies in an alley behind the hotel, and I had to hear it from Basil. Why didn't you tell me?"

"I forgot." Which was partly true. The whole thing about the paranormals not giving off energy had kind of thrown me.

"You should have told me," said the giant, his tone a little harder now.

Should've. Could've. Didn't. "I told you, I forgot. Things got a bit strange."

"Strange, how?" His eyes flicked to my computer screen and then back at me. "What did you find?"

Valen had been hired by the Twilight Hotel and was responsible for ensuring the safety of its para-normals and the paranormals in Manhattan. We were both employed by the hotel, and we shared the responsibility. I had a duty to tell him, just like he would if he'd discovered the bodies. He needed to know.

I moved my hands over the keyboard and pulled up the images I'd taken of the dead. "What you see are two dead vamps and a dead werewolf female."

Valen's eyes were fixed on the screen. "Okay."

"No cause of death that we could see. And they didn't give off any energies. No paranormal vibes. It was almost like they were human. But obviously, they're not human. See my dilemma?"

I searched his face for traces of recognition.

Possibly he'd seen something like this before, but nothing was there. "Have you seen this before?" I figured I'd give it a shot.

Valen flicked his eyes over to me. "Never. First I've ever heard of something like this. Where are the bodies now?"

"At some paranormal morgue," I answered. "I told Basil to inform them that I wanted autopsies performed on them. I want a cause of death. See if maybe the way they were killed could explain the no-vibes thing. And it wasn't a glamour. I checked. No IDs on them either. I checked my Merlin database for missing persons and got nothing." I let out a sigh. "We have no idea who these people are."

Valen was silent for a moment, giving me a chance to look over his face. His features rippled like he was struggling with something internal, like he wanted to tell me something but couldn't.

"I could have helped you," he said finally, a softness to his voice. "You didn't have to do it alone."

I looked away from his luscious lips, which were seriously distracting me. "I wasn't alone. My friends were with me. Besides, I'm used to working alone. I get my best work done when I'm alone."

Valen let out a breath through his nose, his jaw clenching. "You're angry with me? Why?"

Because you kissed me, and now you're with someone else? "I'm not. Just tired." I gave him a quick smile. I was a horrible liar. But I seriously needed to get my head straight.

Valen's gaze intensified, like he could read my

thoughts and knew I was lying. Could giants read minds? God, I hoped not. 'Cause *that* would be embarrassing.

"You came by the restaurant," said Valen. "You didn't stay. Were you looking for me?"

My heart jumped as a new wave of heat rushed from my neck up to my face. Ah, crap. I couldn't lie myself out of this one. "I was. But your hostess—whatever her name is…"

"Simone."

"Told me that you were busy," I continued, watching his reaction, which was nothing apart from staring at me. "So I left."

Valen's face was carefully blank. "What did you need?"

I noticed how he didn't specify what he was busy with, like that pretty blonde. "I'm being investigated by the Gray Council. Someone… someone of high ranking made a complaint."

"And you think it's Adele," said the giant, pulling the words out of my mouth.

I nodded. "It's the only explanation. I did ruin her plans and expose her."

"It wasn't just you." Valen's eyes traced my face and settled on my lips, sending a jolt of electricity rippling through me.

I cleared my throat. "Maybe not. But she's focused her hatred on me. I think it has to do with me being different, being a Starlight witch. Listen, I came to ask you if you knew of any investigators. I thought if you knew any, it might give me a better chance at being prepared."

Valen ran his fingers through his hair. "The only one I know is Drax. And he's retired now. Moved to Florida."

I let out a breath of air, disappointment running through me. "Okay. Well. Thanks, I guess." I'd just have to wait and see who they were going to send and hope Adele's influence wouldn't be a factor.

An awkward silence followed for a while, my heart making music in my ears in the swirl of conflicting feelings while my entire body thrummed with heat that had nothing to do with my warm apartment.

Part of me wanted to ask about the blonde, but I knew it wasn't my business. Plus, the moment those words left my lips, he'd know I liked him. Liked him a lot.

It didn't help that the giant had saved my ass twice. He was gallant, strong, and sexy as hell… but he wasn't mine. And I didn't share my men.

Valen stepped forward until his knees brushed up against my thigh. "Something else is wrong. What is it?"

I looked away from the giant. How could I tell him without betraying myself? Because I thought I felt something between us, something real. But I wasn't going to be that woman. I was too old for this.

And that's when Jade came in.

The witch hurried through my apartment, took

one look between Valen and me, and halted, hands in the air. "Sorry, am I interrupting something?"

"No," Valen and I said at the same time.

"Oookaay," said Jade. "Well, Basil sent me to fetch you. Says he needs you in the lobby, pronto."

"Great. Sounds like fun." Without looking at Valen, I grabbed my bag and jacket and headed out of my apartment behind Jade. I needed to put some space between Valen and me, which would be nearly impossible since he lived next door, at least until I got over these feelings.

But something made me turn around just before exiting the door. I looked over.

Valen stood there next to the table, staring at the floor. His features were tight and guarded, but I could tell he was worried about what I'd just told him. I was concerned too.

Because I had a horrible feeling this was just the beginning.

CHAPTER 5

The lobby didn't look at all like it did an hour ago when I strolled through and hit the elevators. Instead of being sparsely inhabited by guests, it was packed.

Paranormals stood in little knots, talking while drinking from their glasses. Some even sat in comfortable chairs as soft music played with a steady rhythm. But most sat behind the game tables or clustered around the slot machines. The smell of cigarettes reached me, and somewhere in the middle of all that, I felt a quiet, quivering pulse of energies—paranormal vibes.

I recognized a few faces. Barb, the elderly witch, sat at a poker table. She wore sunglasses to help hide her eyes as she held her cards, and she looked like a pro. This was not her first time gambling. I didn't recognize the others sitting at her table.

I saw Luke, our thirteenth-floor cat-man with a big, fluffy orange tabby cat sitting on his lap as he pulled the lever from one of the slot machines. Olga, the chain-smoking witch, who had the hots for Julian, sat at a roulette table. She had a cigarette in one hand while she held a short glass with what could be water in the other. I doubted it was water. Her purple eyeshadow was a bad call. But I wasn't going to tell her.

Hands waved in the air, and I saw Basil gesturing me over next to a tall male and a female shorter than him. Possibly a hobbit.

"She's the Merlin. That's right. Leana Fairchild. The Starlight witch who…"

I ducked behind a large, beefy man with hairy hands. I was tired of being Basil's star of the moment and found myself face-to-face with the front counter.

Movement caught my eye, and for a fraction of a second, I saw a fly sitting on the countertop. Then, with a blur, Errol's hand came out of nowhere. I blinked. The fly had disappeared, and a flick of Errol's gray tongue told me where it had gone.

"Did you just eat a bug?" I stared at him, wide-eyed. Now that was gross, even for him. Or was it?

The concierge glowered at me. "Are you mad?" he spat at me. "You're being especially stupid today. You should stop taking those meds. Now, go away. You're disturbing me."

I smiled at him. "You did, you nasty little creature. You ate that fly. I saw you." What? I had to have a little bit of fun.

Errol's pale face darkened, and he splayed his fingers on the counter. "I don't know why you're still here. The hotel made a mistake hiring you back. I would have thrown you out on your ass. You don't belong here."

I leaned over the counter, right in his face, and waved my finger at him. "Don't change the subject. You ate that fly. You know it. I know it. What else do you eat? Cockroaches? I bet you *love* those. All those juicy cockroach guts. Like gravy."

"Cockroaches? Ew." Jade appeared at my side and leaned on the counter. "I thought the hotel took care of that last year. Without Luke's cats, it would have been an infestation." Her eyes widened. "They were everywhere."

I grinned at Errol. "I'm sure Errol took care of that. Didn't you, Errol?"

Errol's face was practically purple with anger. "I can assure you, there are no cockroaches in the hotel."

"Of course not. You took care of them." I couldn't stop smiling. He was so easy.

I pulled Jade away with me before the concierge's head exploded.

"You like to torture him. Don't you?" asked Jade, yanking up her sleeves. The plastic bracelets tinkled around her wrist.

"A girl's gotta have fun sometimes." I looked around the lobby. It was full of people I'd never seen before. Some were my age, but most of them were older, hovering at Elsa's age and older. They talked and laughed and drank. All seemed pleasantly cheery to be here. "The hotel's pretty full tonight. It's nice." More than nice. It was great. It meant I could easily hide from Basil.

Jade's gaze shifted from side to side. "It is. Looks like most people like to gamble at night."

"Possibly. I don't gamble, so I wouldn't know." I worked hard for my money. The idea of throwing it away on a "possible" win sounded foreign to me. I wasn't rich, and every dime counted. Trust me. I counted them.

Jade gave a laugh. "Look. There's Elsa."

I followed her pointing and saw a frustrated red-haired sixty-five-year-old woman with a drink in one hand as she kicked a slot machine and was apparently cursing at it.

"Let's go help her before she breaks her foot." Jade hooked her arm in mine, and together we joined a crimson-faced Elsa.

The older witch's eyes rounded as she saw us. "That damn machine took my money!" she howled. "Give it back!"

I pressed my lips together. "That's what they do. People rarely win."

Elsa made a fist with her free hand and raised it. "It took all of it. All of it. And it won't give it back. I've tried a reverse number spell, a magical jackpot sigil, and a pandora lottery curse. Nothing worked."

Jade shared a look with me. "That's because the machines are warded against cheaters."

Elsa sucked in a breath, looking scandalized. "Are you calling me a cheater?"

Jade shrugged. "Well, you lost, and now you're

trying to spell the machine to give you back your cash. I'd say that's kinda cheating."

Elsa clamped her mouth shut. Then she took a swig of her amber-colored drink, finished it, and said, "You're right. I'm an asshole."

I spurted out a laugh. "Never imagined that word coming out of your mouth. I like it."

Elsa wiped a strand of hair from her sweaty brow. "Have you discovered anything about the bodies?"

"Yeah. Do you know who they are?" pressed Jade.

"Ah," I said as a waiter walked forward and lowered his tray of wineglasses for us. Jade and I each snatched up a glass of red. "I couldn't find any files on any missing persons," I told them. "Now, I'm waiting to hear from the autopsy. Hopefully, that'll shed some light as to what killed them."

"True." Jade took a mouthful of her wine and winced. "Not as good as Valen's house wine."

She was right about that. The wine tasted very strongly of alcohol and had a vinegar taint.

"Basil doesn't seem too concerned about it," added Elsa with a frown. "He seems more concerned about the turnout of his Casino Week than those poor dead souls."

I cast my gaze over the crowd and found Basil chatting with an important-looking man in a dark suit. When I turned around, Elsa was mumbling another spell at the slot machine under her breath, thinking we didn't see her.

Jade caught me looking and twirled a finger near her temple.

I snorted and looked away before Elsa saw me looking. Poor her. She probably lost a lot of money.

My heart leaped when I saw a pair of dark eyes watching me across the lobby.

Valen stood with a predatory grace that commanded attention. Those surrounding him gave him a wide berth, a king among his peers. Even in his more diminutive human form, he was huge, at least a head taller than anyone. He was all confident and destructive with his arms crossed over his ample chest, making his broad shoulders stand out, and his pecs bulge—a virile man-beast.

Even from a distance, I could see an intensity in his gaze as he watched me and the hair on the back of my neck prickled. The feeling was intoxicating.

Finally, he pulled his gaze away as Jimmy joined him, and the two men started a conversation.

"Did you and Valen have a fight?" asked Jade, which made Elsa stop cursing the slot machine and turn to face me.

"What? No. What made you think that?"

"So why the cold shoulder?" pressed the eighties-loving witch. "You practically wanted an excuse to ditch him to come with me. What's up?"

I contemplated telling them about the kiss I'd shared with Valen but decided against it. The fewer people who knew about it, the better. "I was an idiot," I told her. "I thought… I thought there was something between us. But I was wrong. There's nothing," I said, thinking of the blonde I'd seen with him. "We're just friends."

Jade cocked her head to the side. "What makes you say that?"

"I saw him with someone today." I thought I might as well tell them. They'd find out eventually. "A very pretty blonde. They were holding hands, sort of, and sharing an intimate moment. There was definitely something between them."

"You saw him with another woman. So what?" Jade pressed her free hand on her hip. "Valen knows a lot of women."

I shook my head. "I know what I saw, and what I saw was a man and a woman really into each other. There's nothing between Valen and me." At least, not on his part. "Why are you looking at me like that? It's fine. We didn't even go on a date. I imagined something between us… and now I realize I was wrong. That's it."

"Pfff." Elsa downed the last of her drink and slammed it on the top of the slot machine, her cheeks redder than usual. "Nonsense. We all see the way you two look at each other. Like you want to rip each other's clothes off. Something is definitely there. Don't you try to deny it."

"She's right, you know." Jade took a sip of her wine. "I remember how close he held you when you were dancing at the ball. Just look at the way he's watching you now… like he wants to take you to bed and give you *multiple* orgasms."

My face flamed as Elsa fist-pumped the air and started to sing, "Ah, ha, ha, ha, orgasms, orgasms," to the Bee Gee's "Stayin' Alive" chorus. Clearly, the witch had too much to drink, but she was a fun drunk.

Nearby guests stopped chatting and turned our way, wanting some of the "orgasms" action. They stared at Elsa, who was still chanting and shaking the slot machine with both hands like she'd lost her mind. Maybe they thought orgasms were the secret word to win at the slot machines. I laughed harder.

Jade exhaled long and low. "I wish someone would watch me like that."

I leaned over and noticed Jade staring at Jimmy instead of Valen. Looked like she was still crushing hard on the guy.

Elsa exhaled. "He is a complicated beast. Very handsome beast. But complicated."

"Yeah." I had to agree with that. "Complicated beast."

A sudden cheer filled the air, and I spotted Julian jumping up from his seat and looking rather pleased with himself. "Winner, winner, chicken dinner!" he shouted.

"Julian's having fun." I turned my attention back to Valen, because why the hell not, and saw a woman next to him. Not a woman. A witch. A tall, skinny-ass witch who had my blood boil in not a good way.

"What the *hell* is she doing here?" I growled.

Adele appeared in the lobby wearing a tailored navy pantsuit, a pressed white blouse over her thin frame, and a radiant smile. Her long, blonde hair flowed in loose waves down her back. Her glowing smile reminded me of a ventriloquist puppet's smile

—fake and orchestrated. Eyes bright, she glanced around the room, and when they settled on me, she smiled without showing teeth.

I met Valen's eyes across the room and saw concern cross his features. And then Adele turned her body so her back was to me. I guessed this was an attempt to hide Valen from me, but the guy was huge. She was just a thin pole obstacle standing before him, allowing me to still see him perfectly... along with the frown on his face as he spoke to the witch.

Both Elsa's and Jade's postures stiffened, and Elsa seemed to sober up a bit at the sight of the other witch.

I put my glass of wine on top of one of the slot machines. "I think I'm going to have words with her."

Elsa's hand shot out and grabbed my arm. "No." She gripped me. "Don't. Nothing good will come of it."

I tried to yank my arm free, but Elsa had it in a death grip. "I want to know why she filed a complaint. No. I want to confirm it's her." I knew it was her, but I wanted to hear it from her own thin lips.

"We know it's her," said Elsa, fear making her voice high. "Leave it alone. If you go there, you'll just make things worse. Trust me."

I shook my head, my eyes returning to Adele's skinny back. "How can they be worse than they already are?"

"She can make it worse," agreed Jade, her face pale. "You don't know her like we do."

I narrowed my eyes. "Are you speaking from experience?" I cast my gaze over my friends. "What did she do to you?"

Jade looked at Elsa, and then finally the older witch spoke: "My husband lost his post because of her."

"What?" A flame of anger ignited in my gut.

"Of course, it was a lie," said Elsa, tears brimming her eyes. "My Cedric would never steal anything. She'd just said that to get rid of him. See, he worked as a bookkeeper at the White witch court office here in New York City. He was the only one who stood up against her. She bullied everyone around, but not my Cedric." She wiped her tears with her hands and then smiled down at her locket.

I gritted my teeth at the sudden crazy need to run over there and yank Adele's hair. Then, slowly, I turned my attention back on that horrid witch, imagining her head exploding instead. "Now, I really want to talk to her."

A man came rushing across the lobby and met with Valen. He leaned forward and exchanged a few words. Then I watched as the giant pulled out his phone and put it to his ear.

"What's this?" asked Elsa, leaning forward too much and nearly falling over. She righted herself.

"Not sure." I stared as Valen's face went through a few shades of emotions—shock, anger, and a sense of obligation. His features hardened again, and then he met my eyes.

"Looks like we're about to find out," said Jade. "He's coming over."

I caught sight of Adele's indignant face as Valen left her to come to me. It was a small victory, but I'd take it.

The big, muscular giant came right up to me. "Something's happening in Brooklyn. A group of vampires is attacking humans."

"What?" we all said together.

"Just got confirmation," said the giant. "The head vampire has a team there, but they need help. It's getting out of control. Three deaths already."

Shit. That was bad. "I'll go."

"I'm coming too," said Elsa, hanging on to the edge of a side table so she didn't tip over.

"I think it's better that you stay," I told her, staring at her empty glass.

"I'll stay with her," said Jade, though I had a feeling she wanted to be where Jimmy was.

"Fine." Elsa pressed her hands to her hips. "Then I'll have words with Adele." Before any of us could stop her, Elsa marched across the lobby like she was going off to war, toward Adele.

"Oh, no." Jade looked at me. "I think I better stop her," she said and took off, running behind Elsa.

"Where in Brooklyn?" I asked the giant.

His dark eyes met mine as he said, "Marine Park, near the nature trail. Come. I'll drive."

CHAPTER 6

I t was the most uncomfortable twenty-minute drive of my forty-one years. Not because of the car, though. The black Range Rover Sport SUV was extremely comfortable—luxurious, spacious, sexy, and very manly, just like Valen.

I sat in the front passenger seat, and though the seat was practically molded to my butt, my insides were on a roller-coaster ride. Valen hadn't said a word since we left the hotel. I kind of just followed him to the parking lot behind his restaurant and got in his gleaming SUV.

The last time we'd been this close and alone was the night in his apartment when *he'd* kissed me. And let me say it again—*he* leaned in and kissed me. Yeah, I thought about it, but he was the instigator. And after he'd pulled away from the kiss, he'd also pulled away from me entirely.

But I had a job to do. I knew this would eventually happen where Valen and I would have to work a case together. I had to reel in my emotions, and hormones—let's be honest—and put the safety of our people and the humans first. I had to stop with the naked images of that splendid giant, preferably with me naked too. No wonder I was so horny. I hadn't had sex in over a year, and that had been with Martin, the one-minute man. More like a twenty-second man. Let's be honest here.

As we sat there in silence, my insides kept rearranging themselves in my belly, going from a tango to a somersault, accented by the whoosh of igniting gas, and the come-and-go flashes from the street-lights and cars flashed in my eyes.

Yet I felt his eyes on me. Valen kept throwing covert glances, thinking I couldn't see him. I could see him all right. I just didn't want to look at him right now.

But this was ridiculous. "What can you tell me about the attacks?" I said after I couldn't bear the silence between us anymore.

Valen stopped his SUV at a red light. "Just that a group of vampires is out of control and killing humans. The head vampires are trying to get things under control, but looks like they need our help."

"Have there been other vampire attacks in the city lately?" I asked as the SUV started forward again, pressing me back against my seat.

Vampire attacks were rare, just like werewolf attacks were uncommon, but they did happen occasionally. Usually, the paranormals in question were either sick or had some mental issues, not unlike humans when they had a psychotic break. But it was usually contained to just one vamp or shifter, not a whole gang.

"Three in the last five years since I've been here," answered Valen, handling the steering wheel with one burly hand. "Each time, the heads had the issue under control before it got out of hand or the human police got involved."

I rolled my eyes over his face, watching as the streetlights and shadows raced across his features. "You think these attacks and the dead paranormals are connected?" I didn't believe in coincidences. What were the odds of finding dead paranormals who were stripped of their essences, and now an unusual vampire attack?

Valen's hand gripped the wheel harder. "I don't know. Guess we'll find out when we get there."

"Why do you think they're acting like this? Group psychosis?"

Yeah, that sounded pretty lame, but I couldn't come up with a reason why a bunch of vampires decided to chew on some humans.

A muscle feathered along Valen's jaw. "Could be a sickness? Something contagious to vampires only?"

"Hmmm. It's odd behavior." I stared in front of me, watching the car lights passing us.

I felt Valen's eyes on me again as he said, "I know you've been following me."

Kill. Me. Now.

I cleared my throat. "What?" When in doubt, play dumb.

"For the last three nights in a row, you've been following me," continued the giant. "You think I didn't know?" His lips curled into a smile.

Irritation and embarrassment sizzled inside me. "If you knew, why didn't you say something?"

I felt like an idiot. I thought I'd been clever in my stealth, like Catwoman or something. Guess I wasn't as clever as I thought. The idea that he knew I was following him this whole time was mortifying. I was a big ol' fool.

"And stop you from feeling that you had the upper hand?" teased Valen. "I didn't want to ruin your thunder."

My face flamed. "Well, it is now."

"So, did you find what you were looking for?" asked Valen, humor in his voice.

Shit. Did he think I wanted to see him naked? I played off a shrug. "I'm a curious beast. I'd never met a giant before. I wanted to experience it without you knowing I was watching. It was for work." Partly true. The other part was because he intrigued me.

"Right." Valen turned to look at me, and laughter danced in those damn fine eyes of his.

I raised my hands. "Okay, you found me out. I'm a stalker."

Valen burst out laughing. "At least you're a beautiful one."

Heat rushed over my body, sending little tingles all over my skin. Okay, now I was baffled. Valen wasn't a player. I didn't get that vibe from him. But I knew he dated many women simultaneously—casual dating, if you will. I wasn't that kind of woman.

"If you must know, I won't be stalking you anymore. I got all the information I needed. Thank you very much."

"If you say so," said the giant after a moment, his voice hinting that he didn't believe a word I said. He turned his attention back to the road, a thoughtful expression smoothing his handsome features, his posture confident and strong.

We hit Marine Park after that and continued on until we neared the nature trails. Shadows of tall grasses and shrubbery lined the area. At 10:00 p.m., it was hard to see through the darkness that had settled. The only illumination was the moon and a few streetlights near the parking lot.

Valen pulled up next to another dark SUV and killed the engine. I slipped out of the SUV and looked around.

Oak and ash trees as tall as three-story buildings loomed over us, and acres of marshes spread out all around. Leaves rustled, and a wind blew through the trees—brisk, calm, and unnatural. The smell of moist earth and damp leaves rose with the wind, and for a moment, it almost felt like we were walking through a natural forest. But the thickening scent of blood gave it away. Something was definitely wrong with this nature trail.

I spotted another car parked behind us with the front passenger door open. A man hung from his seat, his legs inside the vehicle while his upper body lay on the ground. I hurried over and slowed my steps as I saw the mess of what was left of his neck. It was like a lion had taken a chunk out of his jugular. Blood was everywhere. The man's lifeless eyes were open, staring at nothing.

I felt Valen come up to me. "I didn't know a human body could bleed this much," I told him. "Don't vampires just drain their victims of blood? I mean, call it a cliché, but why waste fresh blood like this? And look at his freaking neck? Looks like he was mauled to death."

Valen was shaking his head. "I've never seen this before. This looks more like something a werewolf would do or another shifter of some kind. Even then, they'd have to be mad to go this far."

"But your guy said vampires. Right?"

Valen's body hardened in unease. "He did."

I felt bad for the human man. He looked young, not more than thirty, with his whole life ahead of him. "Bad way to go." But we couldn't do anything for him now.

High-pitched screams reverberated somewhere in the marshes. A man's voice let out a ringing, defiant shout.

I looked at Valen. "Let's go."

"Stay sharp," he warned, his stance predatory, emanating a threat. "These are not your regular vamps. Crazed vampires are ruthless. And this feels more like wild animals. There's no thought in the killings. They're just hunting for sport."

I let out a nervous breath. "Got it."

Valen's face was a display of determined rage, sharp like a dagger. "If they come at you, don't think. Just do. Thinking will get you killed."

"Got that too." This wasn't my first rodeo with a mad vampire, but the fact that Valen was clearly edgy about it was making me more nervous. If these attacks were putting a giant on edge, what the hell did that mean?

Without another word, Valen took the lead and ran toward the constant screaming, with me galloping behind him on a sandy path, okay more of a light jog. My legs were already cramping, and the wine I'd had earlier was threatening to come back up.

I didn't know what we'd find once we got there, but I was glad for the clear sky. I tapped into my will and channeled the celestial energy. With my heart hammering, I took a deep breath, tapped into my core, and reached out to the magical energy generated by the power of the stars.

I was ready.

Tall grasses and phragmites as tall as me flanked either side of the path. Valen wasn't much ahead of me. I could tell he wasn't running as fast as he could, more like he was making sure I could keep up. See, things like that only made me like him more. Yup, I was in a mess, but I couldn't think of that right now. This was too important to let my feelings get in the way.

I wondered if he'd change or if he could fight off vamps in his human form. I knew he wanted to keep being a giant secret, or rather private, but I couldn't help but wonder if others knew, apart from me, my new friends, and a handful of others. Did the head of the vampires know? Was that why they called him and asked for his help? I figured I was about to find out.

The giant stopped up ahead and leaned over something in the path.

Breathing hard, I rushed over to him. Lying on the path was another body, female this time. Bile rose in my throat at what I saw. Not only was her throat a stringy mess, but her clothes were shredded, leaving what remained of her chest and stomach exposed. Her jacket, shirt, and jeans had been torn to bloody ribbons along her forearms and legs. I felt ill and angry at the horrific scene.

"This is sick," I said, shaking with adrenaline and anger, knowing we were about to face some seriously messed-up monsters, not vampires. No, these were more like what demons would do to us.

Valen's face was set in anger. "Come." That was all he said as he hurried off again.

I followed the giant, adrenaline pumping through me to help me push with my legs and keep up with him. I didn't have to go much farther.

The moon reflected on a pond, its silvery water rippling in a slight breeze. And there, just on the other side of the pond, were not a handful of vampires, but about a hundred.

"Oh, shit."

CHAPTER 7

The scene was like something out of a horror movie, where a horde of zombies was suddenly upon the frightened humans, who didn't know how to fight or do pretty much anything else but die.

The air shook with the bloodcurdling chorus of battle cries and the shouts of the dying. Bodies—human and nonhuman—lay scattered across the marshes, too many to count and too dark to make out an accurate number.

The vampires were bent from the waist with their taloned hands grazing the ground in an apelike stance. They had a distinctive animal-like gait to them, almost as though they'd lost their humanity and were just animals. Creatures.

I caught sight of a male paranormal with supernatural speed fighting off one of the crazed vampires. He moved with precision, light on his feet. His attack was skilled and organized with deadly grace. This wasn't the movement of a deranged vampire. This was one of the sane ones, for lack of a better word. In a blur, he lashed out with his talons and severed the head of the other vampire.

Now that I knew what to look for to determine the not-crazy ones, I could see about a dozen "normal" vampires battling the other vampires. They were strong and agile with incredible speed, but so were the others. And the so-called crazed vamps fought without any thought process, wild and uncontrolled. They only wanted to kill. To annihilate. The other vampires wouldn't last. They didn't have the numbers.

That's where we came in.

Vamp heads turned at our approach. That drew screams and growls of rage from the mass of vampires. Rows upon rows of sharp white teeth shone in the moonlight. Damn. That was a lot of sharp teeth.

"Stay close," said Valen as he exhaled. The tightness in his voice pulled my eyes back to him. Tension flashed across his features.

"What are you going to do?" A knot formed in my gut at the torment in his eyes.

The muscles along his back tensed. Valen's face was troubled. His features kept flicking from frustration, rage, and uncertainty. He splayed his hands. I could easily see he was struggling with the notion of whether he should Hulk out or not. His secret wouldn't be so secret anymore after this.

"You don't have to change," I said, recognizing

the turmoil. "I can take them." I'd never fought so many at the same time, though, so I would have to pull some serious magic out of my ass. I had a sizeable ass, so it might just work.

Valen clenched his jaw, his eyes on the battle. "I don't have a choice. They're going to die if I don't."

"You always have a choice. I can slow them down and wait for reinforcements."

Valen looked at me, a softness in his eyes that had my throat close. "It's too late. You can't take them all. Look at them. See how they move? You fight off one, and then five more will tear you apart. I can't let that happen. This needs to stop."

With a pull of his muscled arm, Valen ripped off his clothes. In a sudden flash of white light, instead of his normal six-foot-four frame stood his eighteen-foot one. Muscles bulged on arms and thighs as large as tree trunks. His face was different, with a stronger brow bone, more ferocious and harsh, but it was him. Valen was his giant self.

I felt a tautness throughout my chest. Valen was exposing himself to save lives, and it was tough not to like him more after that.

With a powerful thrust of his back legs, the giant shot forward and rushed to meet the onslaught of vampires. I heard a cry and the sound of tearing flesh. The giant tore at the vampires with barbarous rapidity, his mighty body a force to be reckoned with and scary as hell.

I'd forgotten to ask him if I should shoot to kill or

if we were just going to subdue them until we figured out what the hell was happening.

But then I got my answer.

A vampire threw itself at Valen's thigh, its fangs sinking into the giant's flesh as it began to munch on his skin.

Valen reached down, grabbed the vampire by the neck, and lifted him as though he weighed nothing. The vampire looked like a child in the hands of the massive giant. Using both hands, Valen split the vampire in half and tossed it.

Okay, that was kind of gross. But now I had my answer. Definitely shoot to kill, but I'd try to knock them out first.

A flash of dark clothes caught my attention to my right, and I twisted around. A group of three vampires rushed me like a great, black wave of death. It was impossible to distinguish the males from the females with all the blood splattered over their faces and their clothes.

They were fast—damn fast—and a hell of a lot faster than me.

"Stop!" I cried out in desperation. I didn't want to kill them. "Stop right there! Don't come any closer!"

Even as they rushed me, I could see the vacant look in their eyes, nothing but a hunger to kill. Whoever they'd been before was gone.

I yanked on my starlight, feeling the power in the stars' answer as it thrummed through me—and let it go.

Twin balls of brilliant white light fired from my

outstretched hands and crashed into the first two vampires.

The starlight exploded around the vampires, lighting them up in flames of white light. The vamps thrashed, howling in pain as the starlight burned through them. I gagged at the smell of burning, rotting flesh. The air stank of burnt hair and charred fat. These weren't demons I was roasting with my starlight. These were vampires. With a sizzling pop, the vampires crashed to the ground, lifeless. They didn't explode into ash like demons did. Demons didn't belong in this realm, but vampires did.

Two down. One to go.

Not sure how I felt about that, I had a moment of regret, feeling the ramifications of what I'd done. I'd killed those two vampires. I mean, vamps weren't my favorite of the paranormal races. Their good looks kind of pissed me off, and they were arrogant as hell. But I'd been sworn to protect them and all the paranormals. However, when the third vampire came at me, its eyes gleaming with manic hunger, those emotions kind of went away.

The vampire moved with unmatched supernatural speed, much faster than the other two.

Terror-fueled adrenaline rushed through me and kicked me into high gear. I willed my starlight to me and hurled a shoot of brilliant light at the vampire.

And missed.

Oh shit.

The vampire slammed into me with the force of a

moving van. Pain reverberated all the way up my back as I hit the ground with the vamp on top of me.

I smiled at the male vampire, seeing it up close and personal now. "You know, you're moving way too fast for me. I'm not that kind of girl."

I waited for a glimpse of a human-vampire emotion, but all I got was an openmouthed growl, putrid breath, and some thick, stinking drool hitting my face.

"Thanks for that."

The vampire lowered his head as his black eyes found my neck, and he licked its lips.

That was my cue to get the hell out of there.

It was male. And what do males have that we don't? This—

I lifted my knee and smacked it in the vampire-nads.

The vampire's black eyes widened in pain as he rolled over, screeching in agony.

I pushed to my feet. "Be a good vamp and stay down."

Obviously, he didn't listen.

The vamp leaped to his feet, hissed at me—actually hissed like a mad cat—and sprang.

I gathered my starlight, joined my wrists together, and let it rip.

A thick shoot of brilliant white energy lashed out and hit the vamp. The vampire staggered, crying out in sudden agony, his body tightening helplessly as his muscles convulsed just as they would if electrocuted.

The vamp fell to the ground, thrashing his limbs and writhing, but it didn't last long. He flailed around for a moment and then stopped.

I let out a breath. "God, I hate this. See what you made me do? I killed you."

I stepped back and cast my gaze around the ongoing battle, looking for Valen, who wasn't hard to spot.

He swung his great big fists at the crazed vamps with a terrible ferocity. They launched themselves at him like a swarm of wasps, their faces deranged, but Valen brought down his enormous fists. Bones crunched. Heads looked like smashed cherry pies. It was disgusting, but I found I couldn't look away. I was seriously demented. But I was confident that Valen, in his human form, wouldn't have stood a chance at this horde of deranged vampires.

I couldn't distinguish the regular vamps from the deranged ones anymore. All I saw was a blur of teeth, talons, and death.

The sound of something heavy approaching pulled me around. Four more vampires stepped in my line of sight.

The odds weren't exactly in my favor, but I almost always beat the odds.

I was ticked. Pissed that they wanted to kill me, yes, but angrier that I had to kill them too. Clearly, something was wrong with them. I didn't want to kill any of them, but if they came at me, I'd have to defend myself.

Yup. They were coming for me.

The first vamp, a bald one—let's call him Baldy— came at me swinging with a kind of vampire speed that was truly impressive. His swings were fueled with fits of deranged anger instead of any sort of skill or precision. It was the only thing that gave me the advantage. If these were normal vamps, I'm not sure I'd have made it out alive. I still wasn't sure.

Baldy came with a burst of speed, but I slipped aside. His strike went wide before he realized his mistake. I twisted around, pulled on my starlight, and gave a clap of my hands.

Thousands of brilliant mini globe-like stars fired from my hands and surrounded the vamp like frenzied wasps out for revenge.

The starlights danced around the vamp as he howled and flailed his arms in an attempt to stop them from attaching to him. The starlights kept attacking until the vampire was covered in them, wrapped around him like a glowing mummy. He reeled and then keeled over.

My temples throbbed at the giant migraine that had made its appearance. Channeling all that magic so quickly was getting to me, and my body shook with tiredness—payment for the service of conducting all that starlight power.

But there was no rest for the wicked.

Just as the vampire-mummy fell, the three others came at me.

"Seriously?"

Again, I yanked on the powers that came from the emanations. I aimed and sent it free.

A shoot of white energy slammed into the three rushing vamps. It hit the closest one with the tremendous power intended. With a startled cry, the vamp flew back into a pair of his buddies. All three of them went down in a tumble of teeth and taloned limbs.

I heard a snarl to my right.

Willing my starlight magic back to the surface, I spun, and a ball of white light fired out of my hand. It slammed into the oncoming vamp straight in the chest. The vampire shrank back, howling, his body consumed in white flames. It lasted three seconds before the vampire collapsed to the ground.

The smell alone was enough to make me want to vomit. "Damn it. See? See what you made me do again?"

I whirled around at the sound of nearing claws and growls.

Four more vampires lunged at me.

This was becoming ridiculous.

I let out a growl of my own as I swatted the four of them with a blast of my starlight. I winced as waves of pain washed through me, the starlight magic settling and taking payment once again.

Dizzy, I took a breath and steadied myself, wrinkling my nose at the stench of burnt skin and hair. Sweat ran down the sides of my temples and my back. I was tiring. I couldn't keep this up. There were too many. Just too many.

My pulse raced as I spotted Valen. He was covered in vampires. Yup, that's what I said. Maybe thirty were attached to the giant, their fangs and talons biting, cutting. He pulled them off like they were annoying rats, crushing their skulls.

But just as soon as he yanked one off, ten more came.

"Stop this!" I shouted, panting as my magic coursed through my body. "I don't want to hurt you. Listen to me, you idiots. Just stop!"

Another two came—two females, from what I could tell. The two leaped together, flinging themselves at me with their talons extended and jaws open, like I was their midnight buffet.

No rest, then.

I planted my feet as I dove deep into my will and channeled the power from the stars.

And then the two female vamps fell facedown into the dirt.

I stared at my hands. "Weird. I hadn't even fired yet."

I looked over the marshes. Then, like a domino effect, the vampires, one by one, started to collapse. They weren't just collapsing but hitting the ground in convulsions until every last deranged vampire was down. Their limbs jerked and flailed for a moment, like dehydrated fish washed up on the shore. And then they were still.

With my boot, I kicked the nearest one to me. It didn't move. Its black eyes were open but without movement. No breathing. The vampires were dead.

My eyes found six vampires standing amid the sea of dead bodies. Nothing seemed unhinged about them, but they were bent with exhaustion. These were the "normal" vamps. Judging by their lack in numbers, they'd lost a few.

The ground shook, and I saw Valen, the giant, step in next to me. He was bleeding from hundreds of minor cuts and bite marks. Yikes. But the big giant didn't seem to be bothered by it at all.

"What did you do?" came his loud voice.

I'd heard it before, but it was still a little bit shocking and nerve-racking to hear it so close.

I shrugged. "Nothing. I didn't do this. They just… died. All of them. Almost like… it's almost like their time was up. Like they were running on fumes and then poof. They expired."

I scanned the scene, and even if these vampires had tried to kill us, seeing so many of them dead was still disturbing. "What could do such a thing?"

"I don't know. Never seen this before."

"There's no way this many vampires suddenly went crazy," I said, my head throbbing. "Someone did this. Someone did this to them. It's the only thing that makes sense." But why? I had no freaking clue. I had to find out, though, because I had the eerie feeling this wasn't over.

A thought flicked to the forefront of my mind. "Wait a second." I knelt next to the nearest body. The cold, familiar feeling of dread settled in me, and my gut clenched. "I'm not getting any vamp vibes. Nothing."

A growl rumbled deep in the giant's throat. *"I don't like this."*

I crabbed-walked over to the next body, a young

male in his twenties. "Nothing here either." Then moved on to another female. "Yeah. I got nothing." I kept going until I'd checked another twenty bodies. I looked up at Valen and shook my head.

Holy shit. Just like the bodies I'd found next to the dumpster, these vampires had no vamp vibes. No paranormal energies were emitting from them. There was no way they weren't vampires by the way they moved and attacked. Hell, they would have kicked my ass if they hadn't just stopped and died.

But why *did* they die?

"*They're connected,*" said the giant, reading my thoughts. "*These vampires. The bodies you found.*"

I nodded and slowly straightened, my thighs protesting. It'd be worse tomorrow. "They are. Maybe the bodies near the dumpster had run out of time too."

That was so bizarre on many levels, but I couldn't decipher the cause of death, just like these vampires. They just upped and died.

The only thing that could help now was what the autopsy would reveal. "We need to take at least one body to the morgue and have it checked against the other bodies. See if they can tell us how they died."

"*We'll need to take the bodies away before daylight. Before humans start coming through here for their morning jogs.*"

"We wouldn't want that."

Valen's features were twisted in agony. I could tell the whole thing saddened him. It did me too. "*I'll make a call. Phone's in the Range Rover.*"

I nodded. "Right."

Valen watched me for a beat. *"This is bad, Leana."*

I exhaled. "You don't have to tell me." I looked over at the remaining vampires, seeing the distress on their faces and their postures. "I don't know what's going on, but we need to figure it out before it happens again."

Because we all knew in my life, things could *always* get worse.

CHAPTER 8

I looped my hands around the coffee mug and suddenly wished I had some Baileys in it instead of just coffee. I was tired, and at my age, lack of sleep not only made my body ache but made me grumpy.

I'd barely slept the night before with the images of all those dead vampires haunting me. I'd waited with Valen for the vampires' cleanup crew to show up and take the bodies away. It had taken ten nondescript vans, with about ten bodies in each of them, to haul out the dead vampires. All that took a mere twenty minutes. The vampires were highly organized.

According to Valen, one body was to be taken to the paranormal morgue in the city. If the other bodies couldn't be identified, they would be cremated and buried in the vampire cemetery in Queens. Yes, it exists.

After he'd returned to his smaller human size, and grabbed a change of clothes from a duffel bag in the back of his SUV, Valen took me back to the hotel. Neither of us spoke a single word during the ride back. We were both exhausted and possibly a little shocked by the events we had witnessed. No matter how you played it, a hundred dead vampires who had just upped and died was pretty traumatic. Unheard of, actually. And it left us both confused, and let's be honest, a little freaked. Well, I was.

Was this some kind of disease that only affected the paranormals? Was this a vicious attack on us? Three dead the night before and now a hundred? Something was definitely happening in our city, and I was going to find out what.

I wasn't even bothered that the giant hadn't said a word to me as I rolled out of his SUV and shuffled inside the hotel. I was just too damn tired to have a conversation. I just wanted my bed. So I was grateful he drove me back, and I left it at that.

I'd turned as the Range Rover pulled away from the curb and caught a glimpse of the giant. The emotions that darkened Valen's face told me he wasn't ready to talk, either, and I wouldn't push it.

"Tough night?"

I looked at Elsa across from me, her red, frizzy hair higher and fluffier than usual, like she'd fought with her brush this morning. "You can say that."

I took the opportunity to look around, my nose filling with the smells of cooking and spices. We sat around a circular table in the hotel's dining room. A large orange banner above the doorway read CASINO BUFFET.

The soft clink of glasses and the loud racket of conversation wafted around. I'd never seen the hotel's dining room this packed, ever. It seemed Basil was doing something right. Just the smell of the delicious, mouthwatering food would have anyone walk in from the street.

"Are you going to tell us what happened after you left with Valen?" inquired Jade, sitting to my right. She popped a piece of cubed cantaloupe in her mouth. "We're feeling a little left out over here." Her blonde hair was pulled into high pigtails, and she'd rolled the sleeves of her acid-washed denim jacket over her Kate Bush T-shirt.

Elsa put her fork down, where she'd been busy tearing into her spicy Portuguese chicken. "Spill it. Don't leave anything out."

"Don't forget the part where you and Valen rip off your clothes." Jade raised her brows suggestively. "That's the part I want to hear about."

Valen had ripped off his clothes, but it wasn't like that. Just as I opened my mouth to answer, Julian appeared, carrying two plates piled with food. He pulled out a chair with his foot, set the plates down, and sat.

"What'd I miss?" he asked.

I stared at the dark, bruised mark on his neck, just above his collarbone. "Is that a hickey?"

Julian winked. "You bet, darling. I've got more. Wanna see?"

I snorted into my coffee. "No, thanks."

"Don't change the subject," ordered Elsa, giving

me her stink eye. "You look like you haven't slept a wink. I can tell. Something happened. Something that kept you up all night."

"Sex kept me up all night." Julian smiled as he ripped into his thick steak with a knife and fork, looking famished, like whatever—whoever—he'd been doing all night had left him ravenous.

I exhaled and leaned forward. Then, keeping my voice low, I told them all about the deranged vampires, how they all suddenly died, and how they didn't have any vamp vibes. I watched their eyes widening when I was done.

Elsa paled and leaned back in her chair. "Goddess, help us. How horrible."

"Tell me about it. It was much worse in person." I sighed and stared at my grilled cheese sandwich, unable to bring myself to eat. The scent of burnt flesh and blood was just still too fresh in my mind and my nose. The only thing I could keep down was coffee.

Jade was shaking her head. "But how can that be? I don't understand how they all died like that. And so many of them." Her eyes were round with fear. "Is it contagious?"

I shrugged. "I don't know. I don't think so. If it was, I'd be sick or something," I said, remembering my encounters with the crazed vampires. I'd been drooled on and had contact with a lot of them. If it were contagious, I'd have gotten it.

"But I'm hoping the autopsy results will tell us something about what happened to them. They're going to compare the first victims with one of the vampires... see what comes up." I'd been to New York City's paranormal morgue a few times. Maybe I should have gone straight there. Perhaps I would have gotten results if I did.

Julian pointed his fork at me. "But you think it's the same? What killed these vampires and the bodies near the dumpster?"

I took a sip of my coffee. "That's what it feels like. I didn't see how the others died. But my gut is telling me they're related. Valen thinks so too."

Jade's face brightened at the mention of Valen. "Did you ask him about the *other* woman?"

I choked on my coffee. I cleared my throat and said, "Um. No. Wasn't really the time to talk about that. Besides, it's none of my business." It really wasn't. Valen could sleep with as many women as he wanted. He was a grown-ass man with no attachments.

My face flamed at the recollection that the giant knew I'd been following him at night. Clearly, I needed to improve my stealth skills.

"Lovers' quarrel?" said Julian as he shoved a potato in his mouth. "You need me to take care of this *other* woman? It's not a problem."

"Uhh…" I shifted in my seat, not sure what he meant by that. Did he mean he'd poison her? I did not want that to happen. I had some insecurities. I wasn't perfect. But I wasn't a murderer.

The handsome witch winked at me. "I can easily steer her my way. And after spending some time with The Julian, trust me, she won't want anything else. She'll be begging me for more."

I really shouldn't have laughed, but I couldn't help it. "You're crazy, you know that?" But the thing is, he was dead serious. Would I be a bad witch if I was tempted by his offer? Yes. Yes, I would.

Julian waved his fork at me again. "Think about it. I'm always here for you." It would have been touching if I didn't suspect this to be something he rather enjoyed, stealing females from other males, like sport.

A generous woman, who was wider than she was tall, walked to our table. Red splatters that looked suspiciously like blood stained her white chef's coat. It almost looked like she'd just killed a chicken or something. Guests whispered as she walked by, eyeing her with disparaging expressions, but she never took notice.

"Hello, my dear witches," said Polly. She tipped her white hat, and I could see her hair pulled back into a French braid. The same Polly had healed my wounds from my gremlin demon attack and was apparently as good a cook as she was a healer. She bumped her large stomach against our table, a tray of food resting in her left hand and a spoon in the other. "Can I offer you some jambalaya? Or some chicken gumbo? Fresh off the stove."

"Yes, please," said Jade, making room on her plate with her fork.

Polly's smile widened as she plopped two generous helpings of her Cajun dishes on Jade's plate. Her eyes flicked around our table to finally rest on me. "You want some?" Her words came out more like an order than a question.

I shook my head. "I'm not really hungry. But thanks. It does smell delicious."

"It is," moaned Jade as she swallowed. She had some sauce smeared on the side of her mouth. When she took another mouthful, another blot of sauce sullied the opposite side of her face. At least she was consistent.

The chef narrowed her eyes at me. I could see the thoughts moving at the speed of light behind her eyes. Polly pointed her spoon at me, sending chunks of her jambalaya and chicken gumbo splattering on our tablecloth. "Stay out of trouble."

I grinned. "I can't promise anything."

Polly flashed me one of her infectious smiles and pulled away. And with that, the chef moved to the following table of waiting guests just as Jimmy headed our way.

"Basil's looking for you," he said as he joined our table, the distinctive scent of dog rolling off him. I never noticed before. Looked like the longer he was in his human shape, the stronger his paranormal side intensified. Jimmy might be a werewolf. He was some kind of dog. It might explain why the curse took on the shape of a dog. I was going to ask him later.

"Tell him he can find me here," I told Jimmy. I pulled my eyes from his and saw Jade's flushed face as she stared at her plate and did her best to try and shrink down in her seat. Yeah, she had it bad.

Jimmy gave a short laugh. "I will." His eyes moved around our table and settled on Jade. "Oh. You've got something here," he said as he pulled out a handkerchief and carefully dabbed Jade's face with it.

Her arms clamped to her sides as though she'd just been hexed with a solidifying spell. I didn't think she was breathing. And her eyes were wider than I'd ever seen them.

"There. Good as new," said the assistant manager, smiling at what could only be described as a petrified Jade.

Julian snorted at his plate and shook his head.

I looked up at Jimmy, wondering if he was oblivious to Jade's crush or if he knew. But it didn't look like he did.

"Enjoy your meals," he said, and then he was off, probably to find Basil.

"He's gone. You can breathe now," said Elsa, laughter in her voice.

Jade blinked. "I've never been so humiliated in my life. I think I wet myself."

"Stop. That was nothing. Just a bit of sauce," I told her, seeing redness creeping up her face and neck.

Jade shook her head. "I'll never leave my room ever again."

"Don't be ridiculous," snapped Elsa as she wiped her mouth with her napkin. "He was just being nice.

Nothing to be embarrassed about. So what if your face was covered in sauce like a five-year-old."

"I want to die," muttered Jade, and we all started laughing. At first, I thought she'd be furious at us for our shared lack of support, but then she began to laugh too. "I can't believe I just sat there like an idiot as he wiped my face," she said, laughing. "What must he think of me?"

"That you're a wonderful person with a great sense of humor," I told her. When her eyes brimmed at the compliment, I felt a tug around my heart. Jade definitely deserved a good man. And Jimmy, well, you couldn't find any better, in my opinion.

"Leana!"

The sound of my name spun me around in my chair to see Basil marching toward our table.

"Oh dear, he's got his business face on," muttered Elsa. "Wonder what he wants."

"We're about to find out," I said as Basil grabbed an empty chair from the neighboring table.

"I need to speak to you." Basil pulled his chair next to mine and sat. He had a folder in his hand.

"What about?"

"Here." He handed me the folder. "These are the autopsy reports." At that, my friends all leaned in closer.

My pulse spiked as I grabbed the folder and flipped it open. "And?" I asked, my eyes tracking the file.

"Inconclusive," answered the male witch.

"Inconclusive?" I repeated and then glanced back

down and read that exact word at the end of the report—in bold letters, mind you.

"What is it, Leana?" asked Elsa, worry filling her tone.

I looked up and glanced at my friends around the table. "They can't find a cause of death. Not on the ones we found next to the dumpster. Not on the vampires. They don't know how they died."

"But that doesn't make sense?" said Julian. "They died of something."

"Shhh!" hissed Basil, looking over his shoulder. "Keep your voices down," he said as he turned back around.

I stared at the file. I'd hoped to get something back from the autopsy. But now, it was worse than before. It meant that whatever killed these paranormals was untraceable. Undetectable. And that was a hell of a lot worse.

Dread filled my gut like it was loaded with cement. I had no leads, no cause of death, and no explanation as to how they died.

But someone did this.

That I was sure of. Someone killed all these paranormals, and I had to find them before they did it again. Because I knew they would.

Basil leaned over. "Listen. I don't know what's going on, but you need to put a stop to it."

I frowned at him. "I'm trying."

"Try harder," ordered the small witch. "See this?" He gestured around the hotel. "It's never been this busy in twenty years. The hotel needs this. *I* need this. And I want to keep it that way."

"Of course."

He pointed a finger at me, which I didn't exactly appreciate. "Figure it out. I don't want anything to interfere with my Casino Week."

"I get it."

"Do what the hotel pays you for, and fix this." Basil got up, not bothering to put his chair back, and pulled his face into a fake smile as he moseyed over to another table and started a conversation with the guests.

"Sometimes I want to punch him in the face," I said through gritted teeth.

Elsa smiled at me. "We all do."

I understood that Basil was worried about his job. His Casino Week was turning out to be a great idea. I didn't want these mysterious deaths to interfere with that either.

My stomach gave a sudden squeeze, not because of Elsa's comment but because of a certain tall, big, and muscled man-beast who had just walked into the dining room.

My eyes were immediately drawn to him, to his black shirt carved around his thick muscles, broad shoulders, and thin waist. His dark hair was pulled back into a low ponytail, which only emphasized his rugged good looks. It was hard *not* to look. The guy was huge. He commanded respect in a way that only the strongest alphas did.

But then, everyone else was eyeing him. More than usual, that is.

I turned in my seat as the murmurs of voices rose in the dining room. Straining my ears to catch every nuance, I stiffened at the nervous pitch, the rise and fall of their voices mixing with their restless energy.

"…that's him," said a male paranormal from a table to our left.

"…apparently he's a *giant*," said a female paranormal from another table.

"…his name is Valen," stated another voice from behind me somewhere.

"…giant…" came another voice, until the word "giant" echoed all around us, replacing the happy chatter from moments ago with more of an excited, urgent hush, like they were all looking at a freaking unicorn.

"Looks like his secret is out," whispered Elsa, concern etched all over her face. "Everyone knows."

A muscle pulled along Julian's jaw. "The guy looks like he's in hell."

He wasn't off. Valen halted in the dining room, his eyes scanning the space and the people sitting there, pointing at him like he was an animal at the zoo.

I knew this was the result of Valen showing his true self to help the vampires. And now, to thank him, they'd revealed his secret.

Damn it.

Valen's face was tight, and I could see emotions and thoughts flashing behind his eyes. Our eyes met and locked for a beat. I opened my mouth to tell him to come over, but my jaw just hung there, the words evaporating in my throat.

And then he spun around and exited the dining room.

"That's not good," said Jade. "Poor Valen. He didn't look good."

"He didn't." I was torn. Should I go to him? Speak to him? Emotions pulled me every which way until I felt like my limbs were stretching paper-thin. Part of me wanted to go to make sure he was okay. But then the other part felt he'd rather be on his own. He was a solitary creature.

Guess which part won?

The one where I stood up and walked out.

CHAPTER 9

Was I an idiot to go to a man who was most likely seeing other women? Possibly. Yes, I had feelings for him that I had to reel in, but Valen had proven to be a friend to me and had saved my ass more than once. He'd been kind to me, apart from when we'd first met. He'd been a total jerk then, but he'd apologized since. That said a lot. And right now, my friendly giant looked like he needed a friend to talk to.

I knew Valen had been careful to keep his giant nature a well-kept secret. Only a handful of people knew, including me. Probably because the man wanted to avoid all the attention. Not to mention, few giants were probably left in the world. Let's face it. He was a freaking unicorn in the room—a sexy one too.

By the looks of things, the guests in the hotel knew about him, which meant they'd told their friends and their families. Damn. That meant soon, every paranormal in the city would know what Valen was. He'd had to know that one day his secret would be out. He couldn't keep it for long, not with the work he was doing for the hotel.

When I exited the hotel and hit the sidewalk, the giant was nowhere in sight. So, I made for the only place he could be.

With the autopsy folder in one hand, I yanked open the door to his restaurant, After Dark, and strolled in. I cast my gaze over the tables and booths and, not seeing him, went straight to his office.

I went to the first door and pulled.

"Hey! You can't go in there!" cried a voice behind me.

I knew it was the hostess what's-her-name, so I didn't bother turning around. The room turned out to be his office. I'd been right about that. A large wood desk occupied most of the space, the top scattered with papers and a mug. Bookcases flanked each side of the room, but Valen wasn't there.

"I'll have you thrown out!" shouted the hostess, her face flushed with anger, rippling with what looked like fish scales. Yeah, definitely mermaid or some finfolk. She looked like she was about to beast out into whatever fish she was, but I didn't care.

I pushed her out of the way and moved to the only other door, which turned out to be a storage room.

"Valen will know about this," she threatened and yanked out her cell phone.

"Good. You be a good girl and tell him."

I heard her sharp intake of breath, but I wasn't here to fight her. I was already near the front doors when I heard her voice shouting something.

I was back outside, standing in front of the restaurant as my eyes went to the second floor. The building had only two floors, and the entire top floor was Valen's apartment.

Heart pumping, I moved to the right of the building where the side entrance to his apartment was. I yanked open the door, hit the stairs, and when I made it to the landing, I knocked three times.

I moved back, a little out of breath from climbing those stairs so quickly. My heart thrashed in my chest, and I was a little dizzy from not eating. I had a moment of panic then. *What the hell am I doing here?*

I should go. I shouldn't be here. What would he think when he saw me? He'd be irritated because he didn't want to be disturbed, that's what. This was a mistake. I was an idiot.

I whirled around and made to leave just as I heard the door swing open.

"Leana? What are you doing here?" Surprise flashed across Valen's face as I turned back around. His eyes went to the folder that was still clutched in my hand and back at my face.

"Uhh…" Damn it. My mouth wasn't catching up with my thoughts. "I wanted to make sure you were okay." There. At least that came out right.

His dark eyes rolled over my face. "Come." He stepped aside and held the door for me.

Did I go inside? Hell yes.

I stepped in, and the familiar scents of leather and spices filled my nose. I'd only been inside twice, but it looked exactly the same.

"Can I get you a glass of wine?" Valen walked past me to his kitchen and started opening cabinet doors.

I hauled off my boots and followed him. "I really shouldn't. I haven't eaten anything since last night. Can't seem to hold anything down. Just coffee, so far."

"Last night was bad." Valen watched me for a beat longer, but I couldn't tell what he was thinking. "Sit." He gestured at the kitchen island. "I'll make you something that'll help with your stomach."

"I won't say no to that," I said, smiling. He smiled back, and my insides gave a jolt. I pulled my eyes away before my face gave away my feelings. I grabbed one of the stainless-steel stools, which were more comfortable than they looked, let the folder drop next to me on the counter, and sat.

I watched as Valen went to work, staring at his broad shoulders, the way his back muscles danced and pulled as he set pots and pans on his stove. He grabbed some veggies from his fridge that was the size of two of mine and started chopping them on a cutting board. Then he expertly poured the mix into a pot and added seasoning. It was quite the show, and I had front-row seats.

He was so different from the first day I'd assaulted his chest with my face. Then he'd been a man-beast jerk. Now, he was sweet and caring, which didn't help my conflicting emotions.

The last time I was here, he'd kissed me. And it was a hell of a kiss, the kind that made you want to rip off your clothes and shout, "Hallelujah!" The type of kiss that whispered we were about to get our freak on. Which, let's be honest, I would have allowed to happen.

But Valen had pulled away, and I'd seen a sadness in his eyes that had sobered me right up. I'd first thought he wasn't ready to be with anyone. But then Jimmy had told me Valen had many girlfriends, and I'd seen him just yesterday with one of them. So that couldn't be the reason.

It hurt. I wasn't going to lie to myself. Maybe Valen had realized he didn't like me in that way after the kiss. And that was perfectly fine. These things happened. I couldn't be angry at him for it.

I just had to get used to it.

"So," I began, wanting to say what I came here to say. The sooner I did, the sooner I could leave. "The guests were pretty excited to see you. They know. Won't be long before the entire city knows."

My eyes trailed down his back to his very fine behind. His ass looked spectacular in those jeans. "I'm sorry you had to reveal yourself last night." Reluctantly, I yanked my eyes back up to his shoulders. "But if you didn't... I don't think we would have made it."

Without him, those vampires would have reached

Manhattan in no time and killed maybe hundreds of innocent humans.

"I knew it would happen one day," said the giant as he added butter to a frying pan. The scent made my stomach grumble.

I rested my elbows on the counter. "So, you're not upset?"

He shook his head, his attention never leaving his cooking. "I was hoping to stretch it out a bit longer. But after last night, I knew it was over."

I wouldn't say I liked his choice of words there. "So, what does that mean, exactly? Do you still work for the hotel?" God forbid if it meant he'd lose his job. I'd gotten used to the idea of a giant living next door. It made me feel safer knowing he was there, patrolling the streets at night, even when I was stalking him. I might not be his girlfriend, but I didn't want to lose him either.

Valen turned around. A smile touched the corners of his mouth. "Is that why you came? You thought I'd be fired?" His eyes pinned me. They were mesmerizing as they beheld me. It was all I could do not to pull away. Did giants have hypnotizing abilities?

I shrugged, my insides churning, and not because of what I'd seen last night. "I don't know. Basil is a bit of an ass. He doesn't want anything to disrupt his *Casino Week*."

"He puts on a big front, but he's a real softy, that Basil," said the giant as he turned back around. He dumped the contents of the frying pan into the boiling pot. The smell of butter and spices and God knew what else was making me salivate.

"Are those the autopsy reports?" he asked as he whisked the contents into the pot.

I sighed as I grabbed the folder and flipped it open. "Yes. And it's inconclusive. They can't find a cause of death on any of the bodies, which makes absolutely no sense. But there you have it."

At that, the muscles along Valen's back tensed. Obviously, we both knew this was the worst possible outcome.

Without a cause of death, we didn't have much to go on. Basically, we had a whole lot of nothing.

I folded the file shut. "Jade thought it could be a virus or something, which could have accounted for so many of those vampires last night, but the autopsy would have said as much. And we're both fine. So it can't be that. Damn it. I have no freaking clue what did that to all those paranormals." I rested my head on my hands, recalling the scene from last night and trying to pinpoint something. The only thing that stood out was how wild, unfocused, and out of their minds the vampires were.

And they all just died like a mass suicide.

"Here."

I looked up as Valen set a bowl of steaming something with floating vegetables, chicken, and what looked like rice in front of me. Next, he placed a spoon fit for a giant, which made me laugh, and a white napkin.

I stared up at him. "You made me chicken soup?"

My throat contracted. Apart from my mother, no one had ever made me soup or anything. Not even Martin. All he ever made for me was a whole lot of nothin'. Damnit. Why was Valen being so damn nice?

He leaned over the counter until his face was practically over my bowl. "It's my own recipe. It'll help to settle your stomach. You need to eat something."

I narrowed my eyes. "This won't make me drunk. Will it?" I still remembered his special brew of tea, which made me feel like I was drunk.

The giant chuckled. "No. This will make you feel better. Trust me."

I shrugged. "Well, if you say it like that." I stared at the spoon, not sure it would fit inside my mouth. I lifted the massive spoon. "Ready for your spanking?" I laughed and then caught myself. Why did I just say that?

Valen flashed me his perfect teeth. "I'm ready if you are."

Kill. Me. Now.

I lowered my head toward my soup, barely feeling the steam on my hot cheeks. Hell, I probably had some steam of my own shooting out of my ears. I dipped the mega spoon in the bowl, scooped up some of the soup, put the spoon to my lips, and sipped.

"Mmmm, good," I said as I swallowed. "Spicy good. Don't think I've ever had chicken soup that tasted so good."

Valen beamed. He crossed his arms over his chest

and leaned his back on the counter next to his stove, eyeing me. "Glad you like it. It was my wife's favorite."

I froze, spoon halfway in my mouth. "Uh... huh..."

Valen never stopped smiling. I couldn't detect any sadness in his eyes, just warmth. "She was a lot like you, headstrong, fierce, impulsive."

I swallowed. "Was she a giant like you?"

Valen shook his head, losing some of his smile. "A werewolf. We used to shift together at night. She'd lose me the first five minutes. She was too fast for me, and she thought that was hilarious."

My heart clenched at the thought of his wife dying of cancer. "I'm sorry for what happened to her."

"I am too." Valen looked away for a brief moment, but then his eyes were back on mine, bright and softened ever so slightly. I saw something I couldn't put my finger on. "You should start feeling better soon."

He wasn't kidding. As soon as I gulped down another three huge spoonfuls of soup, my stomach wasn't queasy, and the night's aches and pains—both physical and mental—were gone. I felt good. Great.

I eyed the giant in his kitchen. He looked good, edible. "You like taking care of people."

He looked at the floor. "I do. It's in my nature. It's something all giants share."

I waved my spoon at him. "All those muscles have to be put to good use."

Valen laughed, and it sent delicious tingles over me.

"You're not having some?" I asked, shoving another spoon topped with shredded carrots, celery, and some other vegetable I didn't recognize. I didn't care that he heard me slurping and moaning. Once I started with the soup, I couldn't stop. I was ravenous.

"I've eaten."

When I looked up, Valen was still staring at me with a strange smile. "Don't tell Polly." I waved my spoon at him. "She'll freak if she knows you can make a mean chicken soup. Probably'll have you sign an NDA."

Valen laughed, and my heart melted a little. Shit. I had to get out of here. I was not falling for this guy. Nope. No. No siree, Bob.

I grabbed my bowl with both hands, tipped it to my lips, and drank the rest. Every last drop. Why waste a good thing? Am I right?

I set my bowl down and wiped my mouth with my napkin. "Wow. That was good. Thank you so much." I slipped off the stool and grabbed the folder.

"You're leaving?" Valen uncrossed his arms.

"Yeah. Oh. You need help with the dishes?" The man had made me chicken soup from scratch. The least I could do was clean up.

The giant watched me for a long beat, and I thought he would take me up on that offer. But instead, he said, "Have dinner with me tonight."

Uh-oh.

The folder slipped from my hand. Blood rushed to my face as I bent and picked up the file, only to find Valen two inches from me when I straightened.

I raised a brow. "How'd you do that?" The proximity to his hard, muscular chest was making me a little drunk, like he'd given me his special tea again. We were almost touching.

"Have dinner with me," he repeated.

I was hot, flushed, with my body tingly all over. I swallowed hard. "Huh?" Okay, this was not the plan. The plan was to go see the giant, make sure he was okay, and then skedaddle. See? Good plan.

He looked down at me with those dark eyes I could get lost in. "Dinner tonight. I'll have something special prepared for you downstairs."

My heart pounded in my ears. "At your restaurant? You want *me*… to have dinner with *you*?" I sounded like an idiot. But I wanted to make sure he knew what he was saying.

Valen inched closer, his eyes dipping to my lips and then up to my eyes again. "Yes. I'd like to have dinner with you, unless you have other plans."

Images of the pretty blonde flashed in my mind's eye. The way he'd smiled at her, the way they were touching, their closeness… definitely something between them.

What I should have done was tell him no. I licked my lips, preparing to turn him down gently.

"Okay. Sure. What time?" Seemed my mouth had other plans.

"Seven o'clock," said the giant, his eyes gleaming

as they narrowed in on my lips. A cocky smile spread over his own, like hot males got when they knew they had you.

Damn you, hormones.

I spun around before they got me into trouble. I pulled on my boots and headed out.

Only when I was out and had reached the sidewalk did I remember to breathe.

Holy hell. What have I done?

CHAPTER 10

"Not that. You'll look like a slut," said Elsa, grabbing my low-cut black blouse from me and tossing it on my bed. "It screams desperate. You don't want to give him that impression."

"She's right," said Jade, going through my closet. "You don't want to give him the *wrong* impression. You want to be sexy, not slutty. There's a difference."

"I get it," I said as I moved over to my bed and sat. "But I don't have much. I don't have a 'dating' wardrobe. I have a work wardrobe—a killing-baddies wardrobe. I never thought I'd be dating right now after what happened with Martin." The cheating and, of course, the trying-to-kill-me part. That would turn off any woman from dating.

"Things change," said Elsa. "When you know it's right, it's right. Time won't make a difference when the right man comes along. Why do you have so many T-shirts?" She held a cluster of white and gray T-shirts.

I shrugged. "Because I love cotton? I told you I don't have anything worthy of a date." I knew Valen would be wearing something expensive and exquisite on his muscular frame. I hadn't really gone shopping for going-out clothes. The only thing I'd bought recently was that silver gown for the Midnight Ball, and I ended up ripping it so I could maneuver in it. The dress was ruined, and I'd tossed it.

"You know," said Jade, as she poked her head out of my closet, "I have a really nice blue taffeta dress I think would look amazing on you. It makes a swooshing sound when you move!"

I kept my face as blank as possible, not wanting to hurt her feelings because the idea of me in a blue taffeta dress was more horrifying than going on a date with Valen.

"Thanks, but I'd rather wear pants or jeans. I'll be more comfortable. More relaxed. Pants are good. Especially if I have to work after."

Elsa huffed in disapproval. "You need to learn to have fun. Forget about work for just one night and enjoy yourself. Life is short, and the older you get, the faster it goes. Trust me. Do you know how many women wish to be in your shoes, right now?"

"In your pants," laughed Jade.

Elsa nodded. "That too. Do you?" When I didn't answer, she added, "All the single paranormal ladies, that's how many. Valen is the most wanted bachelor in our community. Some women have had the pleasure of being with him, but none of them could tie him down. A wild beast that no one can tame. But something tells me he's serious about you. You'll be the one to tame him."

I shifted my weight on my bed, my white bathrobe pooling around me. "I don't want to tame anyone." Okay, maybe that was a lie. I had the visual of me with a whip and a naked Valen tied to a bed. "I told you about that hot blonde. What makes this any different? I don't have the will or the energy to be Valen's girl of the week. I'm too old for that crap."

"I don't think that's it at all," said Elsa. "Give him some credit."

"How do you know?"

Elsa gave me a knowing smile. "I just know." She twisted around and started shuffling through my clothes on hangers. "Just like I knew Cedric was meant for me. Sure, Katie and Samantha were all over him, but he was mine. And it's the same with you. Valen is your guy… or should I say your *giant*," she added, laughing at her own joke.

Jade pulled her pigtails tighter as she stared at herself in the full-length mirror on the wall. "You practically told everyone how you felt about him, earlier. The entire hotel is talking about it."

I leaned forward. "I'm sorry? What?" I felt a burst of heat rolling up my body in waves.

Jade spun around to face me. "The way you ran after him. Everyone saw."

Another rush of heat settled around my face. "They saw a friend who was concerned," I said, though, by her smile, I knew she didn't believe me. "I saw his reaction when everyone in the dining room was talking about him—pointing and whispering like he was some rare animal at the zoo. I would hate that too. I wanted to make sure he was okay."

Yes, I cared for him more than I should, but I had honestly gone to make sure he was okay. The guests' reaction to him had angered me. And then, well, things just got more complicated after that.

"And that won you a date," called Elsa from inside my closet. I couldn't see her face, but I could hear the smile in her voice.

Something occurred to me. "What do you think will happen now that everyone knows about him?"

"What do you mean?" asked Jade.

I shrugged. "I don't know… maybe he won't stay. Maybe he'll start getting better job offers than working for the hotel. Giants are rare, assumed nonexistent. I'm pretty sure lots of people in power want a piece of him now."

Jade pinched her lips together, shaking her head. "He'll never leave. No. I don't believe it."

Elsa poked her head out of my closet. She didn't say anything, but from the frown on her face, I knew some of what I'd just said rang true. I mean, who wouldn't want a giant on their team or as a soldier somewhere? Not only was he the most wanted bachelor, but he was also the most wanted paranormal.

I watched as Elsa whirled around and continued going through the clothes that hung in my closet, with purpose. "Should I ask him about the blonde?"

"No," chorused Elsa and Jade, making me jerk.

"But—"

"Are you crazy? Do you want to ruin things before they even start?" Elsa stuck her head out from my closet again. One of my hangers was sticking out of her hair, but I wasn't about to interrupt her. "Not on the first date. Look, even if he was dating her, that's his business. That was before you agreed to go on a date with him. So why torture him about that? Trust me. Don't go there. Just see where things lead. After tonight, I'm sure that's the last you'll ever see of that mystery blonde."

I wasn't sure about that. Something in the way they were looking at each other. Call it my witchy instincts, but I had a feeling I'd see her again.

"And he cooked for you," said Jade, beaming. She let out a sigh. "I've never had a man cook for me. That says a lot."

"Jade's right," agreed Elsa. "You said he made a special soup from scratch just for you."

"From *scratch*," repeated Jade, her eyes wide like that was the key ingredient here.

"Men just don't whip up food for women they don't care about," said Elsa, and she tapped her nose with her finger like that was supposed to mean something to me.

"Right." Maybe they were right, but Valen's predisposition was that he took care of others. I had a feeling if Jade or Elsa had been sitting at his kitchen island earlier, he would have made that soup for them too. Yeah, he was that kind of man.

Jade pulled a pair of yellow earphones from her

vintage yellow Sony Walkman that hung from her jeans' waistband. She positioned the earphones over her head, pressed down the play button on her Walkman, and bobbed her head at whatever music she was listening to. She caught me smiling at her through the reflection of the mirror.

"Best of Journey!" she yelled, oblivious to how loud her voice was.

I laughed, hearing Elsa's muffled chuckle from the closet. "You think Jimmy knows how she feels?" I asked Elsa. I chose this moment to ask the question I'd been meaning to ask, knowing Jade couldn't hear me.

"I'm not sure." Elsa's face was set in a frown as she stared down at my leather knee-high boots. "Seeing him as a man takes some getting used to. We were all so used to him as a toy dog. It's different now. But if he doesn't know, he's an idiot. Everyone with a brain can see the woman is in love with him."

I snorted and looked at Jade, who was now twirling on the spot, her lips moving to whatever song was playing in her ears. I loved her free spirit and her happy attitude. I needed some of that in my life.

I sighed and rubbed my sweaty palms on my thighs. "I haven't been on a date in over fifteen years. I'll probably end up just talking about work or the weather. Something un-date like."

My heart kept skipping whenever I thought of Valen and me sitting across from each other at his restaurant, the lights dim and romantic. I didn't like that he was making me nervous. Why the hell did I put myself in this position?

I grabbed my phone. The screen said 6:47. "I've got about thirteen minutes to get ready." I'd already done my makeup, which consisted a bit of black liner over my upper and lower lids along with a bit of lip gloss. I didn't need blush. My face was red enough without adding more. My hair was down in soft waves around my shoulders.

"Plenty of time," said Elsa, pulling out a pair of dark jeans. She observed them and then folded them over her left arm and kept going through my closet.

Jade pulled out her yellow earphones and looped them around her neck. "Don't forget to wear sexy undies," she said, her eyebrows high.

I shook my head. "Yeah. I don't think so. Just dinner. That's it."

Jade's eyes rounded. "Sure. Whatever you say."

Part of me felt like I should just call him and cancel. Valen was a work colleague, and you should never mix relationships with work. Someone always got hurt, and the work relationship suffered. I didn't want to risk my job. I loved where I lived, and my new friends were like family. I didn't want to lose them either.

"Maybe I should just cancel," I said. My friends were more important to me than any man—even sexy man-beasts—and the idea of losing them scared me.

"Don't be a coward. You're going," ordered Elsa.

Jade snorted but sobered up at what she saw on

my face. She came to join me on the side of the bed, and I could hear the faint music from her earphones around her neck. "Why are you so worried? Valen's a great guy."

"I'm sure he is. But if… whatever this is, doesn't work out… I don't want things to be awkward. We have to work together. And he lives next door."

Jade patted my hand. "Valen is a gentleman. I'm sure he can handle whatever happens." Her face went serious. "Any news on those dead vampires?"

"Nothing I haven't told you. Don't worry. Whatever killed them isn't contagious." I could tell she was still thinking about it.

"And you still don't know who they are?" Jade's blue eyes were filled with sorrow. "I can't imagine dying without anyone knowing who you were."

"It's rough. Hopefully, with more investigation, we'll find out who they are. Doesn't seem right to bury them in unmarked graves." I thought of all those vampires. "I was really hoping the autopsy would have revealed something. Now, we're still in the dark."

Jade fumbled with her fingers on her lap. "You think there'll be more. Don't you?"

I looked at her. "If I said no, I'd be lying. This is someone's twisted idea. Their sick joke. Why they're doing it? I don't know. These victims were robbed of their inherent paranormal energies."

"Do you think that's what killed them?"

"It makes sense. But why didn't the autopsy say so? And why did they die all at once?" The memory of all those vampires suddenly keeling over was still fresh in my mind, and it would probably haunt me for a good while.

Jade shifted on my bed. "You know, they could be from out of town. You said there were no missing persons in our community. What if they're not from here?"

I nodded. "Yeah. I hadn't thought of that. I'll check with the other Merlin groups. I have pictures of the three I found behind the dumpster. I'll start with that."

Jade and I were silent after that. The only sounds came from my closet, as hangers were being dragged along the metal pole.

Finally, Elsa came out of my closet looking flushed. The same pair of dark jeans hung from her left arm. "You've got nothing in here. How's that possible?"

"I told you. I've got nothing to wear. I should just go naked," I added with a laugh.

Elsa didn't laugh. The witch's face was pinched as she moved over to my bed and dropped the jeans on my lap. "Do you have a black cami?"

I nodded. "Yes."

"Okay then." Elsa sighed. "Bring out the slut blouse."

CHAPTER 11

My phone read 7:06 by the time I pulled open the restaurant doors and walked in. So I was a little late. Six minutes wouldn't kill the guy. I was late because I had to wait for Elsa to bring me a black leather clutch since my shoulder bag was a "horrible idea," according to her.

So with her clutch, a nice pair of black kitten heels borrowed from Jade—oddly, we wore the same size of shoes even though I was significantly taller—and the slut blouse that was not so slutty with a nice cami covering the girls, I thought I looked pretty good. Causal chic or whatever it was called. My dress code was I usually went with whatever was clean.

The restaurant door clicked behind me, and I strolled into the lobby. The same hostess, the one who *loved* me, had her face set into a glare as I walked past her, searching for Valen. The restaurant was packed. I couldn't see an empty seat in the whole place. I also couldn't see Valen. Shit. Did he leave because I was a few minutes late?

"The restaurant is full," said the hostess whose name I still couldn't remember, not that I cared to. She smiled at me, her eyes rolling over me slowly like she wasn't sure if she liked what I was wearing. "You can try maybe one of the human restaurants and see if they'll let you in."

"Good one," I said, suddenly feeling awkward holding a clutch and secretly wishing I had my shoulder bag with me.

"Leana."

I spun at the sound of my name to find Valen walking over.

Va-va-voom!

The light reflected off his sun-kissed skin, and his tall frame was covered in an expensive-looking, dark-gray shirt and snug black pants, showing off his fantastic physique. His dark locks were pulled into a low ponytail. In the dim light, his rugged beauty was startling, like an ageless elven king—graceful, menacing, and ruthless.

Why he wanted to date me was a mystery. I was seriously rethinking my ordinary jeans. Maybe I should have taken Jade up on her taffeta dress? Yeah, maybe not. The key point here was comfort, and I was comfortable in my jeans, albeit not as fancy.

"You look beautiful," he purred. Or did I purr? Hard to tell.

My guts were doing a jig. "Thank you." I tried to

pry my lips open to tell him how amazing he looked, but they seemed to be superglued together.

"This way." The giant gestured and took my hand, gently leading me into the sea of tables. My skin tingled at his rough, calloused hand. His grip, though gentle, was just hard enough.

I looked over my shoulder and gave that uptight hostess, with a stick up her ass, my best smile. I really shouldn't have, but it was so damn fun. And totally worth it by the look of pure hatred with a smidgen of jealousy I recognized flashing behind those eyes.

I let Valen pull me with him as he led me across the restaurant to the front end, where the tall windows lined the entire front of the restaurant. A table with an arrangement of every color rose you could think of sat empty. I glanced around. The other tables didn't have flowers, just this one.

It was also, I noticed, pushed farther back from the other tables to give it more privacy.

Valen let me go and pulled out a chair for me. Yeah, ladies. He was *that* kind of man.

Smiling like a fool, I sat down and enjoyed the feeling of the giant pushing in my chair for me.

My eyes stared at his fine ass as he made his way around the table and sat in the chair directly in front of me. My eyes drifted down to his chest, where his muscles were screaming to be let out of the confining fabric, and I was willing to oblige them. Was this the hormones talking? I was acting like a schoolgirl with a crush, not a mature woman.

His dark eyes sparkled. "You should let your hair down more often. You look gorgeous."

My instant flush-o-meter soared to my face. Rolls of heat spiraled over me like a hot flash. "Enough with the compliments," I teased, though I didn't want him to stop. "But you do clean up real nice." There. I said it.

Valen's handsome face creased into a smile. "I try."

Cue in another hot flash. Hell, at this rate, I would melt before the food arrived.

Just then a male waiter with a shaved head bumped his thigh against our table. In his hands was a bottle of red wine. "Is this the wine you requested, boss?"

"Boss?" I snorted and then immediately regretted it. But Valen's smile only blossomed over his entire face. It was really hard not to like this guy.

"It is," Valen answered. The waiter poured some into his wineglass, waiting patiently for him to taste it.

After Valen gave the waiter a nod, he poured some into my glass and then proceeded to fill Valen's. I could feel the giant's eyes on me, but I pretended not to notice as I reached out, grabbed my wineglass, and took a sip.

Something was incredibly intimate about us having dinner together and him being so close.

"I'll be back with the entrées," said the waiter before he took off, winding his way through the tables and chairs.

"Cheers, Leana," said the giant, his voice low and sultry. He lifted his glass and held it over to me.

Shit. I'd already taken a sip. Nice one. My heart raced. I was nervous and felt like every nerve ending in my body pulsed into a burn. I wasn't exactly sure why I was nervous, though.

"Cheers," I said and gently tapped my glass to his. I took another sip, letting the fruity flavors sink into my taste buds. "Very good wine. Probably costs more than I make in a month."

A tiny smile crept along his full lips. "Not that much."

I frowned. "You know how much I make in a month?" I wasn't sure how I felt about that.

Valen set his wineglass down. "Basil mentioned it to me when he was having a bit of a meltdown. Does that bother you?"

I thought about it. "No. But now you need to tell me how much profit a year this place makes," I smiled, teasing. "You know. So that we're even."

Valen matched my smile. A shiver of delight went through me. He licked his lips, sending a wave of heat right to my core and pulling my stomach into knots of nerves.

"I think we'll be even when I see you naked," said the giant.

Holy shit.

A rush of heat flared from my middle to my face at the intensity of his eyes. He wasn't joking, either, and it sent butterflies in a boxing match in my belly.

Yes, I'd seen him naked many times when he

changed into his giant form. And yes, I looked, a lot. I couldn't help it. Any warm-blooded female would.

"Well," I said, my heart thumping in my chest. "Let's see how this evening goes first." I could play this game too. It wasn't like I was *planning* on having sex with the giant later, but I was totally thinking about it. "You could think about having some custom shorts or something to wear… you know… when you change."

Valen's eyes crinkled in amusement. "Being naked doesn't bother me."

"I've noticed."

"It's just skin."

"Lots and lots of skin."

"When I'm out patrolling the streets at night, humans can't see me." He shrugged and leaned back. "It's like I'm not even there."

"But there's still a huge, naked man walking around," I said. "Admit it. You're a nudist."

Valen laughed hard this time, and I got a glimpse of that part of him that wasn't so serious, grumpy, or sad. It was wonderful to watch.

I took another sip of wine, enjoying my little victory. I was making this hot guy laugh. Nothing was better than that.

I turned my head and found the hostess watching us, especially me. Her face was a mask of hatred. Okay, that was definitely better.

"If it'll make you feel better, I can have some clothes made for me," said Valen.

I stared at the giant, wondering why he cared so much about how I felt. This date, or whatever it was, had all the elements of something more serious in the long run. But I was confused, mainly about the blonde I'd seen with him.

He wasn't giving off player vibes. His focus was solely on me. His eyes never wandered. I quickly glanced around and saw at least five women openly staring at him with lust in their eyes. They most probably knew what he was and were wondering what it must be like to get into bed with a giant.

Valen was a natural protector, a mighty powerful one, especially for those he cared for. It was an extremely attractive quality. What woman didn't desire a robust and protective type? It was a total turn-on, and I could understand the desire in those women's eyes.

The truth was, Valen could have any of these women if he wanted to. But either he didn't notice, or he didn't care. I'll admit. That felt nice, more than nice.

But I couldn't ignore the fact that I barely knew this man. I had to be careful and had to protect my heart. And although I really, really, really wanted to ask about the blonde, I forced myself not to.

"I'll leave that to you," I said instead.

Valen pulled his handsome face into a grin. "Tell me about yourself. What was your life like before you moved to New York City."

I took a larger-than-necessary gulp of wine and

swallowed. "My mother and I lived in my grand-mother's house. And after my grandma died, it was just Mom and me for a long time." I sighed. The memory of my mother's passing was still an ache inside. "Then my mother got sick. After she died, I was a mess for about a year. I lost twenty-five pounds. I wasn't eating and drank too much. Lost my hair. I couldn't live in that house anymore. So I sold it and then I met Martin. I was still a mess. But back then, he was kinder. And I needed that. The rest, well, the rest, you know. The bastard tried to kill me."

Valen cocked a brow. "Because you broke his penis."

I laughed into my wineglass. "Good times."

A deep chuckle rumbled through Valen. "That's what I like about you," said the giant, making my pulse race. "You're real. You're not afraid of anything or anyone. You don't take bullshit. You're exactly what I see across from me."

"A middle-aged, divorced witch?"

"A badass witch," answered Valen. "The fact that you're beautiful is just icing on the cake."

Yup. I was purring now. "If you think flirting with me will get me in bed with you, you're dead wrong." Yes. It was working!

A slip of teeth showed through Valen's lips. "I'm just saying how it is. I like a headstrong woman who knows what she wants. It's sexy as hell." He stared at me. "If it'll get you in my bed, I'm all for it."

Ask him about the blonde! Ask him about the blonde!

"Let's see how this date—dinner goes first. We might hate each other after."

Valen gave me a look that said that would never happen. "That won't happen."

"You never know. After a few more dates and sleepovers, when we let our true selves out, we might end up despising each other."

Valen leaned forward and surprised me when he took my hand. "You've seen me at my worst. The very first time I laid eyes on you, I was a bastard. Yet. Here you are."

"Here I am." I was very aware of his touch, his rough, calloused thumb rubbing my hand, and it sent a spike of desire through me.

Valen's smile was sly, and it went right to my gut and tightened. "You could have said no to tonight."

"I could have," I answered, my voice tight with desire. He kept rubbing my hand, and I could barely think. It didn't help that I hadn't been with a man in a very long time. My hormones were in overdrive.

A smile hovered over his features, and his gaze became more intent. A thick stubble peppered his face, black and sexy. My gaze slid down to his broad chest, muscles bulging from his fitted gray shirt.

I could have pulled my hand away, but I didn't. I let him caress it as I stared into those deep, dark eyes of his, trying to peel away some of the complex layers and get a peek of the softer, more vulnerable man.

But I also let him because it felt freaking amazing.

"Here we are." The same bald waiter arrived with

plates topped with a variety of foods, and I pulled my hand away from Valen's, my heart hammering at what had just transpired between us. He was watching me with a look that made my breath catch in my throat.

The sexy-as-sin giant. The big, strong type who'd save you from killer ex-husbands and demons. It hit me like a warm wave, ready to sweep me away. Damn.

I flicked my eyes back to the waiter as he settled the two plates, gave a nod to his boss, and then was gone again.

Food. Good. This would be a welcomed distraction to the hot, very hot attraction we'd had going just a few moments ago.

"What's all this?" I asked, knowing Valen had said he'd have something prepared for us, for me.

He pointed to the plates. "Melted calumet cheese, caramel with an emulsion of dried tomatoes and pecans. I hope you like it."

I leaned forward and took a sniff. "If it tastes as good as it smells, I might have to lick my plate."

His laugh echoed around us. "I'd like to see that."

I grabbed my fork and pointed it at him. "You just might."

At first, I tried not to moan whenever my fork reached my mouth, mainly because people were watching. But after the second mouthful, I let it all out.

"Oh, my God, this is good," I moaned, enjoying

the blasts of caramel and cheese in my mouth. "You should package it up and sell it."

Valen flashed me his teeth as he took a sip of wine. "Glad you like it."

"Like it? If I could make love to it, I would."

In my twenties, with all those insecurities that came when you were younger, I would have been embarrassed to eat in front of him, concerned about how I chewed and whether I'd get some food stuck between my teeth. At forty-one, I couldn't care less. I wouldn't let a meal this good go to waste. I'd eat it. I'd eat it all.

We spent the rest of the evening laughing, talking, and enjoying each other's company. I felt at ease and comfortable, something I had never felt before with a man, not even Martin. Especially Martin. I felt myself relax, knowing I could tell him anything and he wouldn't judge me. I made sure not to talk about the blonde, though the thought did creep up on me more than once.

Before I knew it, he was walking me back to the hotel. He held the door open for me, and I walked in, seeing the hotel buzzing with guests enjoying Casino Week.

My skin tingled at his closeness, my mind fluttering with ways of how or if I should ask him back to my place. I'd have to figure out how to lock the door. Shit. What if the gang was there? No way could I have some private time alone with the giant.

"Good night, Leana," said Valen, and I turned as he took my hand. "I had a lovely time."

I smiled. "Me too." My insides fluttered in disappointment.

Valen dipped his head and kissed me. The slip of his tongue over my bottom lip sent bolts of ripples across my skin until heat pooled into my middle. He pulled back, his eyes tracing my lips. He looked at me and smiled, a glimmer of desire in his eyes, and then he walked away.

The kiss had been quick, but it screamed with need and desire, making my knees almost buckle.

I let out a breath and made my way toward the elevator across the lobby. I'd need a cold shower after that.

"You've got a message," called a voice. I turned to see Errol behind the front desk, his face pinched in a mask of derision while holding out a small message card.

I walked over to the front desk. "I've never gotten a message before."

"I don't care." Errol dropped the message on the counter and moved away.

"Who's it from?"

The concierge sighed and turned around. "I don't know. It was a phone message. No name. Just wanted to leave a message. He sounded nervous. Now, go away."

"Always a pleasure, you lizard *bastard*," I mumbled the last bit.

My insides twisted. What if this was a message from the Gray Council's investigator? Curious, I took the message card and inspected it:

Go to 501 West 16th Street.
Look inside the warehouse, and you will find what you're
looking for.

Okay. Definitely not from the Gray Council.
Now, I was *really* curious.

CHAPTER 12

I sat in the front passenger seat of Valen's Range Rover Sport, the message card in my hands as I stared at the darkened street before us.

"How much farther?" came Julian's voice from the back seat.

I leaned over and stared at the SUV's built-in GPS screen. "Says about six minutes, and we'll be there."

The sound of leather pulling reached me. "I wonder who left that message," pondered Jade. "It almost sounded like a riddle. Or it could be a song? What do you think it means?"

"We'll know when we get there," came Elsa's voice right behind me.

My gut told me it had to do with the dead paranormals. It was the only crazy thing that was happening right now. I was looking for answers, and whoever had left that message card knew it. I just hoped I was right.

After receiving the message, I went up to my

apartment, grabbed my shoulder bag and jacket, pulled on some flat boots, and searched for the gang. I'd found Elsa and Jade at the slot machines and Julian in the elevator with a gorgeous redhead, on my way down. After I'd filled them in, I called Valen.

"Miss me already," the giant had said on the first ring.

"You wish," I laughed. "Listen. I got this message just now." Once I'd read the message to him and expressed how I felt that it was somehow connected to the paranormal deaths, the giant had said, "Stay there. I'm coming to get you. We'll go together."

Tonight was a clear night, and although I could handle myself, having the giant with me was a bonus. Not to mention the three other witches. We'd face whatever this was together.

"You think it has something to do with the dumpster deaths and the other vampires?" came Julian's voice.

"Really?" expressed Jade, the surprise high in her tone. "How?"

I turned in my seat to face them better. "I do. Just a feeling. But don't you think it's weird that after I found those dead paranormals, and then the vampires last night, I get this message? I don't believe in coincidences. I think they're connected."

"It could also be a trap," said Valen. "If they've been watching you for a while, they'd know you'd come to investigate. It's how you operate."

I frowned. "Watching me?" I didn't like the sound of that. Following a giant patrolling the streets at night was one thing, but having some creepy stalker spying on me gave me the willies.

Elsa reached out and wrapped her hands around my car seat's headrest. "You think someone wants to hurt Leana?"

"Who wants to hurt Leana?" asked Jade. Her voice hitched, sounding paranoid.

Valen's jaw clenched. "I don't know, but receiving a message like that can't be good news. They didn't leave a name. They gave an address and said to go there. Sounds like a trap."

Nerves pulled my insides tight. I hadn't thought of that. "Well, we'll soon find out." I'd had my share of enemies over the years. I'd put a lot of paranormal "baddies" in jail, but they were still in prison, as far as I knew.

Elsa leaned back into her seat, her hands wrapped around her locket. "I'm glad you told us. I would have been very upset if you'd gone in alone."

I grinned. "I know. It's why I told you." My heart warmed at the feeling that I had these witches looking out for me. Only a few weeks ago, the idea of working with others would have had me walking away from jobs. Now, it felt strangely comforting that they were with me. And that went for Valen too.

"Did Errol say where it came from?" asked Jade. "Maybe he knows who sent it."

I shook my head. "I asked him. He said it came in by phone, and the person wouldn't leave their name. They just wanted to leave a message. He said the voice sounded nervous, and it was male."

Jade pursed her lips, toying with the white plastic bracelets over her wrist. "Hmmm. That is weird. But I'm surprised you got all that from Errol. He's a jerk. Never wants to help with anything if it's not in his job description."

"I had to threaten him to get that much." I smiled, remembering how round his eyes got when I told him I would dump a truckload of cockroaches in the lobby if he didn't give me more information. The actual cockroaches didn't scare him but knowing he wouldn't be able to control himself and would feast on the insects in front of everyone. We all had our demons.

"So," began Elsa, a smile to her tone, "how did the date go?"

Oh. Hell. No.

"We all know you two went on a date," continued the witch. "The entire hotel knows. And we"—she pointed to herself and then to Julian and Jade —"would like to know how it went. So?"

I clamped my mouth shut, and when I cast my gaze over a smiling Valen, a flush crawled up my face. "It went well," I said after a moment. Looked like I was going to have to do the talking.

Julian snorted. "It went *well*? Doing your taxes goes *well*, not a date. Either you knew it sucked after ten seconds and left early, or you stayed for dessert. Looks like you both stayed for dessert," he added with a sneer.

"We're going to find out later, might as well tell us," pressed Jade.

Valen was still smiling as I answered. "It was very nice. The food was perfect. The wine was excellent and the company too." I stared at Valen. "Care to add anything?"

The giant shook his head. "No. You're doing fine."

Elsa, Jade, and Julian all started laughing.

I glowered at them. "Let's talk about something else." I didn't want to talk about my date with Valen, not when I hadn't even had time to think about it myself.

I stared at the GPS. "Should be right there on your left."

The address 501 West 16th Street came into view. It was a giant wall of aluminum boxes—a warehouse. Rust stained the front and sides of the building, making it look like the metal was diseased. There were no windows as far as I could tell.

Valen pulled into the driveway, parked, and we all got out.

Julian walked over and faced the building. "Looks deserted. No lights on from inside."

"It's almost eleven at night," said Elsa, like that explained everything.

Valen walked to the back of his Range Rover and popped the trunk. He yanked out a flashlight from a black duffel bag, tested it, and handed it to me. "Here."

I took the flashlight. "Thanks. What about you? Do giants have night vision?" Vampires did, and so did most of the shifters and weres, so why not giants?

Shadows hid most of his face, though I could see a smirk. "We have better eyesight than most, but not like vampires or other shifters who can see well in the dark." He lifted another flashlight from his bag. "Better come prepared." He handed it over to Elsa, who waved a dismissive hand at him.

"Don't need it." Rummaging through her own bag, she pulled out a small globe the size of an apple —a witch light. I'd seen other witches use them before, though I'd never used one myself. I'd always wished I could do some elemental magic to have a witch light of my own.

Elsa held out her hand and whispered, "Da mihi lux." *Give me light.*

The sphere pulsated against the palm of her hand, and then a light shone through it as though she were holding an LED bulb. The globe soared into the air above her, illuminating the area in a soft yellow glow.

"Show-off," muttered Jade, though she had a huge smile on her face.

I checked the address one last time. "Well, this *is* the place," I said and stuffed the message card into my jeans pocket. "Let's see if the doors are locked."

"If they are, I have a potion for that." Julian strolled next to me, his long duster coat billowing around him as he moved. His hands rested in his jacket pockets, which contained potions and poisons.

"Could be warded and cursed," I said, remembering the sorceress Auria's secret entrance below the bridge. She'd been furious that I had broken through her curse, but even more so that I took her precious book of curses. It made me smile.

Together, we headed for double metal doors, what I assumed was the front entrance. One of the doors was propped open a crack as a silent invitation or a trap, like Valen suggested.

"It's open," I told them, turning around and seeing the worry etched on all their faces.

"I don't like this." Jade shifted on the spot, traces of anxiety on her face and fear in her eyes. "Who would leave it open like that?"

Good question. "I don't know. But it doesn't feel right." I reached out to my starlight. Energy hissed against my skin as the stars' power tingled over me. Hundreds of brilliant white, miniature globes flew out of my hand and hit the double metal doors, wrapping them in a curtain of white light. I waited as the starlights moved around the doors, expecting to feel the familiar cold pricks of a curse, but I felt nothing.

I let my arms fall. The starlights shimmered and then dissolved. "I'm not getting any ward vibes. No curses either."

"I'm not sensing the energies of wards here," commented Elsa as she held out her hands over the doors, like she was warming herself over a campfire.

I sighed. "Well. Looks like someone left it open for us."

Valen's frown and the narrowing of his eyes were

truly scary. He clearly still thought this was a trap, and he probably wasn't wrong. But we'd come all this way. I wanted to know why someone wanted me to come here to see something. I wanted to know what that was.

"Let's go." I pushed on one of the heavy metal doors, and it swung easily to the side with a loud screech. "Let's see what this is all about. Shall we?" I said and walked in.

Valen was at my side in a beat. "Careful. Like I said, we don't know if this is a trap."

I nodded and flicked my flashlight forward, but I didn't need to. Elsa's witch light flew in and hovered above us, casting a soft glow and giving us a great deal of illumination. I still kept the flashlight on anyway, though, for the dark corners.

Still, I wasn't an idiot. Part of me agreed with Valen that this whole thing could well be a trap. I didn't want my friends or Valen hurt. We didn't know what we were up against, and sometimes that was worse.

The warehouse's interior was just as gloomy and stale as the exterior, reeking of disinfectant, like you'd smell at a hospital, with an underlying hint of something acrid like vinegar or blood. With the witch light dancing above us, I could make out racks that reached the ceiling stacked with boxes and what looked like wood crates, with plywood sides warped by moisture and wear.

"Smells disgusting," said Jade as she covered her

nose. "Like a morgue that forgot to turn on the refrigeration switch."

She wasn't wrong. Something smelled ripe in this place.

My eyes flicked over to Valen. His features were set hard, and I could tell by the muscles popping along his shoulders and neck that he was just about to beast-out into his giant alter ego, or whatever it was called.

"Demons?" suggested Elsa.

I pulled on my starlight again, enough to send out my senses. A familiar energy prickled along my skin, the combination of cold-and-warm hum of magic. Magic was here—lots of it.

But something else, something more substantial that I couldn't decipher, was also lingering. It had the typical pulses of magic but was different, like the magical properties had been altered.

"I'm not getting any demon vibes," I said as I walked forward. "But something's here. Something with powerful magic."

"Yeah." Julian nodded. "I feel it too."

"Me too," answered Jade, and Elsa gave a nod.

We continued forward in silence, our boots clattering on the cement floor. I had no idea what to expect or what we would find, apart from mountains of crates. But someone had sent me here for a reason. Could be a trap. Could be anything, really.

We kept moving. My heart was a drum, pounding to a wild rhythm I couldn't stop. Valen stood next to me, a silent, powerful presence.

I couldn't see very well into the rest of the building because of the racks of giant crates, but whispers of energy rolled from the shadows around me. An entrance to another room came into view, and we made for it.

Just as we crept into the large workroom, the energy hit me with a full-on blast.

It was roughly the size of the Twilight Hotel lobby, teeming with computers, filing cabinets, and metal tables topped with microscopes and glass vials. I felt like I'd just stepped into a B-rated science fiction movie where mad scientists were manufacturing human and alien babies. The space looked and felt evil, wrong, and unnatural, as though whatever was happening here shouldn't be happening at all.

I halted as my eyes settled on rows of giant aquarium-like tanks. However, the tanks weren't what had me freezing in place but the people floating inside them. Tubes and wires wound from areas hooked to their naked bodies and connected to machines next to the tanks.

"What in the name of the goddess is this?" cursed Julian.

I rushed forward to the closest tank, feeling the constant thrum of magic and seeing a male floating inside. His eyes were closed. "The tanks are spelled." I stared at the tube of dark red liquid being pumped into him like a dialysis machine, but those machines didn't have magic coursing through them. These did.

"They're alive," came Valen's voice next to one of the machines. "They all have constant heartbeats."

"I don't get it. Is this a clinic?" Jade looked around. "Are they being treated for something? And why here?"

"Good question. They're being kept alive for a reason." I went to grab a file I saw resting on one of the machines when a whimper caught my attention.

I turned to my left, and my breath exploded out of me.

There, in a metal cage, was a person. No, not just one, but three terrified-looking people.

They sat, hunched in a cage fit for a large dog, their wrists and feet bound with rope. A piece of duct tape was strewn across their mouths, wet with tears. One of them, a female, met my eyes, and my chest clenched at the fear I saw.

I rushed over to the cage. "What the hell is going on here?" Anger soared as I looked for the door to the cage and found a lock. "Motherfu—"

"I got it." Julian hauled me back as he poured yellow liquid over the lock. It sizzled as the potion ate away at the metal like acid. The smell of copper filled my nose. The rattling of metal echoed around us as Julian pulled the door open.

"Thanks." I reached in and, with Julian's help, hauled out the female first, followed by the two males. As soon as we cut away their bonds and removed the duct tape, I knew something was off.

"Oh, shit," I said, staring at their scared faces. "They're human."

"What?" Valen stood next to me, his eyes inspecting the three *very* human captives. The female shrank away from Valen, and so did one of the men. I didn't blame them. The guy was still large and imposing, even in his smaller human shape.

Elsa pulled what looked like candy from her bag and offered it to them. "Here. Take this. It'll make you feel better."

The three humans huddled together and cringed from Elsa, like she was about to poison them.

She turned to look at me. "This is very odd. What were they doing in those cages?"

These were all excellent questions that needed answering. "Who did this to you?" I asked them in my most gentle voice, though a bit hurried. "Who brought you here?" I waited for a moment or two, searching their frightened faces, but I didn't think they were going to answer me.

Jade wrapped her arms around herself, staring at the tanks. "What's going on here? What the hell is this place?"

My eyes flashed to the tanks, and then I was moving. Yanking up my jacket's sleeve, I shoved my hand into the tank with a suspended female, trying not to think of what was in the water, and touched her arm. Then I moved to the front of the tank and carefully pulled back her top lip to reveal sharp canines.

I yanked it back, a cold sort of panic rushing through me.

Valen was right there, looking down at me, his eyes narrowing dangerously. "What is it? What did you find?"

I waited to have all my friends listening before I said, "She's human. I'm willing to bet every single person in those tanks is human."

Jade was shaking her head. "But I don't understand. I can sense magic here. We all can."

I shared a look with Valen. "I think… no… I *know* what's happening here. It's all starting to make sense."

"Please tell us before I have a heart attack," said Elsa, glancing over at the huddled humans with pity in her eyes.

Bile rose in my throat at what I was about to say. "These humans are being transformed into paranormals."

My friends all just stared at me like I was nuts.

"Look around you," I continued. "I'm willing to bet that blood in there," I said, pointing to the contraption that reminded me of a dialysis machine, "is paranormal blood. They're making paranormals out of humans."

"It's not that simple." Julian examined the machine I'd pointed to. "You can't just pump in some of our blood, and then you become a paranormal. It's not how it works."

"I have to agree with Julian," said Elsa. "I've never heard of humans being turned this way. Well, not if you count them being bitten by a rogue vampire or werewolf. Even then, it doesn't always take. It usually ends up with the human dying."

"I know," I answered. "But maybe all you need is a powerful spell and magic to complete the transformation. I feel it. You all can feel it. There's a spell here attached to this equipment, or maybe it's in the blood." Yeah, definitely in the blood.

Elsa's face was wrinkled in pity and disgust. "Goddess, help us all, if that's true."

I looked at Valen. He was quiet, his features carefully guarded. But I could tell by the stiffness of his posture he was upset. We all were.

"It gets worse," I said, my eyes tracing over the three terrified humans who looked like they were about to bolt any minute. I wouldn't blame them. They'd been privy to our conversation this whole time, which wasn't allowed. I'd worry about that later.

Jade rubbed her hands over her arms. "What'd you mean?"

My heart pounded as I was filled with dread and horror. "It means all those vampires we fought and those people I found near the dumpster… were human. That's why I never felt any paranormal vibes," I said as the realization hit me. "Because they were never paranormals to begin with. They were humans." I looked at my friends' shocked faces and said, "Humans that came from this place."

CHAPTER 13

Including the three terrified humans we'd freed, another fifteen were floating in the tanks being carefully carried out by the Gray Council's healers and placed on mats. I watched as the tenth human male was lifted out of his tank, the tubes and wires still attached to him. The healers, all dressed in white lab coats, proceeded to pull the wires and tubes from him.

Another group of officers dressed in gray uniforms—the Gray Council's tactical security, the equivalent of their police squad—watched from the doorway. I didn't care for them. They were arrogant and considered themselves above any laws but their own, so I stayed the hell away from them.

The warehouse lights were on now. No point in trying to be inconspicuous anymore, so I had a good view of the interior and the horror that inhabited inside.

I flicked my eyes back to the man on the mat.

His skin had a grayish tint to it and was wrinkled, like that of a newborn. The hum of magic pulsed in the air as the healers mumbled some spells. The man's eyes flicked open for a second, and then they fluttered back closed. He looked like he was sleeping.

The healers were eerily silent as they worked like a group of monks after taking a vow of silence.

The sound of wheels pulled my head around to see another healer pushing a gurney toward the human man. Together, the two healers lifted the man and placed him on the gurney. Then he was hauled away out the door to a waiting van.

"Where are you taking them?" I asked the closest healer, a female about my age.

"Where they tell us to take them," she answered, her eyes flicking over to the gray officers. And then, before I could ask her more questions, she moved to the next waiting tank.

"The three humans are asleep now." Elsa and Jade came to join me.

I let out a breath. "Good. That's good. What about what they saw and heard? It's enough to traumatize them for life."

"The healers performed a very powerful memory charm on them," answered the older witch. "They won't remember a thing. Thank the goddess."

"Better that way." Jade let out a long sigh. "Some humans can go mad after witnessing something like this. It's too much too soon for them, especially since they've never had any dealings with the paranormal world, and they think we don't exist. Better to keep it that way."

"I agree." I looked over to see Valen and Julian both listening to a healer who was pointing to those weird dialysis machines. Valen's big, muscular arms were crossed over his chest, and he had that look in his eye that said I'm not sure if I like you or not.

Jade rubbed her eyes. "Well, I'm glad it's over."

I looked at Jade. "I don't think it's over. Yeah, we discovered their lab, but how do we know there's just one?"

Elsa's face paled. "You don't think there's more. Do you?"

I nodded. "I do. This was all carefully thought out and planned. It took time and effort. Probably months and years to come up with a spell to make the transition from human to paranormal work. There's no way this is over."

"But why? Why do this?" Jade's face was wrinkled in sorrow as another human was hauled out on a gurney.

I cast my gaze around the lab to the tanks and the equipment. "Looks like they're trying to make an army of some kind." As the words left my lips, they rang true.

"An army?" gasped Elsa, her voice loud enough to have Valen's head snapping in our direction.

I met the giant's eyes for a moment before pulling my attention back to Elsa. "That's what it feels like to me. Why wait years for a paranormal army when you can create one from humans?"

Jade made a disgusted sound in her throat. "Some people are just crazy."

"They are. But their army is faulty. It doesn't last. Whatever morphing is happening doesn't stay. It's not permanent. The vampires we fought last night all died when their time ran out. That's why I think this isn't over. We'll see a lot more of this before it's over because they're still perfecting the transformation. They'll keep doing it until their newly created paranormals stay alive."

This was Dr. Frankenstein stuff. But Jade was right. The person or persons who were doing this were clearly insane—psychopaths with no empathy or regard for human life.

"Why an army?" Elsa watched me for a moment.

I shrugged. "Armies are built to fight. Fight what? I don't know yet. But I'm going to find out."

Another gurney rolled our way with a female human resting on it. Dark blue veins were peeking through dangerously pale skin. She looked in worse condition than the others.

"Wait," I said and rushed over. "Will she live?"

The healer, a black male, looked at me. "I doubt it."

My mouth fell open. A heavy lump of dread formed in my chest. "No. Really? There's nothing you can do to help her?"

The healer shook his head, pursing his lips. "She's too far gone in the transformation. There's nothing we can do."

"Can't you reverse what was done to them?" My

throat was tight with emotions, and I didn't care to hide it.

"We can't," answered the healer. "There's no turning back from this."

"But…" I looked at the remaining tanks with a floating human. "That means all those humans you guys pulled out are going to die?"

The healer looked at me, and I could tell he was trying to be kind. "Yes. We'll keep them as comfortable as we can. But they *will* die. All of them. Only those who haven't been subjected to the blood mixture will live."

"The three in the cages," said Elsa, standing next to me. "Oh, dear. How horrible."

My hands fell to my sides, and my eyes burned with both sorrow and anger as I watched the healer haul away the woman.

"What's going on?"

I turned my head to find Valen walking over. "The healers say that none of the humans will survive." My anger soared, forming into something as hot, brutal, and destructive as I felt inside.

"I'm not surprised," answered the giant. "Our blood is poisonous to humans. And with the amount they were given, you can't flush it out with liquids or with more human blood."

I clenched my fingers into fists. "It shouldn't have happened in the first place. This is someone's sick, twisted idea of creating paranormals."

I felt a hand on my arm. "But you saved three." Elsa's face was filled with compassion. "Think of those lives. They would have died if we hadn't come here."

She was right, but I still felt like I'd failed these people. "Who left me that message? Who left the door unlocked?"

"Someone with conflicting emotions," said Jade, casting her gaze around. "Probably worked here."

I stared at Jade. "You're right. Someone who participated in this nightmare… suddenly got their conscience back." And they'd reached out anonymously. But still, without them, we'd never have discovered this lab and saved those three human lives.

"There must be records of those people working here. Something." I looked over the machines at some metal tables piled with papers and files. "Let's see if we can find anything. Clues. All we need is a name. One name, and we'd have a lead."

We all started to go through discarded papers and files, Valen included. But after about fifteen minutes, all I'd found were just notes and data about the human patients. There were no bills, no receipts of any kind. It seemed those responsible had been very careful to keep their identities hidden.

"Nothing is here," I said as I shut a filing cabinet.

Jade held a tiny slip of paper. "I've got a McDonald's receipt. Two Big Mac combo meals. No credit card number. They paid cash."

"How will we find who's responsible without a name or something?" asked Elsa.

"Maybe whoever sent me that message will send

me another one?" Yeah, I didn't think so, but if one person had a conscience, I was hoping others would too.

I turned and watched as the three surviving humans were hauled away on gurneys. Their terrified reaction to us was justified. They'd been kidnapped and forced to watch as other humans were subjected to this maniac transformation, knowing it would soon be done to them. If I'd been in that cage, I would probably have shit myself.

The only comfort I got from this cold, stale, nightmarish place was that they wouldn't remember a thing.

"Where are you taking those?" Julian's loud voice twisted me around.

The magical dialysis machines—not sure what else to call them—were being pushed and hauled out by the healers. He met my eyes across the room and lifted his arms over his head like he was making an offering to the goddess.

"What the hell?"

I rushed to meet them. "What's going on here?" I asked, putting myself in front of one of the machines, blocking their way. I was suddenly not thrilled about the healers taking the so-called magical dialysis machines. What if they could study them and reproduce the spells? Nope. Not going to happen.

Looks passed between the healers until one of them, a young male, answered. "We're following orders."

"Whose orders?" Valen was suddenly next to me,

his hands on his hips. And from the deep frown on his face and the expectant glare in his eye, he was envisioning an answer.

Fear flashed in the same healer's eyes as he peered at Valen through his eyelashes, no doubt the result of knowing who and what he was. "The Gray Council gave specific instructions to bring the devices back," he answered, speaking fast, like the faster he answered, the quicker he'd be away from Valen.

I frowned. "The Gray Council?" I looked over their heads and saw another group of healers shoving all the files in those ready-made cardboard boxes with handles. "And the files? All the data? That too?"

"Yes," answered the same healer. His gaze flicked to the gray officers still standing around the doorway. "We were ordered to bring everything back."

"Back? Back where?" I asked, my pulse suddenly racing.

The healer swallowed, his body tense, and I could tell he was wondering if we were about to kick his ass. Sweat beaded his forehead, and a large vein throbbed on the side of his temple. "Headquarters."

"To be destroyed. Right? Not to study?" I waited for an answer, but the healers weren't talking.

When no one answered after a few moments, Valen stepped forward. "Answer her. Now. Or I will *make* you." The muscles on his neck and shoulders bulged in a show of strength and dominance. Not sure how he did that, but it worked.

The healer looked like he might have crapped his pants before he answered. "I… I don't know. They didn't tell us," he said, his voice quivering. "But we were told to be careful with the equipment and not to leave anything behind. Absolutely everything was to be brought back." The whites of his eyes shone as they darted from me to Valen.

I looked at the giant, seeing the same distrustful expression that I was feeling. But it's not like we could stop them.

Reluctantly, I dragged my body away, stepped aside, and let them pass. "Fine. Go on."

I crossed my arms over my chest as I watched the last of the gurneys with humans being hauled out of the warehouse a little faster than before, thanks to Valen.

Elsa stood next to me. "You've got that frown again. What's going on? What is it?"

I clenched my jaw. "I don't have a good feeling about this. Them taking all this back. It doesn't feel right." No. It felt like the Gray Council was about to set up a lab of their own.

"What do you mean?" asked Jade. "Can't be worse than all this."

I met Jade's face. "The Gray Council should have asked to have the machines destroyed."

"Yeah. They should have torched the place with everything inside," said Julian, his hands in his coat pockets. I met his eyes, and I knew he'd come to the same conclusion I had.

"But they've been given specific instructions to bring everything back," I said.

"And?" Jade shrugged. She was shaking her head, anxiety written all over her face and in her eyes. "It's better that way. Right?"

I shook my head. "These machines, with the blood mixture and the magic still in them, is not better. It means they can study the magic and the procedure. It means they can replicate it."

I let this information sink in a little while, watching the silent, collective horror spreading across their expressions.

Elsa was the first to break the silence. "You don't think... No... I don't believe the Gray Council would do that."

"I do," said Julian, his face tight. "They would."

"I do too." I stared at the now-empty warehouse. The last evidence was carefully packed in boxes as the remaining healers walked in a line out the door, the gray officers following them out. Nothing was left of the lab we'd come across. "If they ever need to build an army for whatever reason... to fight demons or whatever... now they have the tools to do it. The procedure still needs work, but I came face-to-face with the result. It worked. What happened here, to these humans, is way too valuable to destroy."

"Maybe you're wrong," said Elsa, but the tone in her voice suggested otherwise, like she didn't believe it herself.

"Maybe," I answered. But my gut was pulling me

in the opposite direction. Nope. The Gray Council was keeping all of it for a reason.

Elsa sighed. "Well, it's late. I think we should all get some sleep and speak about it in the morning."

"It's already the morning," said Julian. "Like three-ish."

"Then, the afternoon," she snapped. "I don't know about you, but my old bones need rest, especially after a night like this. We'll reconvene tomorrow afternoon. I'm sure things will be clearer after we all get some sleep."

She wasn't wrong. We were all high on emotions and adrenaline. It had been a strange night. I'd gone on a date with Valen and even contemplated asking him back to my place. And now this. I needed to sleep for a few days just to get rid of this eerie dread that had stuck to me like a cold sweat since we arrived.

Because I was pretty sure things would get worse before they got better.

They always did.

CHAPTER 14

"What are you doing still in bed!" shouted a familiar voice. "Get up. Up! Up! Up!"

Even though my eyes were closed, I knew it was Elsa, and she sounded annoyingly chirpy and giddy.

"Go away. I'm still sleeping." I lifted my comforter over my head, trying to shut out her voice. My head pounded with a migraine, feeling like I had a massive hangover but without the fun of the actual drinking part.

I barely slept a wink. How could I when we still had a demented mad scientist or *scientists* on the loose in the city somewhere? I kept waking up in a sweat, my heart pounding in my chest as I kept replaying the scene over and over again. My stomach quailed at the thought of all those humans floating in those tanks back at the warehouse, the way the humans cringed from us in that cage, like we were monsters about to devour them. The notion of what these humans had endured had my guts rolling and my eyes burning every time. It had seemed their lives meant nothing. They were just vessels, their bodies used for a single purpose. To kill? That was still unclear.

I think I started to doze off just as Elsa barged into my room.

I felt a tug, and fresh air assaulted my face as my comforter disappeared. "Up," ordered Elsa. "You're not sleeping. You're having a conversation with me. That's not sleeping." She let out a sigh. "You're exactly like my son, Dylan. I could never get that one out of bed. Slept the day away."

I blinked the crust from my eyes. "You have a son? You never said?"

Elsa smiled proudly. "Yes. He lives in Scotland with his wife. Very much like his dad." She lost her smile. "Don't change the subject. Up you go. Come on. It's nearly six o'clock."

"What?" I reached out, fumbling with my side table, and grabbed my phone. "Damn. It felt more like noonish." Crap, I really had slept the day away. Well, not exactly slept. I only dozed off here and there. Not exactly a good sleep.

Concern flashed across her face. "I know. I don't think any of us slept much. All those poor souls. Dreadful what's happened to them."

I sat up, feeling a little dizzy. My eyes rolled over Elsa, noticing her wild, red hair was carefully pulled back with a barrette, though some loose strands framed her face. Red leather boots peeped from under her flowing, striped-green-and-orange skirt.

"You look nice. Why all dressed up?"

Before she could answer, Jade came gliding into my room on roller skates. She wore pink tights under a black sweaterdress with a white belt wrapped around her waist. Long faux-pearl necklaces looped around her neck and dangled past her stomach. Her hair was scrunched up into a high ponytail like she'd done it without a mirror.

"Oh, my God, she's still in bed?" laughed Jade as she did a pirouette, settled, and braced herself on my dresser. "We're going to be late."

I sat straighter. "Late for what?"

"Hurry up and shower." Elsa pulled me to my feet. My long T-shirt was the only thing I had on me. "The hotel's throwing a special dinner. Casino dinner for the guests and tenants."

"That means us," said Jade, pointing at herself as though I hadn't gotten that part.

"Drinks start at six," said Elsa, looking at my closet like a ghoul was hiding in there about to jump out. "Find whatever you have that's appropriate, and we'll meet you downstairs."

"Okay, okay." I waved at them. "Going to shower now."

Jade laughed and rolled out of my room. "Hurry up, old lady," she called over her head at Elsa.

"Call me that one more time, and you're going to lose a wheel," threatened Elsa.

With my phone in my hand, I rushed over to the bathroom and turned on the hot water in the shower. It took a while for the water to get hot, so I took the opportunity to scroll through my phone and see if Valen had written to me or called. Nope. Nothing.

Last night had been a weird night. First dinner with the giant and then off to the warehouse. Still, I thought he would have reached out.

I stared at his name on the screen, my finger hovering above it as I contemplated calling him. No. I was not going to be *that* woman. If he wanted to call me, he knew where to reach me.

After showering in record time, I pulled on a pair of black pants and a black sweater. I brushed my hair up in a messy ponytail, dabbed on a bit of black eyeliner and clear lip gloss, slipped on my ankle boots, grabbed my bag, and headed toward the elevator.

My stomach growled as I hit the lobby button. Dinner sounded really good at the moment. Food to heal the soul seemed about right. Hopefully, they'd have cheesecake for dessert. That would flush away all sorrows.

I hit the lobby, maneuvered around the gaming tables and slot machines, and made my way toward my favorite concierge in the history of concierges.

Errol looked up as I approached, and his face twisted in what I could only describe as a constipated look.

"What do you want?" he snapped, his upper lip twitching in a snarl, and I got a slip of his gray-forked tongue. I noticed he did that when he was upset or nervous.

I leaned over the counter and got as close as

possible to him. "Any more messages for me?" It was a long shot that the person would send me another, but it was the only lead I had. Their conscience led them to me once. Maybe it would do it again.

"No." He smiled, seeing my disappointment.

"You sure?"

"Positive."

I tapped the counter with my finger. "You're not holding out on me. Are you? Because that would be bad. Bad for you."

Errol gave me an annoyed stare. "I would rather slit my own throat. Now… go away."

I raised a brow. "Ooookay. Good talk."

I pushed off the counter and made my way to the dining room that only yesterday had been set up as a lunch buffet.

The tables were placed the same, but they had a more elegant feel with white tablecloths and short candles as centerpieces. White gleaming plates rested neatly over the tables, flanked by shining cutlery and expensive-looking white napkins with gold etching.

I let my gaze travel over the room, looking for that particular wall of a man with dark, fine eyes and never-ending muscles. But I didn't see the giant anywhere. Maybe he didn't want to experience the same thing he did yesterday when everyone ogled him like he'd just arrived from Mars.

I yanked out my phone and stared at the screen. No new calls. No messages. I struggled for a moment, my fingers itching to text him but figuring the man probably needed space, so I shoved my phone back in my bag.

"Pretty, isn't it?" Elsa joined me, a wineglass in her hand, and by the pink on her cheeks, I knew this wasn't her first.

"It is." I spotted Basil across from us, waving his hands at an annoyed Polly, who was holding on to a meat mallet like she was about to use it on the small witch. "That doesn't look good. Doesn't he know never to insult the chef? Insult the chef, and you'll have spit or worse in your food."

Elsa chuckled. "Basil is a fool. The tables are already designated with tiny name cards on each plate. That's our table." She pointed across the room to where Julian was standing. He picked up a small, white, rectangular folded piece of paper and stared at it.

Jade was already sitting at the table, her head down and her chin rubbing her chest. She looked like she wanted to slide down her chair and hide under the table.

"What's the matter with Jade? She looks sick." Her usual pink complexion had that unearthly pallor of those near death.

Elsa snorted. "She asked Jimmy out."

"Noooo." I pulled my eyes back on Jade. "Atta-girl." She might look like she was about to puke, but I was proud of her.

"Come. Let's sit. Everyone's starting to take their seats." Elsa pulled me with her as the dining room suddenly filled with guests and tenants, the sound of conversation and happy babble loud.

I saw Barb, the elderly witch, standing before a table. She grabbed the name cards, pulled them to her face, and smelled each of them. Okay. Not going there.

Elsa let me go, and I bumped my hip against the chair next to Jade. "I heard what you did," I said, wrapping my hands around the chair's backrest and doing my best not to laugh.

"I think I'm gonna be sick," muttered Jade, her face tight.

Julian pulled out his chair across from Jade and sat. "It took balls to do what you did. Not a lot of women ask men out. I wish they did it more. It's such a turn-on. And it would take some of the pressure off. You know what I mean?"

I laughed. "Not really." I turned back to Jade. "When did this happen?" It couldn't have been that long ago. I'd just seen her a few minutes before in my apartment.

"Like, five minutes ago," said Jade. "Right here. In front of everyone. I want to die."

"No, you don't. It'll be all right."

Jade slid farther down her chair, her eyes brimming brightly like she was about to cry. "No, it won't. I can't believe I did what I did. I'm such an idiot. Big, stupid idiot."

I felt for the witch. I'd seen the powerful crush she had on Jimmy. I swept my gaze over the room and spotted him looking sharp in a blue suit, talking to Basil. I waited to see if he would make eye contact, but he didn't. Some guys were total dicks when dealing with things from the heart, but not our Jimmy. He was a good, kind man who'd been stuck in a damn toy dog for longer than I had been alive. If anyone was sensitive to the feelings of others, it was our Jimmy.

I turned my attention back to Jade. "What did he say?" The worst that could happen to my friend was if Jimmy said no. There was a fifty-fifty chance that he would. But from her reaction, I was guessing he turned her down. Gently, I was sure, but still a blow to one's ego.

Jade's face took on a paler shade, if that were even possible. "Nothing."

I frowned and leaned closer. "Nothing? What do you mean, nothing?"

"Nothing," she repeated, staring at a spot on the table. "Who does that? It means he's not interested. It means he was so *disgusted* by my asking that he didn't even have the words to turn me down."

"Oh, dear." Elsa let herself fall into an empty chair. "Here we go."

I shook my head. "Wait a second. He didn't say anything? He just stood there and said nothing? What did his face look like?" That was strange, even for Jimmy.

"Like he was in hell," muttered Jade, making Julian laugh.

A tug pulled on my heart at the pain in her voice. "Okay, so you asked a guy out, and he didn't answer.

It's not the end of the world. There are worse things in life." But right now, I could tell there weren't. Not for her.

Jade only shook her head. "I knew it was a mistake. My inner Jade told me not to do it."

"Your *inner* Jade?" Okay, I had to laugh this time. So did Julian. So did Elsa. Yeah, we were terrible friends.

"But did I listen?" continued Jade as though I'd never spoken. "Noooo. And look what happened. He'll probably never speak to me again. He'll avoid me like I'm diseased. I've seen it happen before."

"Jimmy's not like that," I told her. "He's one of the good ones." I knew she knew this, too, part of why she had such a crush on him. "Listen. He was cursed as a toy dog for a really long time. Maybe he's just not ready."

"Doubt that," said Julian. "If it were me, I'd be getting laid with as many lovely ladies as I could after being a toy."

I glared at Julian. "Not helping."

Julian shrugged. "Just saying how it is."

The truth was the only person who knew what it was like to be cursed into a toy and then turned back into themselves was Jimmy. Maybe he wanted time alone, and maybe Jade just wasn't his type.

Jade pulled at the strands of hair around her face. "It's humiliating. And now I have to look for a new place to live."

"Don't be ridiculous," snapped Elsa. "It's not like

you were dating for a while and you caught him cheating."

I nodded. "Good point."

"Pull yourself together, and let's enjoy the evening," said Elsa, winning a glare from Jade. "It'll all get sorted out. Things have a way of doing that when you least expect it."

Jade pulled the elastic band from her hair and, with her fingers, combed the strands forward around her face, like she was using her hair as a shield to hide behind.

I grabbed the last empty chair, but I scanned the table before I pulled it out. "Where's my name? I'm not seeing it anywhere. And there are only three table settings."

Elsa put her wineglass down and grabbed the three name cards, rereading them as though the others were illiterate. "Your name's not here."

"I know." I felt a flash of irritation that they'd forgotten to print out my name. But it was nothing compared to how Jade felt.

"Who cares? Sit. We'll get Polly to get another place setting," offered Julian.

"That won't be necessary." Basil stood next to our table, scrubbing his glasses with a corner of his navy jacket.

"Why's that?" I asked him, inspecting his face for a clue as to what he was hinting at but finding nothing.

Basil put his glasses on, straightened, and puffed

out his chest like a proud peacock. "Because you're sitting at the *important* table with me."

I clamped my jaw tightly and tried hard not to laugh. "I am?" Maybe hotel employees sat together. Okay. I could do that. It wouldn't be as fun as enjoying a good meal with my friends, but I knew by taking on the job full time, I'd have to make some sacrifices in the name of the Twilight Hotel. Sitting and having dinner with Basil was apparently one of them.

"That's right," answered Basil. "By special request."

I frowned. "Special request?" Not sure I liked the sound of that.

Basil's face stretched into a smile that was far too wide to be considered normal as he looked across the room. "Yes. Adele asked for you to be seated next to her at her table."

Hell no.

A flame of anger ignited in my chest as I followed his gaze. There, sitting at a table toward the far end of the room, was none other than that skinny witch bitch who had nearly destroyed the hotel and cost Jimmy his life.

The one who sat on the White witch council. The one I'd bet my life made that complaint about me.

Adele.

CHAPTER 15

"Hurry up. We don't want to make Adele wait." Basil grabbed me by the arm and hauled me beside him with surprising strength for such a tiny witch.

I glanced over my shoulder at my friends, seeing their faces cast in worry. They looked petrified, like I was being dragged to the center of the village to be hanged. Even Jade looked like she'd forgotten her troubles for a second and was staring at me wide-eyed and fearful.

"Here we are," said Basil as we arrived at the said important table.

A quick glance around the "important table," and I spotted a large centerpiece of a mix of glass candles and white flowers. The white tablecloth was made of some expensive silk material with golden symbols etched into the fabric, unlike the ordinary white cotton cloth that covered all the other dining room tables.

Adele looked up from her seat where she was currently the only one sitting at the "important table." She wore a white tweed-knit belted jacket over her thin shoulders, a piece of clothing that screamed haute couture and probably cost more than what I made in a month. Diamonds fell from around her ears and neck, taking up more space than they should. Her blonde hair was styled in a chignon on top of her head, adding a catlike resemblance to her already sharp features. Her light eyes tracked me slowly, and I couldn't help but feel goose bumps rise over my skin.

I yanked my arm free. "I didn't need an escort." I glared at the male witch, my fingers twitching as a part of me wanted to wring his little neck.

"Yes, well..." Basil cleared his throat and bowed slightly from the waist. "I must see to the kitchen. Don't worry, Adele. I will make sure your lamb is cooked just right."

Adele gave Basil a patronizing smile. "Thank you."

Still, Basil seemed pleased and rushed away, heading for the double doors to the right, which I knew was the hotel's main kitchen, Polly's domain. I wasn't sure she'd take kindly to being told by Basil how to do her job. The thought made me smile on the inside.

I could feel the older witch's eyes on me, but I refused to look at her. I spotted my name on the name card placed above the table setting, next to hers.

I stood there contemplating whether I should just leave. I didn't want to be here. Sitting next to a hateful witch whose ass happened to sit on the White witch council wasn't exactly my idea of a nice dinner. This witch had cost Elsa's husband his job, had made a complaint about me to the Gray Council, and had nearly killed Jimmy. I would never forget that.

If I left, Adele would probably make my life a hell of a lot worse after everyone saw I'd slighted her in public. Yeah, she'd hate that. I didn't care. She could hate me all she wanted. At least we'd have that in common. But I did care about my job here at the hotel, and I wasn't ready to let that go. Not yet.

Gritting my teeth, I yanked out the chair and sat. I had a good view of my friends' table. They were all huddled together, talking and throwing concerned looks my way. If I didn't know any better, it looked like they were planning my rescue. Loved these guys.

"Hello, Leana," said Adele, her voice dripping with the kind of fakeness that made my skin crawl. "You know, it's very rude to ignore your guests."

"Guests?" I said, though still not looking at her. "I don't get it. You don't like me. I don't like you. So why did you want me to sit here? To torture me? Want to pretend for the world that we're besties?"

The witch gave a phony laugh. "Why are you so hostile, Stardud? Is it a crime now to want to get to know you better? I just want to share a pleasant meal in your company."

I cringed and swung my eyes to her. "Cut the

crap. Why am I here? Payback? Is that it? Your revenge?"

Adele's pale face pulled into a pointed smile. She was even uglier up close. "Trust me. If I wanted revenge for that little stunt you pulled with the Gray Council, this wouldn't be it. You have it all wrong, Stardud."

I narrowed my eyes at the warning in her tone. "You nearly killed my friend Jimmy. I'm very glad my so-called stunt saved his life and ruined your plans. I'd do it again in a heartbeat."

Adele's pale eyes tracked the room and fell on Jimmy. "I heard you removed his curse. How did you achieve that?"

"Wouldn't you like to know?" Ah-ha. So, this was more of an interrogation dinner. She wanted to know how I'd managed to remove Jimmy's curse. She could ask all she wanted. I wasn't about to tell her.

Adele picked up her glass of white wine and took a sip. "The hotel's hired you full time. I find that interesting since you were an epic failure. But that's what you are. Isn't it, Stardud? A failure sort of witch. But *is* it witch? Not exactly sure you fit the bill, as they say. Your magical abilities are somewhat wanting."

If she thought she was going to upset me by dragging out my unusual and, yes, sometimes lacking, magical skill, she was sadly mistaken.

"Well, they did," I answered, keeping my voice from showing any emotion. "Must have done something right. But I'm very surprised your ass still sits on the White witch council. Especially after going behind the Gray Council and trying to have the hotel, *their* hotel, destroyed. How is that?"

Her face was screwed up with irritation, and her eyes almost seemed to glow in frustration. But then it was gone in a blink, replaced by her usual arrogant, contemptible visage. "Careful, Stardud. This ass can take everything away from you. This place. This job. Your friends. I can take it all."

I didn't like the way she said that. My voice twisted with bitter anger when I looked at her. "Is that a threat? Are you threatening my friends? Threaten me all you like, but leave my friends out of it."

Again, she plastered that fake smile on her face, the one that never reached her eyes. "You're *sooo* sensitive. I would never hurt your friends. What kind of witch do you think I am? But you should know something. In this line of work, you need to have thicker skin, Stardud. Or you'll never make it."

I frowned. "You're not as good a liar as you think. Need to work on that." I pulled my eyes away from her face before I lost control and punched her. Or made her eat her stupid diamonds.

"Has anyone ever told you what an insolent and vile witch you are?"

"So I'm a witch again now?" I shrugged. "If you're feeling agitated and frustrated, my work is done." If she thought I'd just sit here and be polite, she didn't know me as well as she thought she did.

"I guess that's what happens when you grow up

with the wrong witch family," she added conversationally.

"What the hell do you want?" I was going to punch her before dinner was served.

"For starters, a pleasant conversation would be nice."

She was so full of crap, I was starting to smell it on her. "Sure. Whatever."

"Good. I heard it was quite the show on the hotel's roof," said Adele. "You defeated many demons. Closed a large Rift as well, if I'm not mistaken."

I nodded. "That's right." She'd let on that my magic was worthless, that I was a dud, practically human, yet here she was, intrigued by it. She was so easy to read.

From the corner of my eye, I saw her watching me. It was creepy. "And you did that on your own?"

Ah. Now I knew where this was going. "No," I said, looking at her. "I had help. My friends helped me."

A strange smile pulled at her lips. "I hear you and Valen are getting close. You were on a date last night. Is it serious?"

My anger resurfaced. "You spying on me?"

Adele gave a laugh. "If you wanted it to be secret, you shouldn't have dinner in a restaurant filled with people."

A waiter came then and held a bottle of white wine in one hand and a bottle of red in the other. He looked at me and said, "Can I offer you some wine?"

I nodded and pushed my empty wineglass forward. "Red, please."

When he was done, I grabbed my glass and took a sip, thinking about why Adele was so interested in my love life. Maybe not even my love life but Valen. I'd seen how she looked at him like he was sex on a stick. Obviously, she had the hots for him. She was jealous that I'd been on a date with him. Now she wanted to know if it was serious or not.

"You want my advice?" asked Adele after a moment.

I laughed. "No."

"He's not the settling-down type. He's been with many, *many* women over the last few years. But to my knowledge, he's never found any of them worthy enough to be serious with. To settle down with. Not one. And there've been many."

"Yes, you said that already." I took another gulp of wine. "Are you hoping he's going to ask you out? Is that it?"

"You like him. Don't you?" continued the witch in that same condescending tone she'd used on Elsa. "You think you have what it takes to tame him. You think you can tie him down?"

"He's not a wild dog. He's a man," I said, irritation flowing in my tone.

"A giant," corrected the witch.

I narrowed my eyes at her. "What's your point?"

Adele leaned back in her chair, balancing her wineglass in her hand. "A giant and a Stardud. Interesting pair. One would never imagine that sort of *union*."

Damn. She could really piss me off. I could feel my blood pressure skyrocketing until it pounded behind my eyeballs in anger—beautiful, hot anger. I was furious, really.

Movement caught my eye, and I saw Elsa standing up from her chair, looking like she was about to come over here. Probably to rescue me.

Our eyes met, and I shook my head. I waited until she sat down and smoothed out my emotions. I didn't want Adele to know this line of conversation had such an effect on me.

Instead, my heart warmed at how a small group of people had become part of my family. And as family, they cared and were worried about me. Even though Adele terrified Elsa, she was willing to come over and help. That was true friendship.

"Call it whatever you want," I told the other witch. "It was a date. Just a date."

"That's not what I heard."

I whipped my head around. "What have you *heard*?"

At that, Adele smiled evilly, and it took an enormous amount of self-control not to grab that diamond necklace and shove it down her throat. "That the giant is falling for you. That he can't keep his eyes off you when you're in a room." She paused like she was hinting that the big news was coming. "That he saved you from a brutal beating from your ex."

My lips parted, and my heart slammed into my chest. "Who told you that?" How the hell did she know about that? As far as I knew, only Valen, Martin, and I knew. Okay, maybe I'd told my friends too. And maybe word had gotten out. Damn. This was not the kind of news I wanted Adele to be privy to.

I kept my face from betraying the emotions fluttering through me like I had butterflies instead of blood flowing through my veins. "That was a personal situation, which is none of your business."

Adele threw back her head and laughed. "Oh, Stardud. Don't you know? Everything that happens here is my business." She leaned forward and placed her glass on the table. "But I can't say I'm surprised. Human males are often filled with uncontrollable emotions. They're weak. Under my council, witches are forbidden to marry out of their race. I would have never allowed it if you were in New York then."

I snorted. "Wow. That itty bit of power really got to your head."

Adele's eyes gleamed. "Power is power. Nothing else matters."

"Hmmm. I'm guessing you're rooting for a spot on the Gray Council. Is that it? You really think they'll give you a chair? The crazy witch who wanted to destroy their hotel?"

"I'll let you in on a secret since… well… since you're so interested and all," said Adele, as though speaking to a five-year-old child. "The thing with the Gray Council… they don't care about you. Witches, vampires, and werewolves all are disposable. One dies and is easily replaced. But the Gray Council, well, it will always stand, and it will always come first."

I shook my head, wishing I was sitting with my friends instead of this crazy bitch. "Quit the Yoda talk. Say what you mean."

A hint of devilry lay in her voice as she said, "Not yet. Soon. Soon you will understand."

I rolled my eyes. "This is going to be a long night."

Just when I thought about excusing myself to the bathroom with a case of intestinal failure, Jimmy showed up at our table.

"Hey, Jimmy." I perked up at the sight of him. "Please tell me you're sitting at this table."

"Uh…" Jimmy's eyes flicked over to Adele and then back to me. "Yes. But that's not why I'm here. Someone's at the front desk asking for you."

Saved by the bell, or rather, the assistant manager. I sat straighter. "Who?" Thinking this must be one of Julian's schemes to get me away from Adele, I flicked my gaze to my friends' table, and my heart sank. They were all still sitting there. Staring over here, but still all present. Jade was staring at Jimmy like she was about to hurl.

"I don't know," answered the assistant manager. "Never seen him before. I told him you were at a dinner party, but he won't leave a message. He's really adamant about speaking to you in person. He's a bit of a twitchy fella."

I beamed at Adele. "Duty calls." I took the last swig of my drink and left, not bothering to say anything else to that icy bitch. The more distance between us, the better.

"You're pretty cool around her," I muttered once we were out of earshot.

Jimmy stopped when we reached the end of the dining room. "I don't let her get to me. You should do the same."

"Touché." I looked him over. "You gonna tell me what happened with Jade?"

Jimmy's face twitched, and then he grimaced. "I... I gotta go."

My mouth was still open as I watched the assistant manager hurrying away from me, like he was late for a meeting.

"What is up with those two?" Shaking my head, I made my way back to the lobby to the front desk. My best pal, Errol, was there. And for the first time, he was looking at someone else the same way he looked at me—like they were walking poop.

The someone was a middle-aged man with reddish-blond hair. He was heavyset, short, with a white shirt halfway tucked into the belt of dark pants that were too long for him. He looked like a mess, which explained why Errol was glaring at him.

The stranger's eyes widened when he saw me approaching. "Leana? Leana Fairchild? The Merlin?" he said in an accent I couldn't place.

"Yes." I came to stand next to him. "Do I know

you?" He had a forgettable face, kind of like Raymond.

He grabbed my arm and pulled me with him.

"Hey!" I yanked out of his grip, pulling on my magic as I felt a burst of nervous energy coming from him. Okay. He was a witch too.

"Grab me like that again, and you'll be kissing the floor," I growled.

He let go, pulled out a handkerchief, and started to dab the sweat from his face and forehead. "Apologies. I just"—he looked over his shoulder, his eyes darting nervously around and not settling on anything—"I don't want to be overheard."

I crossed my arms over my chest. "What's this about? Who are you?"

The man leaned forward and muttered, "My name is Bellamy Boudreaux. I'm the one who left you the message about the warehouse."

Okay, then.

CHAPTER 16

I took Bellamy back through the hotel lobby to one of the slot-machine areas that was now vacant and away from Errol's eavesdropping.

Once I was sure we were alone, I turned to the witch. "You're a witch?" I had to be sure.

"Yes." Bellamy nodded. "I'm the chief—*was* the chief—witch scientist on the HTO project." At my bewildered expression, he added, "Human Transference Origins."

"Wait—there're witch scientists?" Of course, there would be. I don't know why I said that.

Bellamy nodded. He looked over his shoulder. "Yes, well, as you have probably guessed by now, after seeing the warehouse, I was charged with altering humans' genetic material. To transform them into us. Into paranormals."

"I noticed. It worked."

The witch shook his head, his body twitching like he had a spasm. "No, not always. What you saw was a small percentage of humans that survived the actual transference."

Dread clenched my chest as the images of those floating people came back, slamming into me like a physical blow. I cocked my head to the side. "So you're saying a lot more humans have died for this?"

I thought it strange that I hadn't found any mention of masses of humans disappearing in the human news. I made it a habit of checking social media for anything suspicious.

"Unfortunately"—Bellamy pulled out his handkerchief to dab his sweaty forehead and face and then shoved it back into his pocket—"mostly prostitutes and the homeless."

I didn't like the casual way he'd said that, like they didn't matter somehow, as though that made them lesser humans. "Still people. Still humans. Still illegal to harm them." Every paranormal child knew that harming a human was forbidden. We were all raised to know our laws inside and out.

"They didn't all take to the paranormal transference," said the witch, and he blew out a heavy breath like that had been highly tedious for him.

"You said that." I was starting to dislike this witch scientist, possibly more than Adele at the moment.

Bellamy seemed to cower at my heavy glare. "No. What I mean is we were able, more or less, to administer modified werewolf blood into a human host. Vampire blood worked, too, but we were not able to manipulate the blood of a witch. I still don't know why, but the witch gene could not be transferred."

"Good." The idea of a bunch of crazy, brand-new witches loose in the city was not a good thing. It was horrible enough we had a bad case of crazed vampires. But witches? Witches could do magic. And I didn't want to think of the horrors they would have bestowed on the human population.

The witch scientist sighed. "Even then, it was not enough. It was never enough."

I stared at him for a second. It seemed like whoever he was working for had high expectations. "But your science project has flaws," I told him, seeing him narrow his eyes at me. "I fought a horde of newly created vampires and then they all just died. Like they had an expiration date. Care to explain?"

"Another unfortunate consequence of the trans-ference," said Bellamy, shifting his weight. "We tried to have them last longer. At first, it was only a few seconds. Then a few minutes. Hours. But we couldn't get them to last more than six hours."

A cold sliver of dread slid through me at the thought of all those test subjects. Human test subjects.

But in an instant, my anger took over my dread. I didn't like this guy. Yes, he'd given us the location of the warehouse, but he'd still participated. He made this happen. You'd have to be pretty demented to work on something like this and call it science. It wasn't even fringe science. It was barbaric.

I swallowed, feeling the tension rise in me. "Why did you do it? *How* could you do it?"

Bellamy clenched his jaw and swallowed. It

looked painful. "Money. Power. Prestige. I thought I'd be published in our science journals. But I quickly realized that would never be the case." He hesitated. "There's no excuse. I just… couldn't do it anymore. Couldn't. All those humans. Terrible. I had to tell someone. Now, I'm on the run."

I stared at him, still wondering if I should punch him. "Telling me was the only good thing you did about this whole situation."

Bellamy's pale eyes rounded, and he reached out and grabbed my arm. "You have to protect me! They're going to kill me!"

I peeled his hands from my arm. I did not want this guy touching me. Ever. "Take it easy. You're safe here."

"No. No. No. They have spies everywhere." His head spun around as he surveyed the lobby, like he thought we were being watched. "They're after me. They know what I did. I'm a dead witch if you don't protect me!"

"Who? Who's after you? Who's behind all of this?" I had my suspicions, but I wanted to hear it from him.

Bellamy's bottom lip trembled. "Never got a name. But they just sent instructions to be followed by their mediators. They have lots of money and power. I think… I think it has to be someone on the Gray Council."

I let out a breath through my nose. "My thoughts exactly."

Bellamy paled at the mention of the council. "It's

why I couldn't go to them. What if I was right, and then they'd just kill me to silence me." His wide eyes flicked behind me. "They have eyes and ears everywhere. Everywhere!"

Right. He was a bit of a drama queen, but I knew he was scared. He had intel, the only intel about this whole nasty operation. He was my key witness. My only witness. I had to keep him safe.

"You're a Merlin," said the witch scientist. "You're sworn to protect the vulnerable. Those who need help. That's me."

Not exactly. But I wasn't about to explain my role as a Merlin.

"I'll protect you," I told him and saw tension leaving his posture. "First, I need to find a safe place for you, like a safe house. Somewhere they won't think of to look for you."

"Here?" Bellamy looked around, not at all that comfortable with the idea of staying in a hotel owned by those he was allegedly running from.

"No. I don't think here is a good idea." I stared at him, wondering if I should find him a hoodie or a hat to hide his face, but I decided we didn't have time for that. "Come with me."

I grabbed Bellamy, and together we exited the hotel. I looked over my shoulder when we got to the front entrance to see if anyone was following us, but no one was there.

"Where are we going?" asked the witch scientist, who was now sweating profusely in the cool September weather.

"A friend's place," I answered.

I yanked out my phone and called Valen. After the fourth ring, it went to voicemail. I hung up. It wasn't ideal, but Bellamy would be a lot safer in Valen's apartment than he would in the hotel. And I didn't think the giant would refuse to let him stay, either, as a protector and all.

Besides, Valen needed to know what was happening.

Exhaust fumes and the stench of garbage displaced the night air as I hauled Bellamy with me to the building next door. The gathering dark rushed in to fill the spaces where the streetlights couldn't reach.

When we arrived at the storefront, I looked up and found Valen's apartment windows black as night. I didn't think he was there.

"Are you taking me out to eat?" asked Bellamy, squinting his eyes at the glass like he was trying to get a better view of the restaurant inside. "I am kinda hungry."

I rolled my eyes. "Come on." Grabbing Bellamy by the arm, I hauled him through the restaurant doors and came face-to-face with none other than Valen.

And the mystery blonde.

"Oh," I said, jumping back and pulling Bellamy with me.

"Leana?" Surprise flashed across Valen's face. "What are you doing here?"

I narrowed my eyes at his reaction. I'd expected a

"What's the matter" or a "Are you okay." Instead, I got a "What are you doing here?" Yeah, something was definitely up with him and the blonde.

Speaking of said blonde, I took my time to really look at her. She was about my height, but with a more voluptuous body and curves in all the right places. Her lean figure was perfectly enclosed in a snug black pantsuit under a black cashmere coat. She wore her hair in a slicked-back, low ponytail, which only accentuated her pretty features. She was classy and put together, the total opposite of me. If I were to guess, I'd say she was a paranormal lawyer.

Annoyingly, she was even more beautiful than I remembered, with large blue-green eyes and full lips, reminding me of a young Christie Brinkley. Seeing her up close was playing with my insecurities, but I could also see her horizontal pupils. She was a shifter.

But I couldn't let my imagination get in the way. I came here for a reason. I waited for Valen to introduce us, but he just stood there, looking slightly awkward and, did I dare say… guilty?

Bellamy leaned forward. "What are we doing here? Are we eating or not? I'd go for a large steak with fries. Smells decent in here. But you can never tell what's really going on in the kitchens. You know what I mean? You can never be too careful when picking out a restaurant."

Valen watched me and then moved his gaze over to Bellamy, sizing him up. A slow frown creased his brow.

I ignored Bellamy and spoke to Valen. "Are you going to introduce us?" I should have gone straight to the issue at hand, but I couldn't help myself. I'd wanted to know who she was for days. Now, she was right here in front of me.

At that, the mystery blonde raised her perfectly manicured brows, and a coy smile reached her lips. She thought I was hilarious. Great.

I heard a snort and looked past Valen to see my favorite hostess smiling at me, the kind of winning smile like she knew I'd been played. Either that or she knew something I didn't.

Two people thought I was hilarious. Fantastic.

Valen's eyes darted between Bellamy and me. He gestured toward the blonde. "This is Thana. A friend."

I looked over at the woman called "Thana. A friend," expecting to see her hand out for a shake, but she just stood there with that amused look in her eyes.

Okay, either she didn't want to shake my hand because she thought I was beneath her, or maybe she didn't want to shake it because I was the competition?

My gaze fell back to the giant, expecting him to say something else, but he just stood there, looking more uncomfortable than anything.

A painful silence settled in, and my anger welled.

"That's it?" I looked at him. "That's all I get?" Okay, so maybe I wasn't exactly entitled to know all about his personal life and whether he was dating other women, because it certainly looked like it. It's not like we'd made what we were—what were we, exactly?—exclusive.

But it still pissed me off.

"Let's go." I grabbed Bellamy and hauled him out of the restaurant with more force than necessary.

Valen didn't call out my name. He didn't come after me either.

Nope. He let me leave.

It hurt. I'm not going to lie. It hurt a lot. But that was my own damn fault.

I should have never let myself fall for a man I barely knew. That was all on me.

CHAPTER 17

"You think I'll be safe here?" asked Bellamy, staring at all the open doors on the thirteenth floor, like he thought a monster was going to sprout out and grab him.

I snickered. "Don't worry. Everyone's downstairs at the special dinner. No one's here but us."

"But is it safe?" pressed the witch scientist, the whites of his eyes showing.

I had no clue. "It's the safest place we've got for now."

Valen's place would have been ideal, but it looked like he was going to use his space for some sexy time with the blonde later.

I cringed on the inside, trying not to think about it, but it pounded against my skull like a migraine. I wasn't perfect. I still had those insecurities that crept up from time to time, and having lived with a cheating husband didn't help them from springing up again. It just brought them all back with force.

My eyes burned. No. I would not cry. Not for any man. Not anymore.

It was my own damn fault I'd let a stranger into my heart. And now I had to pull up my big-girl panties and get to work. I had a job to do, something more important than my personal life. Besides, I would get over it. I always did.

"Why are all the doors open?" asked the witch, walking a little faster whenever we got to a doorway and then slower when we hit the hallway wall. "Is that normal? It's like everyone left in a hurry. Maybe there's a fire?"

"No fire. Trust me. This is how it is here. This entire floor is kinda like one big apartment," I said, feeling a warmth creeping in and filling that little part of my heart that was aching. "I was a little taken aback at first too. But I love it now. Everyone's amazing. We all look out for each other. Like a family."

"Hmm." Bellamy's face was screwed up in irritation, his shoulders going stiff. Clearly, he didn't think this was a good idea. I didn't care. I didn't really care about his feelings. The witch had been involved in torturing humans and had subjected them to horrible experiments. He could be *bothered* all he wanted.

"Right here," I said when we'd reached the end of the hallway and my apartment. I gestured to Bellamy to follow me inside.

I took five steps and then halted. "What are you guys doing here?"

Elsa, Jade, and Julian looked up from the living room as we entered.

"Waiting for you," said Elsa, her eyes on Bellamy with a questioning frown.

Jade stood up and rolled over to me in her skates. "Who's your friend? And why is he sweating like he's in a sauna?"

Bellamy let out a squeal like a frightened mouse, doubled back, and started for the doorway.

Good thing I caught him.

I grabbed a fistful of his shirt, spun him around, and dragged him forward, helping with a little shove. "This here is Bellamy. He's a witch scientist with the ho project."

Julian grinned as he leaned forward. "The ho project? Count me in."

"HTO project," corrected Bellamy, enunciating every letter.

I cocked a brow. "Whatever. He's one of the witches who performed those experiments on the humans."

At that, I watched as my friends' faces darkened with a mistrustful cast. Yeah, they liked him as much as I did.

"He's the one who left me the message about the warehouse."

Bellamy looked at me, horror written all over his face. "What are you doing?" he hissed. "I came to you for protection! And now you're telling them everything about me. Might as well kill me now."

I rolled my eyes and heard a chuckle from Julian. "Bellamy has a flair for drama."

Bellamy scowled at me. "This was *not* the plan."

"These are my friends," I told the witch scientist, scowling right back at him. "I trust them with my life. So, you can trust them with yours. Okay?"

Bellamy didn't answer, but he really didn't have a choice. If he wanted my protection, well, it came with my friends.

I looked back at my friends. "What about dinner? It can't be over so soon?"

"We left before dinner was served," said Elsa as she stood from the couch. She saw my disappointed look and added, "It just didn't feel right. We saw how uncomfortable you were sitting with… her. I didn't think it fair that we would have a good time while you looked…"

"Like your guts were being pulled out of your mouth," said Jade, smiling. Her face stretched into a bigger smile as she caught Bellamy looking at her, but the witch scientist pulled his face into a glower and quickly looked away as though someone like Jade shouldn't be ogling him. What a tool.

"It got better when you left," informed Julian, piquing my curiosity.

"What do you mean?"

"Adele was furious you just left her like that," he said, and I saw Bellamy stiffen at the mention of that witch's name. Guess he didn't like her either. "She started to scream at Basil to go get you back. Poor bastard. He tried, but you weren't in the hotel."

Ah, hell. I didn't want Basil to get mixed up in my mess. "So, what happened?"

"He found someone else for her to torture." Julian shared a look with the others.

"Who?" I didn't like the sound of that.

"Jimmy," he answered, and I felt a wash of anger flow over me. "Don't worry. Jimmy can handle himself. He was all smiles when he sat down too. Probably gonna try to get some info out of that cold bitch. He was still with her and Basil when we left." Julian stretched and crossed his ankles on my coffee table. "I can't wait to hear all about it."

"Me too," said Jade, and she rolled off to the kitchen to pour herself a glass of water.

Bellamy leaned forward and whispered in my ear, "Isn't she a little old for roller skates?" His voice was filled with mockery. "She looks ridiculous. And look at her hair?"

"No, she's not," I snapped. I leaned forward until I got right in his face. "Another comment like that about my friends, and I'll personally send you to the Gray Council wrapped up in a bow. You got that?" I wasn't kidding either.

Bellamy's face went from shock to irritation, but he was smart and kept his mouth shut after that.

Seems my little encounter with Valen still had me on edge.

"Why are you so tense?" Elsa's eyes inspected my face. "You look flushed. Did something else happen?"

I shook my head while grabbing Bellamy and pushing him into the armchairs. I wasn't about to relay what had happened with Valen. It wasn't the time. And I didn't want to bring up all those feelings.

"More humans died than we first thought," I told them instead and began to communicate everything Bellamy had told me about their experiments.

"I think I need to sit down." Elsa's face was pale as she fell back onto the couch.

Julian pressed his feet on the floor and leaned forward, resting his elbows on his knees with his attention on Bellamy. "And you don't know who's behind this?"

Bellamy swallowed hard. "I believe it's someone on the Gray Council. But I don't have any proof. We never met them. They paid really well and just gave out orders through other people."

"And you kept killing humans because it paid well?" came Jade's voice as she rolled back into the living room.

The witch scientist's face flushed red, and he wiped it with his handkerchief again. "We believed it was for the greater good. For our people."

"Who's we?" I crossed my arms over my chest, staring down at him.

"The other witch scientists," he said. "That's what we were told. We believed them."

"Through these mediators?" I pressed.

Bellamy nodded. "Yes. Through phone calls and emails. It was something they kept repeating." He hesitated like he was trying to recollect a memory. *"The time of the paranormals has come. We must rise and protect our people.* It was repeated constantly. Texts. Emails. It just became normal."

"When did this all start?" Elsa's voice was filled with anger. "When did you…" She gestured with her hands.

"About a year ago," answered Bellamy. "At first, it was just to get the lab going. People don't realize how much work it takes just for pre-op. And then we got our first human subject."

I cringed at how excited he sounded at the prospect of using a human for his experiment. "So, what you're saying," I began, "is basically you've killed what… hundreds? Maybe thousands of innocent humans?"

Bellamy's mouth dropped, his eyes darting around the room but not settling on any of us. I could tell he was quickly trying to find a way to defend his actions. "We thought—"

"It was for the greater good of our people." I felt bile rise in the back of my throat. I really hated what he'd done. I despised him for it. But so far, he was our only proof that the Gray Council, or someone in it, was responsible for killing those humans. It could never happen again. I had to stop it. And for that, I needed more.

"I'm going to need names."

Bellamy shook his head. "I told you. I don't know who they are."

"Names of the other witch scientists you worked with," I told him, seeing his eyes rounding. "And a copy of all those emails and texts. You still have them. Right?"

"Yes," answered the witch scientist, dribbles of sweat running down his temples. "What will happen to them? To me?"

"Well, first, we need to keep you safe and alive," I said with a sigh. "You did come forward. I'm sure that will swing in your favor when your case goes to trial. You'll probably get off with maybe six months to a year in prison."

"Prison! I can't go to prison," cried Bellamy. "I have an IQ of two hundred and five!"

Julian snorted. "Anyone else feel really stupid at the moment?"

Elsa pressed her hands to her hips and glared at Bellamy. "Well, you should have thought about that before you started torturing humans if you're so smart."

Jade rolled over to him. "That doesn't sound smart."

Bellamy stared up at Jade like she was an annoying child. "I told a Merlin. I stopped. I gave you the message. That has to mean something. I cannot go to jail."

"That's not up to me to decide," I told the witch scientist. "Once we have all the evidence and a solid case against the Gray Council member or members responsible, you'll know. I wouldn't be surprised if your colleagues get life in prison."

Bellamy's complexion went a tad green at that

point. "That *cannot* happen to me. I still have plans, projects that need pursuing."

I didn't think Bellamy should be anywhere near another lab in his lifetime. Not after what he'd done. He was dangerous. What he did was unethical. Yeah, okay, so he had a teeny conscience, which was the only thing that would save him right now.

"There's more," said Bellamy into the sudden silence.

My pulse was fast and still rising, and I felt my anxiety pulling me stiff. "What?"

The witch scientist wiped his forehead and face again with his damp, sweat-covered handkerchief. So gross. "If I tell you, do you promise to keep me out of jail?"

I clenched my jaw. The nerve of that little bastard. And then I realized this was his plan all along—string us along, and when he knew it was the best time, play his only card. His "get out of jail free" card.

When my gaze traveled over the others, they were all looking at me. Waiting. Fear echoed in their faces. Fear of something worse. It rattled them.

I stepped closer until my thigh bumped against Bellamy's chair. "What is it?"

"Promise," he said, pointing a trembling finger at me. "Promise me, or I won't tell you."

"We could just beat it out of him," suggested Julian, staring at Bellamy like he wanted to test one of his newest potions on the witch. "He kinda deserves a beating. And worse."

I couldn't agree with him more, but seeing his resolute face, I had a feeling he wanted to tell me. And I knew how to do it without a well-deserved beating.

"Fine." I kept my face from showing any emotion. "I promise to keep you from jail. Tell me." Total lie. And for once, I felt like I'd pulled it off, but only Bellamy's reaction would tell.

The witch scientist relaxed and leaned back into his chair. He believed me. "Thank you." He let out a breath, met my eyes, and said, "There's another lab in the city."

Ah, hell.

CHAPTER 18

The cab ride to Upper Manhattan was silent and uncomfortable. First, well, because we had a human driver, and second, we were all dreading what we were going to find. Would it be worse? A more extensive lab with more humans being experimented on?

I'd really hoped the lab we'd discovered yesterday had been the only one. I'd never imagined we'd find more of these human workshops around the city. Bellamy knew of one more, but what if there were more than he knew? The thought sent pricks of fear through me.

I'd left the witch scientist back at my apartment. No way was I going to risk his life. He was too important—a bastard, yes, but a bastard I still needed.

"You stay here and lock the door behind us," I told him about five minutes after he'd given us the news of another lab. "Don't let anyone you don't know in. Got it?"

Bellamy gave a nod. "I'm hungry. Do you have any gluten-free food in that contraption you call a fridge? Something of quality?"

I'd slammed the door in his face. I was protecting him. I didn't have to like him or be nice to him.

The silence was suddenly interrupted by the loud ringing of my phone. Damn. I'd forgotten to put it on vibrate.

The cab driver looked at me. "You gonna answer that?" He was a middle-aged white male with a scruffy beard and a receding hairline. At first, he'd refused to take us all in his cab since there were four of us and the back of his sedan only fit three. Although Julian offered, I was not going to sit on his lap. The cabbie finally agreed after I'd pulled out a hundred-dollar bill.

I gave the cab driver a look, pulled out my phone, and switched it to vibrate mode.

"Who was that?" asked Jade from the back seat.

I turned my head and stared out the front, blinking at all the oncoming car lights. "Nothing important."

I heard the pulling of leather and then Elsa's voice. "The same *nothing important* as the restaurant owner next door?"

"Possibly." I was going to tell them about my abrupt visit with Valen earlier. They were going to find out anyway, just not right now in a dingy cab with a human stranger sitting so close and staring at me more than was considered comfortable.

After another ten minutes, the cab pulled inside a long driveway and stopped his car. "That'll be a hundred and thirty-two bucks," said the driver, a grin on his face.

Julian whistled. "Expensive ride."

I paid the cab driver. "Maybe. Still cheaper than owning a car." With the gas prices up and all the insurance and maintenance of a car, I didn't think I was going to buy my own anytime soon. "Can you wait for us?" I didn't feel like waving down another cabbie who might not want all of us in the cab.

The driver flashed me a toothy grin with more spaces than teeth. "It'll cost ya."

"Fine."

Still smiling, the driver pressed on his meter box and turned it on. "What are you guys, anyway? You're not cops. You ghost hunters or something?"

I winked at him. "Or something."

The driver gave me a look like he thought I was full of crap and started to scroll through his phone.

I got out and shut the door just as the others climbed out. I glanced around to see we stood on a tight street stacked with warehouses and apartment buildings that looked like they'd survived a world war. Across from us an empty lot was blocked off with a sagging chain-link fence, and tall grass grew through the fissures in the pavement.

Before us loomed a lengthy gray building with a flat metal roof and no windows. It looked more like a container than a building, like the mother of all containers.

"Looks like someone left the door open *again*," said Julian as he moved closer to the container-like warehouse and headed for the large metal door.

"Just as charming as the one we found last night," muttered Jade, rolling beside me. She was still in her roller skates.

I frowned, unease rippling through me. "Stay close and be alert. We don't know what other *things* they're creating in here."

"I don't like the sound of that," said Elsa, hanging on to her bag.

Julian was the first at the entrance, a vial clasped in his hand as he pulled open the door with the other. After a loud screech, we all stepped into line behind him—you guessed it, in complete darkness.

"Hang on," said Elsa as she whispered an incantation and drew a glowing, silver witch light from her hand before tossing it in the air. The globe rose above our heads, illuminating the space in a nice soft yellow glow.

We stood in a sort of entrance, if you wanted to call two metal walls with an opening an entry.

Jade reached out and steadied herself on the side of the metal wall. "What do we do if we meet any of these witch scientists?"

"Probably have to fight them." I hadn't thought about that. I was hoping they wouldn't be quick on the magical draw. We could also face some opposition with those mediators Bellamy talked about.

As a precaution, I tapped into my will and called my power to the stars, my starlight magic. A cool tingle of magic washed over me, and I held it. If these intermediaries came at us, I'd be ready for them.

I didn't sense any other magic, either, but I didn't think it odd. The other human subjects hadn't emitted any paranormal vibes either.

"I need something that'll connect this lab to the Gray Council," I said, keeping my voice low in case we weren't alone. "The entire warehouse is a big evidence pile. This time we'll be taking some of the evidence back."

I wouldn't be putting out a call to the Gray Council until I knew who among them was in on it. And if they were all corrupt, I would talk to the head of each paranormal council and show them the evidence. It might even cause an overthrow of our government. The thought had my guts in a twist, but what choice did I have? None.

"If only one of those transformed humans had stayed alive," said Jade, pulling that thought right out of my head. "We could have nailed them with that. That's all the proof you'll ever need."

"Or those we found in that cage, if they hadn't wiped their memories," commented Elsa, her face pinched in thought.

With my temper rising like a fever at the idea of finding more transformed humans, we walked past the entrance and stepped into a much larger space— the only space since there were no signs of doors, hallways, or other compartments in the massive container.

As soon as the reek of disinfectant and bleach reached me, I knew something was wrong.

I swept my gaze around the area. I saw no signs of wood crates that had littered the other warehouse, and the racks that reached the ceiling were empty. I saw no tanks with floating humans in them and no cages with terrified humans. Not one of those magical dialysis machines. Not even a single file remained. Nothing. It was as though the lab had never been operational. Either that, or it had been wiped clean.

"That son of a bitch lied to us," cursed Julian, pacing until he reached the middle of the warehouse, his voice echoing off the walls of the space. "He's dead. He's fucking dead."

I felt the air move next to me as Jade rolled ahead. The screech of her wheels reverberated over the concrete floor. "Why would he lie? What purpose would it serve?" she called as she took on speed, clearly enjoying the empty space.

"To throw us off, maybe?" Elsa had a frown on her face as she placed her hands on her hips, looking very much like a mom about to scold one of her kids.

I looked around. "Throw us off from what?" I didn't think Bellamy had lied. He wanted to stay out of prison too much.

My phone vibrated in my bag, but I ignored it.

"You know you can share with us," called Jade

from the other side of the warehouse. "We won't judge."

How did she hear my phone? "I know. Just don't want to think about that right now." I crossed to the other side of the container warehouse and then turned around and did the same, walking the length of the structure and hoping to find something, anything. But there was nothing.

I began agreeing with Julian about Bellamy lying to us until something caught my attention. It was small, a miracle I even saw it in the dim light.

A drop of blood.

I grabbed my phone and switched on the flashlight mode, carefully shining it on the spot. "Definitely blood."

"What? You got something?" Elsa joined me, Julian following closely behind, her witch light hovering and bathing us in enough light for me to see.

"Not just a drop. A *trail* of blood," I said, seeing it clearly with the witch light. A long splatter of blood led to the door we came from.

"What?" Jade came speeding toward us, tried to stop, missed, and just kept rolling by.

Not wanting to take any chances, I tapped into my starlight. A ball of white light, the size of an apple, hovered over my palm, and I blew out a breath, causing the ball to burst into a hundred smaller globes. They flew over the trail of blood and fell on it like an illuminated walkway.

As soon as the starlight hit the blood, I felt it—the

pricks of paranormal energy and something else I couldn't decode.

"He didn't lie." I watched as my starlight vanished. "That's paranormal blood. Shifter blood. And it's been tampered with." I knew in my gut this was the same type of blood that had been pumping into those humans at the other lab.

Jade came rolling back and this time managed to slow to a stop. "Did I hear you say you found shifter blood?"

"I did." I pointed to the trail of blood. "Bellamy told the truth. This was the same kind of lab he worked in. My guess was they knew about the raid on the other one and packed everything up."

Elsa sighed. "There goes our evidence."

"Not necessarily," I said, looking at my friends. "We still have a witch scientist."

And now, more than ever, I knew I needed to keep him safe.

CHAPTER 19

O f course, when I got back to my place, Bellamy was gone.

My eyes went from my open apartment door, the door I distinctively remember Bellamy locking behind us, to the living room area just off the hallway. I strode through, dread clenching my chest as I already knew I wouldn't find him even before I checked the other rooms.

The witch scientist was gone.

A series of curses flew out of my mouth as I rubbed my temples and my eyes. The night proving to be one of the worst in my career—first with the empty warehouse and now with the only witness disappearing.

"He split," said Julian, stating the obvious. He started to laugh. "That little shit just took off. He's dead. He's so dead."

"He left?" Elsa sounded incredulous. "Why?

Doesn't he know you're the only one he can trust? Who will protect him? What an odd thing to do."

I shook my head, frustration filling me. "I don't know. Maybe he got spooked. He didn't want to stay here. He didn't trust the hotel. But I never imagined he'd leave." He'd come to me to protect him, so why did he just leave?

"Maybe he just got bored and decided to gamble some of his blood money downstairs." Jade walked into the kitchen barefoot. Her roller skates hung down from her neck, tied with their laces. She grabbed a glass and filled it with water.

"Yeah. That's it," said Julian, his hands on his hips as he gave the room a final glance. "Let me go check." Before I could stop him, Julian strolled out of the apartment and disappeared.

"More like there are a few ladies he wants to go see," laughed Elsa. She sounded tired as she leaned on one of the dining chairs.

I let out a sigh. "I should have left someone with him. Damnit. I shouldn't have left him alone. Now the only person who can expose those on the Gray Council is missing." I was angry with myself. If I could kick my own ass, I would. This mistake would cost me. It was a rookie mistake, and I wasn't a rookie.

I'd screwed up because I wasn't focused. My head had been filled with Valen and that blonde. I'd been hurt and angry at the giant but mostly at myself for letting my heart fall for this man. I'd tried to clear my head of him and focus, but I'd failed. And that had cost me my only witness.

Crap. This was bad. I rubbed my eyes, looking over the room for clues, anything that would give me an indication as to where Bellamy had gone.

My pulse raced as something else occurred to me. In a burst of speed, I rushed around the living room, checking the side tables, sofas, and chairs, trying to look at everything all at once.

"What are you looking for?" Jade put her empty glass of water in the sink.

"I'm not sure." I spun on the spot, not seeing anything out of place. "I was wondering if maybe Bellamy was taken."

Elsa sucked in a breath. "You think?"

"Possibly. I'm not seeing any signs of a struggle, but that doesn't mean they didn't put a gun to his head." More like a magical gun or something to threaten him with. The more I thought about it, the more it started to make sense. Someone had come here and had taken Bellamy. But who? And where did they take him?

"But how did they know he was even here?" asked Jade, coming around the kitchen to where I stood in the living room.

Elsa let herself fall into the chair with a flop. "They must have recognized him with Leana. They must have seen him downstairs. The hotel is filled with guests and strangers. I'm willing to bet they saw Leana with him."

"And they put two and two together. They knew I'd put him in my apartment, and then they just had to wait for us to leave and…"

"They took him," added Jade. She looked at me, determination on her face. "Then let's go find him and bring him back."

I gave her a weak smile. "I wouldn't even know where to look first. I'd say to check his house or apartment, but I'm sure those who are after him have already been there. And he'd come here, knowing his home was compromised." I flicked my gaze between the two of them, seeing dark circles under their eyes. They were drained. "Besides, you guys look exhausted. I'm not going to make you run around the city looking for a scared witch scientist, when we don't even know where to look."

"I'm not that tired," said Jade, though her droopy eyelids said otherwise.

"I still have about three hours of investigation left in me," said Elsa. "If I don't have to run, I'll be fine."

I smiled at her. "There'll be no running tonight." I moved to the coffee machine, flicked it on, and went to fill it with water. I wasn't tired at all. Quite the opposite. I'd slept half the day, so I was still running on adrenaline and energy. "This is my fault. My mess." I had to find him. And I wouldn't rest until I did.

"Fine," said Jade, moving next to Elsa by the table. She wrapped her hands around her roller skates that hung from her neck. "We'll go. But only if you tell us what happened between you and Valen."

I cringed as I turned around and rested my back on the counter. "Do I have to?"

"Yes," they chorused.

"When I first found Bellamy, I took him to Valen's restaurant. I figured it was a better place to hide him than the hotel."

"Makes sense," said Elsa. "No one would have thought to look there."

"That was what I was thinking," I continued, seeing their focus on me, their eyes gleaming with interest.

"You didn't find Valen?" asked Jade. "Is that why you brought Bellamy back here?"

I turned and poured myself a fresh cup of coffee. "Oh, I found him, all right. I found him with that pretty blonde."

"You caught them having sex!" Jade smacked her roller skates together, looking positively thrilled.

I sighed. "No. They were leaving the restaurant when we got there."

"And you think he's dating you both? Is that it? Is that why you're angry with him?" Elsa watched me, her lips pressed in a tight line.

I took a sip of coffee. "I know what you're getting at. I have no right to be upset. We've only been on one date." The fact that he hadn't reached out after that date did sting. "But I reacted. I didn't use my head."

A slow smile worked Jade's lips. "What did you do?"

"I didn't do anything. Bellamy was with me. I left and brought Bellamy here."

"Leana," began Elsa. "It doesn't mean he doesn't care for you. I mean, you don't know who that blonde woman is."

I thought about when I asked him to introduce us, the way Valen didn't want to elaborate on who she was. It only cemented my belief that he was in a relationship with her.

"It doesn't matter. That's it. That's all that happened. And you know the rest." I was done talking about it. I needed to find Bellamy, and I wouldn't let my emotions get in the way of work. I wouldn't make that mistake again. "Off to bed, you guys," I said as I ushered them out of my apartment.

When we reached the doorway, Jade turned. "What are you going to do?"

"I'm going to start downstairs and ask around to see if anyone saw anything. If he was taken by force, someone must have seen something." I wasn't sure I'd be so lucky, but I had to start somewhere. I had to do something. I couldn't just sit here and wait for Bellamy to show up, because I doubted he would.

"You come and get us if you find anything," ordered Elsa, her back hunched with tiredness.

"Sure," I lied. My friends had done enough tonight. I was going to drag Bellamy by the ears on my own when I found him. *If* I found him. "Who knows, maybe Julian has something."

We said our good nights, and I headed to the

elevator. When the doors slid open to reveal a lobby, loud with the murmurs of people, the clanking of chips, and the binging of slot machines, I made my way to the front desk.

"You still here?" I leaned over the counter, knowing it would anger Errol that I was contaminating his space with my dirty witch DNA.

The concierge lifted his lips into a snarl. "The night shift is late. Happens all the time. What do you want?"

"Any messages for me?"

"No."

"You sure?"

"Do I have three eyes?"

I grinned. "Maybe? It's hard to tell sometimes under that frown."

Errol grimaced. "Go away."

"Did you see a short, heavyset male, kinda disheveled looking with a white shirt, by any chance?"

Errol gave me a mock laugh. "Lots of dirty-looking guests fit that description."

I raised a brow. "He might have been with someone else. Being dragged by force? Anyone like that?" I knew Errol watched the lobby. He might be a lizard shifter, but he had the keen eyes of a hawk.

"No," he said. "You stink." He moved away from me to the other side of the front desk, where a female guest in a short red cocktail dress was waiting.

I gave my armpits twin covert sniffs. They

weren't shower-fresh but nowhere near as bad as Errol led me to believe, especially after the night I was having.

Disappointed, I pushed off the counter and went in search of Julian. He was pretty easy to spot. You just had to look for the handsome, tall male surrounded by three females.

Julian sat at a blackjack table with a brunette on his lap. A redheaded female stood behind him, rubbing his shoulders, and another darker female whispered things in his ear that kept him grinning like a fool.

Yeah, he didn't look like he was trying hard to find Bellamy. Still, it wasn't his fault we'd lost him. That was on me.

"Julian," I called as I squeezed in. The three females all glared at me. "Got anything on Bellamy?" I asked, ignoring them.

"Oh, hey, Leana," said the witch. "Blow on this for luck, darling," he said to the brunette on his lap as he held his fist with dice toward her. She gave him a lustful smile and blew on his dice. Satisfied, Julian tossed the dice, and from the winning cheers all around, I was guessing it had worked. I didn't really care for those games.

"Julian?" I pressed again.

"Oh." The witch turned to me. "No. Sorry. He's not here."

I wanted to press him with more questions, but the way the three females were staring at me meant it wouldn't be long before their nails came out.

Shaking my head, I left Julian and his harem to search for Jimmy. Maybe he'd know or had seen something. What I did not expect was to see Errol coming my way.

"Here. This came for you." Errol all but threw a message card at me.

I caught it before it hit the floor. "Thanks, gecko."

"You're welcome, *witch*." We all know that's not the word he used.

I laughed because why not. Plus, I was beginning to feel a little bit tired now that the initial rush of losing Bellamy had passed. I flipped the message card over.

Sorry I had to go. Meet me at 599 East 120th Street. Come alone. I don't trust your friends. You are the only one I trust.
—Bellamy.

A wash of relief fell over me. Okay, so he hadn't been kidnapped. The witch scientist had snuck out on his own because he distrusted the hotel and its owners. Now that I knew where he was, I could still build my case. All was not lost.

I frowned at the slight on my friends. But I got it. He was scared. It had taken what courage he had to find me and trust me, as he said. I would have to respect that. Besides, my friends were either preoccupied or already sleeping.

First, I was going to find him, and then I'd figure out where to put him. Even if it meant I had to go back to Valen's, seeing as it was still the perfect spot to stash a critical witness.

And this time, I wouldn't let Bellamy out of my sight.

CHAPTER 20

By the time the cabbie dropped me off at 599 East 120th Street, it was one in the morning. I looked at the massive gray-brick building standing before me with tall chimneys jutting from the top, like a crown of a giant beast. Lines of blackened windows stared back at me, and darkness stretched in the arches and doorways. No lights shone from the inside to give any hint of where Bellamy could be. Not even the soft glow of a candle.

"Why did you come here, Bellamy?" I whispered to myself. "Should've stayed in my apartment."

The fact was, the building gave me the creeps. It was huge. Thousands of square feet. Six stories high and the size of a large hospital. Bellamy could be anywhere. It would take me hours to scout the entire building.

I sighed. "Couldn't you at least have given me a clue?"

My phone vibrated and made me jump. I pulled it

out of my bag, saw Valen's name flashing on the screen, and hung up. The giant was persistent. Maybe his guilt was talking. Either way, I was going to speak to him. But now wasn't the time.

Part of me wondered if I should call Elsa and Jade to see if they were up to searching a creepy building with me. But just the memory of how tired they'd been when I left had me stuffing my phone back in my bag and abandoning that notion with it. Bellamy might not even be here.

No. I was doing this alone.

I crossed the street toward the colossal and grotesque building. The windows from the front entrance shone in the half-light from the distant streetlamps. Graffiti plagued the exterior walls like mismatched murals, but the bright colors did nothing to improve the decrepit structure.

A door lay open, dark and frightening like the mouth of the beast. Yet, even in the semidarkness, I could still make out worn, red letters just above the frame that read ENTRANCE.

I sighed and adjusted the strap of my bag higher on my shoulder. The tightness in my gut reappeared tenfold at the massive, eerie building. If Bellamy was in there, I was going to find him.

I pulled out my phone again, realizing I should have kept it in my hand, given the darkness reflecting inside the building. With a swipe of my finger, I turned on the flashlight mode. A shoot of bright white light bathed fifteen feet beyond in its luminance. Good enough.

I halted just before stepping inside and looked to the sky. It had clouded over, and dark gray-black clouds raced across the night sky. It would be harder to tap into my starlight magic, but I might not have the need to. I might just knock Bellamy over the head and drag his ass back with me.

I stepped through the doorway. A tingling presence of magic and something much stronger hit me like I'd walked face-first into a wall of mist. I took a deep breath and let it out, exhaling anxiety with it before I kept going. I met darkness and shadows and nothing else. Even though my senses weren't as acute as a White or Dark witch was to paranormal energies and the vibrations of magic, I still felt a cold transition of energy as soon as I'd stepped through the entrance. The shift in the air had nothing to do with the wind that moved through the open door behind me.

Magic was here. And a crapload of it.

My pulse raced as I moved inside, holding my cell phone before me like a weapon. After a moment, my eyes adjusted to the darkness until I could make out shapes and familiar-looking objects. *Very* familiar-looking objects.

"Oh… shit."

Similar to the first lab I'd seen with my friends, the space was filled with rows of tanks, crates, and machinery, all hooked up to humans submerged in huge liquid tanks. I could hear the clicks and taps of the machines over the blood pounding in my ears.

This was the same setup but on a much larger

scale. The ceiling was probably thirty feet high or more, and the edge disappeared into shadows. Here, there weren't just a dozen or so tanks paired with a single floating human inside, but hundreds of tanks.

An uneasy feeling settled in my core. This was the mother ship of labs. The other two were just the offspring. This was massive.

"Bellamy?" I called out, my voice echoing around me. I waited about a minute or so, listening, but I didn't hear anything apart from the constant beeping of the machines and my own damn heart. Maybe this was Bellamy's way of telling me there was another lab. Perhaps even where everything originated? Yeah, that had to be it.

I rushed over to the first human-tank setup, snatched up all the files that would fit in my bag, and stuffed them inside. I needed proof. *Proof!* I grabbed my phone, switched off the flashlight mode, and started to take pictures of the tank, the miserable suspended human inside, and everything around it, like a paparazzi on a coffee high. Once I had about thirty pictures or so, I sent copies to myself by email. Just in case.

That's when I heard the footsteps.

Instinctively, I dropped my phone, yanked on my starlight, and spun around with twin balls of star power hovering in my palms.

"Bellamy?" I lowered my hands, my starlight vanishing, but not before I got a clear view of his face. He looked… he looked *off*. The witch scientist shifted his weight like he had ants in his pants or he had a prostate problem.

"Shit." I bent down and picked up my phone. Even in the dim light, I could see a long crack all the way across the screen. Relief washed over me as glowing icons stared back over the multitouch display. It wasn't dead. I stood and switched on the flashlight mode once again. With a flick of my wrist, I shined it in Bellamy's face, and I watched him squint his eyes.

"I told you to stay put." I glowered at him. "It's not safe for you. Especially not here. Please tell me why you thought coming here was a good idea?" When he didn't answer, I kept going. "You could have just told me about this place instead of me chasing you around the city. It would have been a lot easier and cheaper. I'm spending way too much on cab rides." I swept my gaze around the space. "It's huge. It's where it all began. Right? Where it all started?"

Bellamy's hands twitched nervously as he yanked out his dirt-smeared handkerchief and dabbed his face. "Yes. That's right."

I frowned and moved closer to him. "You look nervous. More than usual. Why did you bring me here?" Something was definitely up with him.

Bellamy's face was sweating, and his hair was damp like he'd gone for a dip in a pool before meeting me. "I'm sorry. I had no choice."

My gut tightened at the fear and guilt in his voice. "What are you talking about? What the hell is going on?" I stepped closer. "Start talking. Why did you bring me here?" I looked around again at the gargantuan lab. "I thought you were running away from places like this. That you'd be too afraid to set foot in here again." It didn't make sense that he'd want to meet here.

"I'm... so sorry." Bellamy spun around and ran.

"Wait!" I hurried after him. Adrenaline spiked through my thighs, helping me put on a burst of speed. The witch was in worse physical shape than I was, and I caught up to him in no time. I was going to tackle him like a linebacker.

But then something stepped from the shadows and blocked my way.

I skidded to a stop. Bellamy's shape veered left behind a wall or a tall cabinet, and he was gone.

The said something that had blocked my way wasn't just a something—but *some things*.

Miraculously, I still had my phone in my hand, and I flicked it up.

A group of paranormals teemed before me. And guessing from the smells of wet dog, old blood, and what I thought was feces, I knew I was looking at newly formed vampires, werewolves, and shifters. Some were naked, and some were partially clothed. One male had only a pair of boxers on him. Their hair was damp, and their skin shone with moisture.

Tension tightened my muscles. "Fantastic. Fresh out of the tanks. Am I right?"

I gritted my teeth, anger welling inside my core. Bellamy had set me up! The witch bastard brought me here, hoping these newly created paranormals would kill me. And all after I tried to keep his sweaty ass safe.

Note to self, never trust a profusely sweating individual.

Well, he was wrong about one thing. I wasn't planning on dying tonight.

I dropped my phone in my bag, freeing my hands. "Let me pass," I ordered, pulling on my starlight again and hoping they still had some humanity left in there somewhere. Perhaps their transformation had been successful this time, and they weren't deranged like the previous vampires I'd encountered with Valen.

A dark male flashed me his teeth and did a swipe of his sharp black talons at me in a show of violence and strength.

I guess not. "I don't want to hurt you, but if you come after me… you'll give me no choice." I knew these were humans, tampered with paranormal blood, no less, but still human at the source. I didn't want to kill them, but I wouldn't let them eat me either.

But all notions of guilt evaporated as the first swarm of human subjects threw themselves at me.

"I'll get you, Bellamy!" I shouted as I threw out my hand.

A brilliant ball of starlight hit two paranormals. They lit up like twin white Christmas trees, twitched, and then they collapsed ungracefully to the floor.

"I'll find you, and then you'll get it, Bellamy!" I

cried out. "You're gonna get it!" I didn't know what I'd do to him when I found him again—because I would. I just knew it would involve me smiling and him crying.

Movement caught my attention to my right. My body flooded with the tingling starlight energy that gushed from my core and raced along my hands.

A female vampire rushed toward me, fangs and talons out like she was ready to make me her late supper. Or was it early breakfast?

A burst of white light fired forth from my outstretched fingers, and I directed it at the vampire. It hit her in the chest, covering her body in a sheet of white light.

A shriek of pain came from the vampire, her long limbs flailing like she was attempting a backstroke. And then she fell to the ground in a heap of charcoaled, blackened flesh.

I didn't have time to feel guilty about killing her as another paranormal came at me from behind.

I spun around, my hands ready. A male of considerable size advanced with more muscles than he seemed to know what to do with and crushing fists. He growled, spit dripping from his mouth. My eyes burned at the stench of vomit and something else I didn't want to think about.

"You are mine," he roared, in a voice that was two voices, like the part of blood from whatever paranormal that was used to create this thing had formed its own voice along with the human's. Damn.

"So, you can speak?" I said, surprised.

It appeared as though the newly transformed humans were capable of thought. How much of it was still to be determined. But they weren't mindless zombies.

The male paranormal threw his head back in a deeply amused laugh. "I can do more than just speak." And then he rushed me.

A sledgehammer of flesh and bone barreled my way. He scared the crap out of me. Just as well, fear added fuel to my magic.

Gripping my will, I blasted him with shoots of my starlight. It hit the male human subject on the shoulder, causing him to stagger back. And before I could conjure up my starlight again, his mouth was wrapped around my arm.

I cried out, and tears filled my eyes. His jaw tore into my flesh with his needlelike teeth. I swore as white-hot pain ripped through me, and I felt hot wetness trickling down my arm.

I kicked out with my leg, and my boot vibrated as I made contact with his knee. He stumbled back, but in a flash, he went for me again.

Fear and anger rising, I thrust out my hand and hit him with a single thin burst of starlight, coming at him horizontally like a glowing white blade.

The blade of starlight sliced through him like he was made of butter. I saw a surprised look on his face as he glanced down at himself. And then his upper body slid off his waist and landed in a clump next to his severed lower body.

"I told you to stay back. Damn it," I told him, though I knew he was dead.

I looked up to find a row of paranormals smiling evilly at me, their eyes traveling over my body like they were wondering what part to rip off first or what I tasted like.

Crap. I was seriously regretting not picking up the phone, when Valen called. I could have used the giant's help right about now.

I thought about dialing his number, but that thought died as a shadow sprang at me from the left.

Before I could stop it, we hit the wall together with frightening force. The impact of pain took the breath from my lungs, and I felt my hold on my starlight slip. A shower of wood fragments, and what might have been wires, blasted into the air, falling over my hair as dust blew into my eyes. I was pinned to the wall and couldn't move.

The male vampire shrieked with laughter, and his warm breath assaulted my face as he spoke. "I will tear the skin off your bones slowly until you beg for mercy… and then I'll suck out your blood like water through a straw."

I coughed, blinking the tears away. "That's really gross." I yanked on my starlight, reaching out to the magic of the stars, and let it rip.

A burst of light emanated from me and blasted the vampire, sending him end over end across the lab. A sudden crashing sound seemed like maybe one of the tanks had busted, but I couldn't see that far out in the dark.

I pushed myself forward, staggering as I felt the effects of drawing on my starlight. My body weakened as the magic took its compensation.

Growls echoed, pulling me around. A group of human subjects fell on their hands and knees. Their bones cracked and popped, their arms and legs lengthening. Their faces warped and stretched until their jaws elongated into a hideous blend of human and wolf.

A fluff of silky, thick gray-and-black fur appeared over their skin as their yellow eyes tracked me. Nothing human was left in them, just animal. Their lips curled in a threat with steady growls in a promise of death.

I felt a rush of panicked anger. "Super." I exhaled. "I'm getting too old for this shit. Should have stayed in my apartment. That's what I should've done."

I barely had time to register how quickly my plan had gone down the crapper as the wolves came at me.

I flung myself under one of the tanks, twisting while ducking and rolling until I barely missed a swipe of razor-sharp claws from the black wolf.

But then something grabbed my foot, and I was dragged back out.

Rolling, teeth and claws slashed at me, shredding and tearing at my clothes and skin. It hurt like a sonofabitch, but I was up in a heartbeat. Good ol' adrenaline could do that.

A fist came out of nowhere and down onto my face. Blackness plagued my vision as I stumbled, and my cheekbone screamed in pain. I felt the warm trickle of blood from my nose as I blinked the wetness from my eyes while the shadow of vamps loomed over me. Even with the starlight energy that flowed in me, I was no match for a vampire's supernatural speed. They were still way faster than me and stronger, able to dodge my attacks with fluid ease.

My face throbbed, and I felt it swelling up like a balloon. No need for fillers. A male vamp lunged at me, teeth bared and unnaturally white. I leaped back, but not fast enough, as his fist connected with the side of my head.

I stumbled, bending forward and nauseated as the walls of my skull drummed. I was barely aware of my legs that were miraculously still supporting me. A hand shot out, and the same vamp grabbed me, throwing me to the ground.

I was *so* going to kill Bellamy.

"Playtime is over," said a voice that sounded vaguely familiar.

With my head throbbing, I struggled to sit up, but something grabbed my arms.

"Hold her down," ordered a female voice.

Flashes of white lab coats assaulted me, and the next thing I knew, I was pinned to the cold cement floor, unable to move.

Fear cascaded down me in waves, ice-cold and chronic. I tried hard not to think about the throbbing in my head or the fact that these human subjects were listening to someone.

The sting of a needle prick pinched the side of my neck.

Immediately, I felt a rush of something warm, the feeling of fatigue rushing through my veins. And for some strange reason, I couldn't make my legs or arms move.

Uh-oh.

Straining, I tried to will my legs, arms, even a finger to move, but it was as though I'd been hit with a freezing spell. My body wasn't responding.

Shit. This was really bad.

That fear boosted me with the last burst of adrenaline, keeping me awake. I couldn't move, and that alone terrified me.

The lights flickered on, and I blinked into the light, letting my eyesight adjust to the sudden brightness as the entire warehouse lab was suddenly bathing in bright light.

A shape drew my eye. And then the figure stepped forward into my line of sight.

"Stardud," said Adele, a smile in her voice. "How nice of you to come."

CHAPTER 21

A dele? My mind seemed to be suffering from the effects of whatever they'd given me, because that person looked exactly like Adele. Unless she had an evil twin? Yeah, didn't think so.

Nope, it was her. I'd recognize that demented twinkle in her eye and her false smile anywhere.

"You?" I said, my lips strangely tingly and numb, like when the dentist injects your gums with Novocain. Tendrils of tension squeezed my chest, and all my warning flags went up.

Adele looked down at me. Her white council robe hung on her tall, lean frame, and gold etching weaved around the sleeves and collar in sigils and runes. It was an exquisite robe. Too bad it draped the shoulders of such a cow. "Yes. It's me. Who else?"

"You drugged me." I stared at the syringe she still held in her lengthy, spindly fingers. "What did you give me? What is this?" I tried to move, but it was no use. It was as though my limbs were made of cement, and they were part of the floor.

In a flash of white, I could just make out three people dressed in white lab coats standing above me. Not just people but witch scientists like Bellamy.

"A powerful muscle relaxant," answered Adele, her voice silky and venomous like a snake's. "A neuromuscular-blocking drug, like human doctors give patients to keep them still before operating on them."

Operating on them? I tried to frown, but it seemed my facial muscles were all out of whack too. I might have been smiling. I might have been glowering. "But your bony ass sits on the White witch council. How could you do this?" Yeah, she was just the sort of narcissistic psycho to come up with something so twisted.

"Poor little Stardud, caught in a web." Adele stepped calmly toward me.

The other remaining paranormals stood watching, their faces peering down at me with excitement flashing in their eyes as they anticipated what Adele was about to do. Whatever it was, I was betting it wasn't good.

Straining, I tried to focus on my starlight as I called to it, but it was like something was blocking me. Some kind of invisible wall or obstacle kept me from reaching out to the stars. It felt similar to when the sun cockblocked me, as Julian had said, like it was high noon even though it was, like, one in the morning.

"You can't call on your starlight magic," commented Adele, apparently having seen me struggling with something internally. She glanced at the syringe in her hand. "I made sure to add a magic-barrier component in that shot I gave you. Bellamy prepared it for me. Your magic can't save you now, Stardud."

Damn that Bellamy. I'd never heard of a magical blocker used through a syringe. From what I knew, you could potentially block another witch or any magical practitioner from using their magic with a spell or a hex. I'd even heard of magical handcuffs that could break the magical link. Adele had figured out a new way to jam my starlight frequency.

I tried to grimace, but I'm sure I looked more constipated than anything. "My friends will come looking for me. They know where I am." Total lie. I should have at least texted Jade or Elsa, telling them where I'd gone. The fact was, no one knew where I was except for Errol, who took the message down from Bellamy. I was as good as dead if I expected Errol to come to my rescue.

"It's over," stated Adele. "You think too highly of yourself and your abilities. I noticed that flaw the first time we met. So arrogant. So self-absorbed. You will always be a nothing, a dud. The fact is, you were never going to win this. For the strong to survive... we must rid ourselves of the weak."

"Blah, blah, blah," I muttered. "You really like listening to yourself talk." But that was good in a way. I wanted to know the full extent of this plan of hers. Because when I could move again, I was going to come after her hard. For that, I needed her to keep talking.

Because I would move again, just as soon as this drug wore off, and then her ass was mine. I just didn't know when that was going to happen.

Adele snapped her fingers. "Put her in a chair," she ordered. Those three white-coat idiots picked me up, dragged me, and then dropped me in an office chair none too gently.

My head lolled to the side. Thank God the chair had a high enough headrest to keep my head from snapping off of my neck. I knew technically that wouldn't happen, but that's how it felt. The only good thing about my new chair was that now I had a good view of my surroundings.

I felt a string of drool starting to trickle down the corner of my mouth. Damn. I was drooling. I tried to suck it back in, but that didn't work. I could feel it but could do nothing about it. I was a paralyzed, drooling Starlight witch. Fantastic. The next thought in my head was thank the goddess Valen wasn't here to see this.

I heard the scrape of a shoe on the floor and flicked my eyes to see Bellamy crouching behind one of the human tanks.

"You're dead," I threatened. "You came to me for help, and you do this? I'm coming for you next. Just as soon as I can move, you lying sonofabitch!"

At that, Bellamy's face went from pale to paler. But as he continued to watch me, I could see the realization on his face, the way his posture seemed to relax a bit. He knew I wasn't going to get up anytime soon. Once he found some courage, he came around from his hiding place and stepped forward.

"I'm sorry. But she gave me no choice," said the witch scientist. "It was either my life or yours. And I'll always choose me. You're a Merlin. There're lots of those. But you can't replace me on a whim. I have an IQ of—"

"Shut up, you sweaty little prick," I howled. "When this is over, I'm going to kick your ass. And then I'm gonna do it again because it's fun. You can count on it. I'm a woman of my word."

Bellamy clamped his mouth shut, his eyes darting over to Adele. It was almost as though he wasn't sure who was scarier, me or the skinny witch. Yeah, he was right to be scared.

But Bellamy, the traitor, was the least of my worries.

I turned my gaze to Adele, trying to think of a plan to get myself out of this mess. "This is the revenge you were talking about. Right?" I was glad my voice came out level and strong, even though my stomach was in chaos. "You want to kill me because I stopped you from destroying the hotel? That's a bit extreme, even for you. Don't you think?"

The corners of Adele's mouth twisted at my defiance. She shook her head, looking at me like I was her human subordinate who'd picked out the wrong robe. "The hotel needed to be replaced with something better. Bigger. Bigger is always better." Her thin lips stretched into a terrifying smile. "I will make that happen. One day soon. But I can't be distracted from my work." She moved to one of the desks and dropped the syringe.

I tried to lift a brow, but I might have flapped my upper lip instead. "What's that? Queen bitch? I think you've already achieved that goal." Okay, so this was probably not the best way to talk to my captor who had the means to rip me to shreds. But I hated this witch. And sometimes my mouth got ahead of my brain.

Adele turned and looked at me. "Haven't you been paying attention, Stardud? Look around you. What do you see?"

"If I could move my head, I could help you with that." I blinked. "What I see is your science experiment gone wrong."

The witch walked over to my chair and stared at me. "I thought you were smarter than this, smarter than those fools of witches you call your friends. But your name says it all. Doesn't it, Stardud? You're just an idiot with a pretty face."

At that, Bellamy snorted. He caught me staring, and whatever expression he saw on my face was enough to make him look away.

I flicked my eyes back on the witch. "Very mature." Still, it was clear she wanted me to see something or just validate what she'd done here.

The constant beeping of the machines pulled my eyes toward the tanks and the tubes filled with paranormal blood pumping into the human subjects.

"How did you get all the blood? Volunteers?" The amount of blood pumping through those magical dialysis machines was probably equivalent to ten liters or more. More than half of the average for a human body.

At that, Adele's eyes sparkled. So I was getting somewhere. "For the creation of the races, it required great amounts of blood from specific paranormals. So I took it."

"Meaning what? You killed them?" She was crazy. Not only did she kill humans, but I had no doubt she'd killed some paranormals as well to get what she wanted.

"Not always," answered Adele, coming closer still. She was so close, I could smell the bursts of her rosy perfume and something else like old onions. "Some gave blood in exchange for money. But sometimes, they didn't survive the retraction. Sometimes their bodies couldn't handle it. And well, maybe we took too much. Guess we'll never know."

"I said we were taking too much," expressed Bellamy, the faint tightening of his jaw the only sign of his resentment. "You didn't listen."

Adele gave him an irritated glance before returning her eyes to me again. "They were a means to an end."

"A very excruciating end, no doubt."

The twinge of indignation on Adele's pallid face almost made me smile. Hell. It felt good to piss her off. I should do it more often.

"You still haven't said why you're doing this," I

tried again. And seeing that satisfied gleam in her eyes, I knew she was about to tell me. It looked like Adele wanted to brag about her achievements before she got to the punchline.

A slow, deeply satisfied smile came over the witch. "It's time for the paranormals to rise. Time for us to take back what was ours in the first place."

"What's that?"

She raised her arms. "This world."

Uh-oh.

Adele sneered, her features pulling back and making her look feline. "Humans are weak, greedy, and stupid. Too long have we lived in the shadows of the weaker species. Not anymore."

"If I could throw up, I would."

"See," continued Adele. "We will remove the human race, but we'll keep just enough to sustain our thirst. They will continue to provide us with their blood, you see. We'll contain them. They'll be right where we need them."

"Like a prison?"

"Like a prison," she repeated joyfully. "My dear Stardud." Adele looked down at me. "I'll let you in on a little secret since… well… you're going to die."

I wasn't surprised to hear her say it. "And what's that?"

Adele surveyed my face, like she was making sure she had my complete attention for the full effect of what she was about to say. "There's no room for humans in *my* new world," said Adele, speaking clearly and emphasizing the word *my*. Her eyes traveled to the tanks and back to me.

"*Your* new world?" Yeah, she was most definitely nuts. I felt dizzy. This was too much information. "Holy shit. You're trying to breed out humans. Only you can't wait that long, so you're manufacturing paranormals?" It sounded even more insane as the words left my mouth.

"Vampires, werewolves, every kind of shifter," said the skinny witch. "Some species are more difficult to recreate, but soon we will achieve the impossible. Right, Bellamy?"

Bellamy looked up from a file he was staring at. "Yes. Yes, that's right. Witches are posing a small problem but nothing that we can't adjust for."

"Excellent." Adele's face twisted in a wicked smile.

Heat rushed to my face. I tried to move again, but it was no use. My body was just as useless as Bellamy's trust. "But your experiments are flawed," I spat. "They don't last. All of these… these *things* have an expiration date. It's not going to work."

"Long enough to achieve what I need," said Adele. She glanced at me, her smile widening at what she saw on my face. "The complete and utter destruction of the human world. My *experiments,* as you so delicately put it, are the key. No longer will we be kept in our cages. No longer will we live in secret. Paranormals will walk the earth. This is the end of the human world as you know it. It's a shame you won't be around to see it. Billions of humans will be replaced and will eventually die. No skin off my teeth."

Yikes. A mix of anger and fear rushed through my core. "You're insane."

At that, the witch's cool demeanor seemed to crack on the surface. "And just like everyone here, *you* have a part to play in my new world, Stardud," she added, her eyes gleaming.

My blood went cold as I suddenly understood what I was doing here, paralyzed in the chair, why Bellamy made me come here. He didn't mean to kill me—well, not at first.

"No. You can't take my blood. You can't make other Starlight witches. It doesn't work like that." I gritted my teeth, praying to the goddess to give me the use of my magic again, but as I tried to reach out to the power in the stars, I felt the same blockage as before. I looked at Bellamy. "You can't create witches. Tell her, Bellamy. Tell her!"

Oh, shit. I shouldn't have come here.

Bellamy looked at the other witch scientists, like he was hoping they were going to back him up. But they glanced away and turned their backs on him, looking just as terrified of Adele as he was.

Sweat trickled down Bellamy's temples. "Witch transference is a problem…" His eyes went to Adele. "But nothing we can't overcome. I assure you," he added quickly.

Damn. They were going to take my blood and probably kill me in the process. I couldn't do anything about it.

Worse, no one knew where I was. I felt foolish and terribly alone at the moment. Tears brimmed my eyes.

"Are you crying?" laughed Adele. "I thought you were made of stronger stuff, Stardud. Crying's for losers."

Tears from anger, desperation, and regret fell. I didn't care that they all saw. What did it matter anyway? They were going to use me like a lab rat.

Adele tsked and leaned over me. I heard some rustling, and then she hauled my bag from my head and pulled it to her.

"What are you doing?" I asked as she rummaged through it.

Adele reached in and pulled out my phone. "Like I said. You give yourself way too much credit, Stardud. In a few minutes, you'll be dead," she cooed. "Your life will have never mattered. Soon, no one will even remember Leana Fairchild, the Starlight witch. You're nothing, and you'll die nothing."

My expression warped as I searched for an answer that wasn't coming. Panic redoubled, clouding my mind and my focus. I didn't want to die like this, paralyzed and unable to defend myself.

"It's not going to work," I hissed. "My blood can't help you."

Adele gave a mock laugh. "Oh, Stardud. This isn't about you. It was never about you. You're not that special."

"What?"

"What is the rarest, most special of all of us?"

Oh, fuck…

Adele held my phone in her hand. "I told you. It was never about you. It was always about the giant. To make more giants, well, I need a giant." She smiled wickedly and said, "I need Valen."

CHAPTER 22

I was a fool. The biggest fool in the universe of universes of fools.

The blood left my face. I'd been wrong. I knew where this was going. It all made sense now. Why I was coaxed here and carefully kept alive. Adele was going to use me to lure Valen somehow.

I stared at my phone in her hand. "It's not going to work."

"Yes. Yes, it will."

"It won't."

Adele looked up and said, "He'll come. He'll come for you. I've seen the way the giant looks at you. The way a man desires a woman. You're all he thinks about. He's in love with you, I think."

My face flamed at her comment. "He's not. I know that for a fact. He's seeing other women. Just tonight, he was with someone else. You've got it all wrong." But did she?

Adele's fingers moved over the screen as she

typed. "I don't think so. I've been watching you two for quite some time. It was nauseating, but the work had to be done. He's that handsome, strong, overprotective type of male who will come if he thinks his woman's in trouble."

"I'm not his woman." Though, I liked the sound of it.

She pocketed my phone inside the folds of her white robe. "He cares about you deeply, though I have no idea why. Still, he'll come. I'm always right."

"What do you want from him?" I knew what she wanted, but I wanted to hear her say it.

"With a giant army at my disposal," she said, straightening, "the humans will never be able to resist. There'll be nothing left of the humans after my giants take care of them."

"You're one twisted bitch," I snarled. "You won't get away with this. The Gray Council will stop you." I wasn't entirely sure, not anymore. Even if Adele had orchestrated this lab, I had a feeling she had some admirers within the Gray Council. "And I'm pretty sure you'll get some resistance from the paranormal courts. They won't let you destroy all the humans. Because… well… because that's crazy."

Adele tidied the front of her robe. "You're right. Resistance is inevitable. And they'll be taken care of just like the human resistance. With my giant army."

Dread was a sudden finality. I felt useless and ashamed. No way could I get out of my chair. My body wasn't my own anymore, but I still had the use of my mouth.

"Bellamy, listen to me," I said, talking fast. "Do you hear what's she's saying?" The witch scientist angled his body toward me from one of the workstations, but he wouldn't make eye contact. "Don't you know this is genocide? You can't do it. If you let her, you're part of it. You're just as guilty as her. Even if you manage to get her plans up and running, we will stop you. You hear me! And when we do, you won't make prison. You'll be killed." His shoulders tensed, so I knew I was reaching him. "You can stop her. Just don't do it. Say you won't."

Bellamy finally lifted his eyes to mine. "You don't understand. I have no choice."

I growled as I tried to move, more angry tears leaking from the corners of my eyes. "If I could move, I would kick you in the ass! You *do* have a choice, Bellamy. Don't. That's your choice. Don't do it."

The witch scientist looked away and turned his attention back to whatever he was doing. When he shifted his weight, I got a glimpse of three syringes with fluffy red ends placed carefully in a line next to a dart gun. Not syringes, more like darts filled with whatever they'd used on me. "Are those for Valen?" I practically spat. Yes, I was certain there was moisture there. "You sonofabitch, Bellamy. You're just as nasty as her."

Adele laughed like I was some comic show put on just for her, but the witch scientist hunched his back —whether from guilt, tiredness, or fear, I didn't know. I didn't care. He'd prepared to do the same thing to Valen that he'd done to me. He was just as culpable as Adele in my book. He deserved a good ol' ass whooping.

Anger burned through my misery and my feelings of betrayal. I went somewhere far, far away from myself. Silent tears slid down my face and neck, puddling around my clavicles. Yup, some snot was mixed in there as well, and I could do nothing about that.

My own fury and fear evaporated at the thought of Valen, replaced with an overwhelming need to protect him. So what if he dated other women? Valen wasn't a bad guy. I wouldn't let her hurt him.

"Why don't you take my blood instead? Am I not good enough for your science experiment? I'm right here. Aren't I? Ready for the plucking?"

Adele threw back her head and laughed. "Why would I want more Starduds? You're the weakest sort of witch... you can't call on the power of the goddess or the elements, and even demons won't give you the time of day. I don't think it's accurate to even call you a witch. You're more human than anything else." She let out a breath. "I want a giant, and a giant I will have."

"He's not an object. He's a person."

Adele raised her brows. "He's whatever I want him to be. He's what I want and need at the moment."

My eyes burned as more tears fell down my cheeks. "You're a sick bitch. You know that?"

"I've been called worse."

239

"He won't come," I said. "He's busy." It was true. He was with that hot blonde.

The sounds of voices drifted over to me above the loud humming of my heart in my ears.

My pulse quickened, and I deeply regretted my decision to meet with Bellamy.

Adele's eyes rounded with excitement. "He's already here."

I darted my eyes over and saw some white coats rushing over to the table with the tranquilizing darts. One of them grabbed the gun, and then they all disappeared off to the sides, out of my line of sight. The paranormals were next as they all scattered like frightened rats behind crates and disappeared.

"No!" I clamped down on my jaw as I struggled with all my might and my strength. I might have farted, but it was hopeless. I couldn't move.

Adele snapped her fingers, and to my horror, Bellamy advanced with a roll of duct tape.

"Don't you dare," I growled. "Don't! Valen!" I shouted, looking over Bellamy's shoulders. "Don't come here! It's a—"

Bellamy slapped a piece of duct tape on my mouth. "I'm sorry." He leaned forward like wanted to say more, his lips flapping, and then he just said three words in a whisper, "It won't last."

"Mrrghh!" I cried, my words muffled.

Bellamy pulled away from me, and he moved off somewhere behind my chair.

When I searched for Adele, I couldn't see her

anywhere. Everyone was gone. It was just me, the chair, and… Valen.

Valen strode into the warehouse with a fluid, predatory grace, but his movements had a hurried edge as though he were uncomfortable or anxious. Though his rugged face was warped in worry, he was just as handsome and mesmerizing as ever. A black leather jacket covered his wide shoulders over a snug T-shirt and jeans. Even in the distance of the room, I could see a darkness in his gaze and tension over his face. Such concern lingered there.

Our eyes met, and my heart lurched.

Valen's eyes widened for just a second as he took in the chair, the duct tape over my mouth, my inability to move, and my tear-stricken face.

Raw emotions crossed his features—fear, guilt, and then a deep fury.

"Mmhhh!" More tears leaked out of my eyes as I tried to tell him no with just a stare, but Valen was already closing the distance between us at a sprint.

The tears kept falling, and Valen's speed increased. This was wrong. All wrong.

From the corner of my blurred vision, I saw dark forms fall from the ceiling, and then a blur of shapes surrounded Valen. Their black eyes flashed with a dark hunger, talons thrashing. Vampires.

Valen halted.

The sound of growls pulled my eyes to the left. More shapes came into view with fur and bodies that were too big to be considered normal wolves, their ears pinned and lips curled to show teeth the size of short blades with paws the size of my head.

In a blur of limbs, Valen ripped off his clothes. Next came a flash of light followed by a tearing sound and the breaking of bones. His face and body twisted, enlarging and expanding until he stood at his eighteen-foot giant form.

And then they rushed him.

Hot anger welled over my skin, though I could do nothing but watch.

Vampires and werewolves attacked Valen from each side. The giant moved fluidly and with the skilled grace of a killer. He swatted them with his great arms, sending two vampires crashing into one of the water tanks.

Valen ducked, spun, and came up with a great swipe of his fists, crushing the skulls of about three werewolves at once. They let out choked screams of pain and shock as blood fountained from their bloody stumps.

If I didn't know he was here to help me, I would have been scared shitless.

A thud of metal hit bone, and I saw one of the vampires holding a sword. Valen grabbed the sword, snapped it in half, and then did the same to the vampire.

Damn. That was pretty nasty. But I couldn't look away.

More vampires fell from the ceiling like big, ugly spiders and clung to the giant, sinking their teeth and talons into his flesh.

I heard a cry and the sound of tearing flesh as Valen peeled the vampires from his person, two by two, before smacking their heads together. I heard a sickening sound like the crumpling of bones, and he tossed them.

He crushed their bodies with voracious rapidity, his massive body unstoppable.

A flash of brown fur appeared in my line of sight. With a torrent of paranormal speed, a werewolf sank its teeth into Valen's thigh.

The giant cried out, more in anger than in pain, and with a swipe of his great fist, he pummeled the werewolf's head. The beast slid off the giant's leg and crumpled to the floor.

Another group of werewolves threw themselves at Valen in a flash of fur and teeth. A black werewolf opened its maw as it roared, its yellow eyes glowing while it snapped its huge teeth. It came up behind him. Valen spun and brought down his foot over its head, killing it instantly.

Strangled cries and yelps rang out all around me, followed by the horrid sound of flesh being torn and the fast, thrashing sound of fists pounding on soft flesh. Again. And again. And again.

Then a sudden silence hit me. Blinking through tears, I looked around.

Valen stood in a sea of broken, crushed, lifeless paranormals. Everywhere I looked, bodies of vampires and werewolves lay crumpled and very dead. I pushed aside the guilt that threatened to rise as I knew these were human subjects, well, most of them. But I couldn't know for sure. Some real paranormals could have sided with Adele.

My eyes found Valen again. He met my gaze, and a strange, warm thrill vibrated in my belly.

Glee and hope filled me. Valen had beaten them all, and no one was left. Not alive.

He turned his head to me, and I tried to smile, but the tape was too damn tight.

"*Leana*," said Valen, and my heart cried a little at the worry in his voice. Worry for me.

I heard a sudden loud pop, like the sound of a firework.

A small object flew past me and hit Valen in the chest. The fluff of red feathers stood out against Valen's skin.

Shit. The darts!

My eyes rounded in fear. "Mmgghmm!" I felt the blood leave my body and heard the intake of breaths from behind me. A wisp of panic unfolded like a leaf inside my chest.

Valen reached up and pulled out the dart, staring at it a moment before he crushed it in his hand.

The giant's face rippled in anger. And then he was moving toward me again.

Another pop. And I blinked to see another dart speared in Valen's neck.

The giant pulled that one out, too, and tossed it. He faltered for a moment, and I hissed through my teeth.

He took another step toward me just as a third dart sank into his right bicep.

"*Mmhhmm!*" I cried through my bound mouth.

Valen yanked out the third dart. He teetered and then he fell to his knees, the dart still in his hand. I watched in horror as the dart slid out of his palm.

And then the warehouse walls and floor shook as the giant hit the floor and collapsed on his side.

CHAPTER 23

"Finally." Adele came out from somewhere behind me. Her white robes billowed around her as she crossed over to where Valen lay. His head was turned in the opposite direction, so I couldn't see his face.

Adele stood over the giant for a moment, and then she pulled back her leg and kicked him with her boot.

"*Grrrrrh!*" I shouted.

She glanced over her shoulder at me and smiled. "He's ready."

I heard the muffled sounds of voices followed by the sound of many feet crossing the warehouse floor as the white coats came into view.

I narrowed my eyes at them. *Cheaters*. If they had fought Valen with the other paranormals, they'd be broken and crushed, lying on the floor with the rest of them.

"Don't worry," said Adele as she met my eyes.

"He won't feel a thing," she added with a satisfied smile.

I watched in horror, unable to move or work my magic, as the six white coats dragged a thick chain that looked like the anchor chain from a large boat, from somewhere off to my right. They wrapped the chain around Valen's arms, and then with a sudden click, a machine turned on. Suddenly Valen's large, heavy body was being hauled across the floor.

They dragged him to a lab station and laid him on his back. Then quickly began to stick needles all over his body until he had tubes connected to his neck, wrists, arms, legs, and chest.

The sound of wheels drew my attention to two white coats pushing a cart. Tall glass jars clinked together as they parked the cart next to one of those magical dialysis machines.

"Where's Bellamy?" Adele tossed her head around, her eyes darting across the warehouse.

"He left," said one of the white coats, a male with a short, brown beard. "Couldn't handle it." The others all laughed at that.

"He's a rat," said the only female white coat. "We should have killed him."

"That's not up to you," snapped Adele, and the female white coat's face flushed red. "*I* make the decisions. Bellamy served his purpose." Her eyes moved to Valen on the floor, and then they flicked up to me. "Without his traitorous ways, I wouldn't have my giant." Adele moved to stand next to Valen's head. From my vantage point, I could see only part of his face. He was staring up at the ceiling.

Terror pulled my throat tight. "Hhhhmmm."

"What about her?" The bearded white coat pointed at me. "She knows too much."

"We could perform a memory charm," said another white coat, the oldest one of the group, with his short white hair and a face draped in wrinkles.

The female white coat shook her head. "They never last. She might not remember a year from now. Or maybe in two years, it'd all come back to her. It's too risky. We should kill her."

What was up with that one and the killing? My heart jumped to my throat, and I could feel the beginnings of a panic attack.

"More Starlight witches could come in handy," said the bearded white coat. "We should bleed her. Save her blood for when we're ready for a witch transference."

"Have you not heard a word I said?" Adele leaned her tall frame over the smaller witch scientist. "I make the decisions. Besides"—she looked at me, a curious frown on her face—"Darius wants her alive."

Darius? Who the hell was Darius? Was he the one on the Gray Council calling the shots? I bet he was.

"But…" Adele smiled coolly at me. "He never said we couldn't play with her first."

The white coats all laughed at that, sounding like a pack of wild hyenas, and I saw a flicker of fury cross over Valen's face.

"We're ready," declared one of the white-coat

males standing next to that dialysis machine, his hand next to a large, red button.

Adele let out a sigh of satisfaction. "Let us begin."

The white-coat male pressed the button, and the rumble of a motor came to life, beeps and clicks ringing throughout the warehouse.

I felt sick to my stomach as shoots of Valen's blood rushed through long tubes and disappeared inside the dialysis machine. Then drops of red liquid began to fill the glass jars.

"Quickly," ordered Adele, snapping her fingers. "Bring in the human."

Bring in the human? Was she going to create another giant now?

Yup. I blinked at another group of white coats hauling a heavy, water-filled tank on wheels with a floating, unconscious female inside.

Shit. They were going to try and create a giant with this human female.

I looked over at Adele, trying to tell her with my eyes that she was a demented bitch, but she was just staring at Valen like he was a prized diamond. She was pacing. Her excitement for torturing and killing people was sick.

Bile rose in my throat, and I pressed it down. If I threw up now, with my throat partially paralyzed, I might choke to death.

I pulled my eyes back to Valen, and my breath caught. His skin was pale, sweaty, and almost had a greenish tint. His face was a mask of distress. He looked sick, like he had a fever.

I tried to thrash, giving it my all, but all I did was let out more gas. "*Mmmm!*"

Adele looked at me and flashed me a smile. "You're thinking that we're just wasting her life like the others. That her weak human body can't withstand the transformation." Her smile grew. "We've added a special mix this time. A key element to preserve all magical properties of giants. As though she were born a giantess. If she lives through the mutation, there's a good chance she'll survive. She'll never be human again. She'll be a giantess."

I frowned, or at least I tried to, a feeling of dread filling up to my eyeballs.

"Count yourself lucky. Not many have witnessed the birth of giants."

The birth of giants? She was a freaking lunatic.

The female white coat grabbed tubes attached to the human female and connected them to the same machine that Valen was connected to. They were bleeding him and trying to create a giant at the same time. They were going to kill him.

My eyes rolled over Valen again, seeing his face and body weaken.

The sound of chanting broke over the beeping of machines. The white coats and the witch scientists were working their magic. The chanting took on the edge of fierce, vindictive satisfaction and continued to rise in pitch until it sounded almost like shouting.

The scent of white magic twined around me like a vine. A cold, icy feeling hit me that wasn't from the

September wind. My skin pricked at the shift in the air like tiny electrical currents. I swore as I felt the sting of them mixed with the scent of candy and rotten eggs.

The human in the tank jerked, her limbs flailing as Valen's blood was pumped into her. She looked like she couldn't breathe, like she was being held underwater by force. She turned her face, and we locked eyes for a moment. Through the glass, I saw the fear and despair in them. I wanted to help her, to do something. I got a flash of her frightened human face, and then her eyes went dull, her head hanging. Was she dead?

I'd never witnessed something so terrible, so inhumane and vile in my entire life. I could never unsee it. It was imprinted inside my eyelids forever.

"With my army of giants, I will be invincible!" cried Adele, her face set in a manic smile. "I won't need Darius or any of them. I will crush all who oppose me. I will have my new world. And I will be queen!"

Total psycho.

The witch scientists kept chanting. A blue-white light flashed so brightly, I had to close my eyes for a moment if I didn't want my eyeballs to burn.

Next, came a sizzling sound and then a pop, like a campfire, followed by the overwhelming scent of wet earth mixed with sulfur. The light diminished, and I stared at the human female floating in the tank. She was the same size as before. Nothing had changed as far as I could tell.

Adele snapped her fingers impatiently. "Drain it. Come on. Come on."

Obeying their mistress, one of the white coats pulled on what I could only call a black tub plug, and the water released into a thick, black pipe that stretched all the way to the side of the warehouse.

"Take her out," ordered Adele as soon as the tank was empty of water.

The white coats yanked the naked human female out and placed her on the cold cement floor, wet and most probably dead. Somewhere deep inside of me, I hoped she was.

The anger on Adele's face made me smile. Well, I tried to. Oooooh. She was mad.

The witch stood over the human. "Get up. Up! Get up and change, or I will burn you alive!"

The female human's eyes snapped open. Holy shit, she was alive!

"Get up, you filth." Adele moved and kicked her in the stomach hard.

The human yelped in pain and rolled to her side.

"Rise!" Adele called out, her arms stretched wide. Yeah, total Dr. Frankenstein wannabe.

I took the opportunity to glance at Valen, and fear choked me. His skin was wet and almost transparent. Blue veins shone through that looked as thin and delicate as tissue paper. I could almost see the blood being sucked out of him.

They were killing him. He wasn't going to survive this.

And it was all my fault.

Dread twisted my guts, and more tears spilled down my face as I stared at the man, the giant, who I obviously cared for more than I wanted to admit to myself.

"Up! Get up! You stupid human whore!" Adele kicked the human female again and again. Even her white coats had the smart idea of moving back and giving her space.

The human female let out a scream, and then she started to convulse. At first, I thought this was the end. But then I felt a hum of magic in the air and saw a flash of light.

The human woman went down on all fours, howling as her face and body rippled and stretched to unnatural proportions.

"Yes! *Yes!*" shrieked Adele.

The female subject's face swelled, and so did her limbs until her body was triple her normal size. The floor trembled as she pushed to her new, giant thighs and then feet. She had a prominent brow ridge and a protruding upper jaw, giving her more of an ogre-like look, just like Valen. She wasn't as big as Valen in his giant form, but she was close. Maybe fourteen feet tall. She was frighteningly big and strong.

Adele had done it. The bitch had made a giant.

When I looked back at Valen, his eyes were closed. And his body had returned to its human size. He looked… he looked dead.

My despair worsened. My gut twisted as I let the panic in until it felt like the world dropped out from under me, and I was falling through the chair.

And then something strange happened.

I felt a tingle. A prick. First along my toes and then up toward my knees, sneaking over my skin, like I had thousands of creepy insects crawling inside and out of my body. Totally disgusting. But the tingling continued throughout me until it reached all the way up to my scalp.

The tingle lasted a few seconds, and then I felt a release, like a sudden unbridling of a tight rope that had bound my limbs.

I was free. I could move again.

Bellamy's words made sense now. *It won't last*. He'd meant the paralyzing drug. He'd tampered with it. He'd only given me part of that drug. Enough to fool Adele. Enough to set me free.

I reached out to the stars, to the powerful emanations. The Starlight answered as it hummed through me, waiting to be unleashed.

I ripped off the duct tape and leaped off my chair. "Get away from him!"

And then I let my magic fly.

CHAPTER 24

The anger, the fear, the desperation—all of it consumed me as I hurled my starlight at the machine that was pumping Valen's blood.

A white coat jumped in my line of fire. Too bad.

I blew the fucker into pieces just as I shattered that damn machine in a blast of my starlight.

The metal contraption flew back, end over end, and crashed against a far wall. All the wires and tubes that were connected to Valen were yanked and torn away from him. He still wasn't moving, nor had he opened his eyes. Red rage filled me as I turned slowly and faced my enemies.

"Get her," I heard one of the white coats say and saw the only female, with another syringe in her hand.

"Not this time, bitch." I flung out my hand and fired a brilliant white blade of starlight.

It hit the female just below her jaw. Her eyes went wide. She didn't have time to cry out as her head slipped from her body, and she crumpled to the ground, taking her syringe with her.

The white coats were witches. And they brought their magic down on me.

But I had magic too.

Like a storm of wild magic, the white coats exploded into motion.

"For the new world!" one of the males cried as he vaulted forward with purple flames spewing from his hands.

Anger. Fear. Pain. The tidal surges of my emotions fueled my magic. I would use it.

I planted my feet, pulled on my starlight, and clapped my hands once.

A white, glowing disk sprang in front of me like armor. Purple light flooded around me as the witch's magic hit my shield and then bounced off.

I stood my ground, my starlight pumping through and around me as it bathed me in its brilliance.

The same witch hit me again with a volley of purple flames. The flames angled off my shield, redirecting the magic, and a burst of his own magic slammed into the oncoming witch.

I lowered the shield and looked up in time to see the witch I'd struck flying back. His body sizzled in purple flames. That could have been me.

I saw Adele's shocked expression at my starlight shield. She didn't know I could do that.

Surprise, bitch!

The mumblings of a curse spun me around to face another witch.

He moved awkwardly, stiff like he wasn't entirely sure what he was doing, or maybe he'd never dueled one on one before with another witch.

I smiled. "You ready? I'm ready. Bring it."

He snickered at what he saw on my face, probably a combination of anger and fatigue.

"You're dead," he snarled. Green magic coiled around his arms, and it reminded me of Jade's plastic bracelets. Love her.

"Iqtz M'atx!" he cried, flinging his palms at me.

Green fire rings burst from his outstretched hands, and my face flamed from the heat of his magic.

I flung out my hand as a sheet of starlight knocked his magic rings away, a foot away from my face.

I didn't want to hurt or kill anyone, except for Adele—and maybe Bellamy—but this was self-defense. Kill or be killed. And the witch was trying to fry me.

The witch's lips moved in a dark chant or a hex, I had no idea, but I was way ahead of him.

With my starlight still pounding inside me, I arched my body back and hurled my shield with both hands. It fired straight and true, spinning like a disk and catching the witch on his right side.

He let out a cry of rage, and then I heard nothing but the sound of flames burning his robe and flesh.

I barely had time to catch my breath as two more white coats leaped my way.

"Damn. How many of you are there?" I asked, spotting another two waiting in the shadows, like a wrestling tag team anticipating their turn to pound my head in.

The nearest white coat's eyes met mine, and he smiled lazily as if pleased that we were about to duel. "We're going to bleed you, and then we're going to take you apart… little piece by little piece."

I pursed my lips. "Let me think about it… screw you."

The same white coat's eyes gleamed with orange magic. And then he flicked his wrist, and a flaming orange whip materialized.

Nice trick.

I jumped aside, the end of the whip grazing my hip. I hissed at the pain. But his strike went wide before he realized his mistake. I spun around and fired a ball of starlight at him. It caught him in the chest and sent him stumbling away just as a larger white coat took his place.

He struck more proficiently than his colleague, fireballs whistling as they soared in the air, aimed at my face. I had a split second to whirl before they struck.

I jumped back, his balls going wide—yeah, I know how that sounded. "You guys lack in your defensive magic. You should stick to what you know. Being dicks." It was obvious these witches, these white coats, weren't trained in this type of magic.

They were all over the place, uncalculated, their strikes untrained.

But I was.

The beefy white coat snarled at me, sweating profusely, and he reminded me of Bellamy. "I'm better than you. You're not even a real witch."

"Gotta stop listening to your mistress." Speaking of mistresses, I stole a look to my right and saw that Adele was still standing by the new giantess. The look of pure joy on her face was enough to nearly make me hurl.

"You're going down for a very long nap... the forever kind," said the same white coat, pulling my attention back around. His hands were dripping with orange flames. "I see it now. Your fear. You know you're going to die, and you can't do anything to stop it. Your miserable friends aren't here to help you. You're all alone." His lips curled up almost in a smile, his eyes widened in victory. "And you're going to die alone."

"I'm not dying tonight, buddy." My fear of dying wasn't what spiked the sweet adrenaline in me and through my limbs. It was the horror and the pain of what these assholes did to the innocent. But mostly to Valen.

My pain was lost in my fury. I pulled on my starlight and pushed out. A shoot of white light fired out of my hand—

"Ignitu det!" shouted the white coat, waving his hands, and a sheet of semitransparent orange haze rose before him. My starlight hit the protection shield like it had hit a solid concrete wall and fell away.

The white coat's grin widened at the shock he saw on my face. "See? You're not the only one who can work shield magic."

I shrugged. "And you just said I wasn't a real witch? Which is it?"

He widened his legs, his stance firm with his hands moving confidently. "You're not," he panted, as though that bit of magic took some enormous effort and energy from him. I didn't see him pulling another shield. He was done.

He smiled at me again and opened his mouth to throw another insult.

But I didn't have time for this shit.

I flicked my wrist at him. In a blur of white, a starlight arrow speared his chest.

He stumbled, blood bubbling out of his mouth as he fell to his knees.

I felt a shift in the air behind me, and I whirled to see five white coats approaching, their magic dripping from their hands. From what I could tell, these were the last five.

And I'd had enough.

Straining, I took a deep breath and reached into that spring of magic, to the core of power from the stars. Clamping my jaw, I pulled on my starlight, letting it rip through me until five balls of blazing white light hovered over my hand.

And then I flung them.

Five shoots of starlight magic soared straight and

hit the white coats. Cries erupted with the scent of burning flesh. I blinked at the sudden white light as their bodies were engulfed in the starlight, like they were lit by a million LED lights.

I staggered, feeling a sudden wave of dizziness. The more I pulled on my starlight, the more my body felt like it had been beaten with a two-by-four wood plank.

And then, the last white coats went down in wailing screams of fire and ash.

I bent at the waist, sweat pouring down my back and between my breasts. My lungs felt raw, like I'd just finished a five-K run. I was drained. I needed rest. But first, I needed to take care of Valen.

"Kill her!"

I turned to the sound of the voice and saw Adele pointing at me and motioning to the giantess, her arms beating the air like she was trying to fly.

Crap. I'd forgotten about her. I was exhausted. I'd never fought a giant, or rather a *giantess*, before, and I doubted I'd survive if I did. From what I'd observed with Valen, not much could harm them. I wasn't even sure my magic would serve me against a giant.

Adele's face was red and blotchy as she pointed at me, a slight tremor to her hand. "Kill her! I command you. What are you waiting for? I told you to kill her. Kill her now, you idiot. You will do as I command. I am your god! Obey me!"

Yeah, like I said, total nutjob.

Fear spiked in my chest as I surveyed the giantess's massive hands that could easily bludgeon me to a pulp. Those were some seriously big fists.

"Kill her, you stupid giant!" shouted Adele. "Kill her now, or I will end your miserable life." She stood there, hands on her hips with that same self-satisfied expression, as though she ruled the world and was above all of us peasants. She felt she could do as she pleased with us, which included killing us.

The giantess looked at me from across the warehouse, and I felt my bowels go watery. Her expression was cast in a frown, and I wasn't sure if she was angry or if this was her thinking face.

But what happened next, I did not expect.

The giantess's face rippled with anger as she turned back and looked down upon Adele.

"*No*," she said, her voice loud and deep like Valen's but with a more feminine edge to it, if that were even possible.

"No?" Adele's rage was palpable. "What do you mean, no? I'm your creator! I'm your god, and you will—"

The giantess's hand shot out and wrapped around Adele's neck, pulling her effortlessly off her feet and into the air.

"Oh, shit," I said, unable to look away.

"Let me go!" shrieked Adele as she hit the giantess's hand with her fists. Her lips moved in a chant or a spell, and I saw sparks of orange, green, and red magic slamming into the giantess. But the massive woman didn't even flinch.

The giantess's eyes were filled with anger, but I

could see the anguish, the sorrow, and the hatred there. She hated what Adele had done to her.

The giantess's lips curled into a snarl, and the hand around Adele's throat tightened. The witch's eyes bulged, the whites showing.

I heard a snap like the breaking of a twig, and Adele's head was bent at an unnatural angle. It happened so fast, a part of me thought I'd imagined it.

But then the giantess tossed Adele's body to the floor. Her limbs splayed out. Her head turned my way. I could see her lifeless eyes.

Adele was dead.

CHAPTER 25

I had a somewhat freak-out moment as I stood there staring at the dead witch and the giantess who'd killed her. Who knew what the giantess was thinking right now? She could turn her anger on me and break my neck too.

I could make a run for it, but I wouldn't leave Valen.

I wasn't sure how long I stood there, staring at the massive human woman who looked… lost? But then the giantess looked my way, and all I saw was sorrow and pain. I might have been scared, but I felt her anguish too.

The giantess then lowered herself to the floor and sat, dropping her head to her knees as she sobbed. Damn.

I swallowed, looked over to where Valen still lay, and made a run for it.

I slid to my knees, my thighs bumping into him as I scrambled on the floor and pulled myself next to him. I grabbed his arm and winced at how cold his skin felt. It was like ice.

"Valen?" I shook his arm, big, hot tears spilling down my face. When I didn't get a response, I wrapped my fingers around his wrist. A sigh escaped from me as I felt a pulse. It was weak, but he was alive. He needed help.

The sound of great, slobbering sobs twisted me around. I looked at Adele's dead body and then at the giantess who was still weeping. Her shoulders shook as another cry released from her.

"This is a strange night."

I pushed to my feet, and I was off again. I knelt next to Adele's body, lifting her heavy robe as I searched for my phone and doing my best *not* to look at her bruised neck. Too late. I looked. Damn. It was even worse up close. Deep-purple marks wrapped around the dead witch's throat. A piece of her cervical spine perforated her skin where her head was bent at an unnatural angle. Yikes. I yanked my focus back to search for my phone. I slipped my hand inside Adele's robe and felt something solid and flat. I yanked out my phone and rushed back to Valen's side. I stole a look over my shoulder. The giantess hadn't even looked up.

Valen needed help. He'd lost so much blood. I didn't know if he'd survive.

Fingers shaking, I quickly texted my friends a 9-1-1 to send help and Basil to contact the Gray Council. I knew a so-called Darius was corrupted, but I was hoping the others on the council weren't.

They were going to find out about this sooner or later.

My phone beeped.

Elsa: *On our way. Gray Council too.*

I let out a staggered breath.

"Leana?"

I jerked as I stared at Valen's dark eyes staring up at me.

"Oh, my God, Valen!" I reached down and pulled him over my lap, cradling his head. My vision blurred by the sudden tears. I didn't care that he saw me bawling my eyes out and would know how much I cared. I was over that. This wasn't about me, and he needed help. I cringed as I stared at his face. Blue veins shone through his skin, and his eyes were sunken. He looked weak.

"What can I do? I don't know what to do. Do you need my blood? I know you're not a vampire. I have to do something. I—"

"Not your blood," said Valen, his voice depleted, and it brought a sob over me.

I looked around the room to where the remains of the machine I'd destroyed lay scattered across the floor, not realizing at the time that I'd also destroyed his blood. He could probably use that blood right about now. I'd ruined the only blood that could save him.

What have I done?

Fear rushed through me, stealing my breath at the memory of losing my mother. Tears welled in my eyes, and my throat throbbed. I couldn't lose Valen. Not when this was my fault.

"Why did you come, you fool," I told him, more tears spilling down my face. "You should have stayed at the restaurant."

"You texted… said you were in… trouble… needed me," he said, his voice harsh and weak.

"That wasn't me. It was Adele." I knew she was dead, but I still hated her for what she'd done.

"I figured." A feeble smile pulled his lips, and I felt a stab in my heart.

I wiped my nose on my sleeve. "I'm so sorry. This is all my fault. I shouldn't have come alone. But I wanted to get Bellamy back. That's the guy I was with when I went to your restaurant." My jealous reactions from before felt so foolish. And I regretted them. "You should have stayed on your date with that pretty blonde. Think about it. You missed out on some sex." I flashed him a smile. "Instead, you came here and got… well… this."

Valen blinked slowly. "Wasn't a date. I hired her."

I cocked a brow. "Okay, so she's an escort. I guess you didn't get your money's worth. Sorry about that."

Valen opened his mouth to speak but instead broke into an agonizing, wet cough, sounding like someone who'd smoked three packs a day all their life. Every breath looked painful, like his lungs weren't working properly.

I rubbed his arms with my hands, trying to get

him warmer and his blood flowing. "Don't talk. Keep your strength."

"She's not," Valen cleared his throat. Then he closed his eyes, his face twisted in pain. He opened his eyes again and wheezed, "Not an escort. A private investigator."

I did not expect that. "You're dating a private investigator?"

His face shifted into an expression of effort. When he spoke, his jaws stayed locked together, but I could understand the words. "No. I hired her to look for others like me. Giants. She's been looking for six years."

Now I really felt like a fool. Six years was a long time to get to know someone. It explained what I saw on their faces, a friendship. Not lovers.

So Valen had wanted to find more of his kind. I could understand that, being the only Starlight witch I knew. I knew others like me were out there. I just didn't know where they were at the moment. But it wasn't the same. I was still a witch, and plenty of witches lived in our communities. Not giants.

A weak smile curled his lips. "She found some."

My mouth flapped open, and I let his words sink in. "Giants? She found other giants? Where? Who?" My body warmed at the spark in his eyes.

"Two. Brother and sister. In Germany."

I squeezed his arms tighter, not feeling any warmth in them. Was his skin getting colder? "I'm really happy for you," I said, trying to keep my voice from showing the fear that was redoubling. "If you want… I can be your travel guide to Germany. Though I've never been, I've always wanted to go and see the Neuschwanstein Castle. Pretend it was mine and all." It was true, but I couldn't afford to go anywhere, especially Europe.

Valen let out a breath. "No need. They're coming here."

"That's great." I waited for him to say more, but he didn't. "Then we'll just have to throw a party in their honor when they get here. Oh, wait. Maybe they're secretive like you, right? They won't want us to know."

"They are," said Valen. His voice was so low, I had to lower my head near his lips to hear him properly. His eyes flicked over to the giantess. "Is she… is she all right?"

I followed his gaze. The giantess was still quietly sobbing, her shoulders shaking and her head still hidden between her knees. My eyes watered at seeing her like this.

"No, she's not," I told him. "They took her. Imprisoned her. And transformed her into a different being, a creature she never thought was real. She'll never be all right." Ever. If she'd been a paranormal, it might not have been as traumatizing, though still disturbing to be morphed into another creature. But she was human. Only yesterday, she didn't believe in vampires and ghouls and fairies. And tonight, she was a giant. The woman would probably go insane if she lived long enough. And *if* she lived, she'd need serious therapy. But after seeing what happened to

Adele's science projects, it didn't look like she had a bright future.

"Adele is—*was*—a crazy bitch," I said to Valen, seeing he'd gone silent again, his eyes closed. "She wanted to create a new world without humans, where she wanted to be queen or a god. A goddess? Anyway, the point is, she wasn't alone in her insanity. She was taking orders from someone called Darius. Do you know anyone by that name who sits on the Gray Council? Valen?" I had to keep him awake. I knew if he fell asleep, he might never wake again. "Valen?" I shook him, and his eyes popped open.

"Hmmm?" He blinked at me, his eyes unfocused, like he wasn't sure who I was.

"Do you know someone called Darius? I think he sits on the Gray Council."

Valen's dark eyes searched my face. "No. I don't think so."

Shit. I could barely hear him. His eyelids started to shut. "Got to keep awake, Valen. You hear me. Don't you fall asleep on me."

"So… tired…"

"I know." I rubbed his arms again, I had to keep doing something, or I'd lose it. "But you have to keep fighting. You hear me? Valen? Valen!"

Valen's eyes shut. I shook him and then again harder, but he didn't open his eyes. He looked like he'd gone into a coma. Panicked, I put my ear to his mouth. I heard a soft breath. He was still breathing but barely.

Okay, now I truly did have a freak-out moment. My insides twisted. Raw terror radiated through my guts. I felt sick. My breath caught, and I blinked a few times to keep the room from spinning.

Valen was dying.

By the time the team got here, it would be too late.

CHAPTER 26

I needed to do something. *Think, Leana!*

And then I remembered something. Giants had healing properties that were different than anything I'd ever seen. Maybe… maybe it was worth a shot.

Carefully, I lay Valen's head back on the floor and pushed myself up. With my heart lurching in double time, I ran over to the other giant. A cold sweat trickled down my back as I flung a long strand out of my eyes.

"Excuse me," I said, standing about five feet from her, my pulse hammering. My eyes darted over her hands the size of car wheels. I'd just seen what she could do with those giant hands. I wanted to keep my neck from being crushed.

I took another breath and repeated, "Excuse me—"

The giantess snapped her head up.

"Ah!" I jerked and fell back on my ass hard. I

might have broken my coccyx. Her glare was enough to make me pee my pants, but for some strange reason, I kept my bladder in check. Looks like those kegel exercises weren't so useless after all.

Still on my ass and cowering, I raised my hands. "Please don't kill me. I'm not here to hurt you," I said quickly. "You've got a serious glower, you know? Like big. Um. Listen. My friend is dying. Can you help him?"

The giantess looked over to Valen, but I couldn't read what crossed her face. She was still glowering.

I decided to try another approach. "My name is Leana. What's your name?"

At that, the giantess's features seemed to soften a little. "*Catelyn.*"

I winced at the ferocity of her voice. "Nice to meet you, Catelyn." I waited and then said, "My friend's name is Valen. That evil bitch that did this to you, well, she hurt him too. He's dying. And I think you can help him."

Catelyn stared down at her hands like she couldn't believe they belonged to her. "*I don't want to be like this. I want to be me.*" Her eyes met mine. "*Can you change me back?*"

Oh, shit. "I'm not sure. But I promise you I will do whatever it takes to change you back. Back to you. To the human Catelyn." I wasn't sure if she could change back into her human part. I'd seen Valen do it, so maybe she could. Perhaps she just needed coaching on how to do that.

Catelyn shook her head, tears trickling down her

face. I looked over to Valen. His eyes were still closed, but somehow he looked worse, like thin or thinning.

"Please." I pushed to my feet and faced her. "You saw me tied up in that chair. I know you know I had nothing to do with this. I tried to stop it. I don't want any more people to die. And right now, you're the only person who might be able to save him. Please, Catelyn. Will you help my friend?" Okay, now I was really crying. My voice cracked with emotions.

Catelyn brought her tear-filled eyes to me and said, "*Okay*."

I wiped my tears and rushed over to Valen, trying not to despair at how frail he looked.

"*What do I do*?" asked Catelyn as she pushed to her feet and went to stand over Valen.

"I think you need to touch him," I said, hoping I was right. "If you could lay your hands on him for a bit, I think it'll work." Goddess, let me be right.

Catelyn did as I asked and knelt down next to Valen, who looked tiny in comparison to her massive frame. She placed her hands gently over his chest, her eyes roving over him. I saw confusion there, but I also saw a spark of worry in her eyes for Valen.

After about a minute of Catelyn's hands touching Valen, I was expecting to see something. Maybe sparks. Him opening his eyes. But after two minutes of nothing, I realized I'd been wrong. Catelyn couldn't save him. No one could.

My eyes burned, and I shook my head, dread forming a hard knot in my stomach. "It's not w—"

Valen's skin began to glow, softly at first and then with more intensity.

"Look! It's working! Catelyn, you did it!"

Catelyn flinched, as whatever she was doing surprised her too. The giantess had a determined look on her face now as she kept her hands on Valen's chest. She wanted to help him. Save him. Even after what had been done to her, she still wanted to help. Wow. She was my hero.

Soon, Valen's skin went from a dangerous, deadly pastiness to his natural golden, healthy color. The veins that webbed over his face disappeared, leaving his skin smooth.

I searched his face. "Valen?"

Valen's eyes snapped open. "I'm all right." He looked at Catelyn and smiled. "Thank you."

The giantess blushed and pulled her hands away, realizing she was touching a seriously handsome and seriously naked man.

I pressed my hand on her shoulder. "Thank you. You saved his life."

Catelyn looked at me, her eyes sad. Her lips parted, but she nodded instead, seemingly unable to formulate words.

I felt a little tear in my heart. "Valen," I said, looking at him. "This is Catelyn. She was made from you. Damn, that sounds so strange. Um, listen. Does that mean she can transform back into her smaller version? Like you do?" I knew if she went back to her original body, her human size, it might not be so daunting. Scary still but manageable.

Valen propped himself on his elbows with a small moan on the exhale. "Catelyn. All you need to do is calm yourself. Take deep breaths. Think about yourself before the change. Keep that image, and let the change undo itself. Try it now. You can do it."

I didn't know if I could have been calm after such an ordeal. It would take some serious self-control.

"*I'll try*," said the giantess, and I was genuinely impressed by this woman's inner strength. I thought I was badass, but she was badasser.

I watched as she closed her eyes, seemingly in a meditative state. And then, just as I'd seen Valen change multiple times, with a flash of light, Catelyn's body shrank on itself, smaller and smaller until she was about my height and size.

She did it.

"You can open your eyes now," I told her.

Catelyn's eyes flashed open. They were red from all the crying, her face blotchy. She looked to be about my age, maybe a few years older. She raised her hands slowly up to her face, turning them over as she inspected them. She looked down at herself and then at me. Her mouth started working soundlessly, and her eyes overflowed with tears. It took her several seconds to let out a little choking sound, followed by the words, "I'm me. I can't believe it."

"A very naked you." I laughed and hurried over to one of the dead witch scientists. I yanked off a white coat and gave it to Catelyn so she could cover herself.

"Thanks," she said, wrapping her arms around herself, her eyes wide and anxious.

"I know you must have loads of questions," I began.

"I do," she said. "All this… all this is real. It's a lot to process."

"It is, Catelyn. I think it's best that you stay with us for a while. My friends and I stay at this really nice hotel. You'll be safe there. And you'll have friendly people to talk to. To coach you and explain what's happening. Do you have a family?"

She nodded. "I do."

"Okay, then call them." I handed her my phone. "Tell them you're okay and that you're staying with some friends for a while."

"Will I ever see them again?" Catelyn's bottom lip trembled, catching my heart.

"You'll be able to go see them… once you get your big-girl-self under control." I didn't know what else to call it.

Catelyn's eyes brightened. She took the phone and walked away for some privacy.

A labored breath spun me around. Valen was lying on his back again. He turned his head and looked at me. "I think she's going to be okay."

I nodded. "Yeah. I think so too." Strangely enough, it rang true. I knelt next to him. "She's going to need your help to explain all the"—I waved my hands around his body—"giant stuff."

"She has it."

"Are you cold?" I asked, rolling my eyes over him, our eyes locked.

"No." Valen's face transformed into one of his sexy smiles. He looked just as handsome as ever, naked, no less, his thick, dark hair brushed just above his eyes. But he did look fine.

And the man was still naked. I liked him naked. He rocked, naked. Still, I needed to find something to cover him up before the others got here.

"Just a sec."

I pushed myself to my feet with a tiny moan, my thighs and knees protesting. Still, I moved across the room without falling over. I was tired and still bleeding from some of the wounds bestowed on me by those vampires. I'd have to see Polly later so she could fix me up. But Valen came first.

Finding what I needed, I yanked another lab coat from a dead witch scientist, a little too roughly as his head kept smacking the hard cement floor, but the guy was dead.

"Here you go." I knelt down next to Valen again, and placed the coat over him. Obviously, it was too small, but it did cover the larger-than-average important bits.

His lips curved toward his eyes. "Kiss me."

"What?" My core pooled with warmth, and I whipped my head around to see whether Catelyn had heard, but she was busy talking to someone on my phone.

"Come here and kiss me."

I turned my head back around. He looked at me

expectantly, cocky as hell, like he knew he had me—had me good. Was it wrong that I was turned on?

My heart thumping like an idiot, I leaned over, stared at his dark eyes for a moment, and then lowered my lips to his.

I was expecting a soft kiss. Nope. That's not what I got.

Valen's hands wrapped around my back and my neck, pulling me down farther, closer, as he crushed his lips on mine.

His kiss was different this time. Cautious. But it had an intensity. Emotions poured into it. My breath came fast as he slipped his tongue into my mouth, and a thrust of desire went right to my core. The heat of his mouth, his tongue, was an exquisite kind of torture.

A tiny gasp escaped me, and he moaned. His rough, calloused hands slipped under my shirt and moved around my back, down to my waist.

I never wanted to stop kissing Valen. It felt too damn good, intoxicating, like a sugar buzz after eating four scoops of rocky-road ice cream. But this wasn't the place for such a sensual kiss.

I pulled away, breathless. Waves of desire pulsed through me as I leaned back on my knees. "A guy who was close to death shouldn't be able to kiss like that."

"I can't help myself," he breathed huskily. He winked and added, "Especially with you. I just want to keep kissing you."

Okay, that did all kinds of great things to my ego.

And the way he was staring at me did all kinds of things to my lady bits.

The sound of running feet had me twisting around.

Jimmy came jogging toward us, his lean legs propelling him with speed and his face set in concern.

"Jimmy?" I said, surprised. Behind him came Julian, Elsa, and Jade. The thirteenth-floor gang was here.

Jimmy skidded to a stop. He looked over us and then to the dead white coats sprawled between some of the dead paranormals. "Shit. What the hell happened?"

"Long story."

"Is that Adele?" Elsa was staring down at the dead witch. She wasn't smiling, but she didn't look bothered either. She looked… curious.

"It is," I answered.

"What happened to her neck?" asked Jade as she joined her. "I can see her trachea." She had a pen in her hand, and she poked the witch on the floor like she wasn't sure she was dead and thought she might spring back to life. Not with a neck like that.

My eyes flicked to Catelyn, who was off the phone and staring at my friends like she wasn't sure whether to change into her big-girl form and break their necks too.

"These are the friends I was telling you about," I told Catelyn. I waited for her to make eye contact. "You can trust them."

She gave me a nod, but she still was watching them with uncertainty and fear. It was going to take some work.

"Where's Bellamy?" Julian was staring at one of the tanks with a human floating inside. I saw anger creep over his face as his jaw set, and the veins at his temples stood out.

I shrugged. "He took off just when things got interesting." The bastard had slipped away, but I would find him. He carried the knowledge and the expertise to do this again. He was dangerous, and he would have to deal with the consequences of his actions. He might have tricked Adele and the others by only subjecting me to a part of that paralyzing mixture. But he had betrayed me and lured me here under false pretenses that had nearly killed Valen. Yeah, he needed to be dealt with.

"I bet he did." Julian's eyes locked on Catelyn. He flashed her a smile, but she didn't smile back.

"The Gray Council should be here soon," said Jimmy as he swept his gaze around the room. "This place is creepy."

"Tell me about it," I answered.

"Who is she?" Jimmy was looking at Catelyn, wondering if she was one of the good guys or in alliance with Adele.

"That's Catelyn. She's—*was*—just an ordinary human."

"She's one of the human subjects." Jimmy looked back at me. "A were or a vamp?"

I shook my head. "A giantess."

Jimmy's mouth flapped open as the rest of the gang all looked between Catelyn and me.

"Long story," I told them, smiling at their collectively shocked faces. "I've got lots of them. Catelyn is staying with us for a while. We need to look after her."

"Of course she is," said Elsa, giving Catelyn one of her motherly smiles. "We're going to look after you, Catelyn. Don't you worry. You'll fit right in with the rest of us crazies."

And when Catelyn gave her a weak smile back, I knew she'd be okay.

I let out a breath, tension still ringing through me. Tonight could have turned out to be one of the worst nights of my life, but it didn't.

I was alive. Valen was alive. And the threat, well, Adele was dead. I wasn't a fool. I knew this wasn't over. I still needed to find this Darius, but I'd take this as a win for tonight.

"You ready to go? Valen?"

When I looked back down, Valen's eyes were closed. A light snore emitted from him, and he had the tiniest of smiles on his face.

CHAPTER 27

I stood in the lobby of the Twilight Hotel, a glass of red wine in my hand as I cast my gaze around. The air smelled like grilling meat and buzzed with happy chatters. The clanking of chips echoed from the multitude of game tables splayed around the lobby and neighboring rooms. I peeked through the door to the dining room and saw long tables stacked with food and every alcoholic beverage you could think of. Polly stood behind the table with the meats, a pair of metal tongs in her hand, and her white toque over her head as she served happy, hungry-looking guests.

I'd never seen the hotel so cramped before with so many guests. Basil's idea to hold a Casino Week had helped revive the hotel. No one spoke of demons and devils in the rooms. Everywhere I looked, I saw happy, smiling faces peering back.

It was the final night, and it looked like he'd gone all out.

"Not a bad turnout." Jimmy came to join me, looking dashing in a dark-gray, three-piece suit, his hair styled in the 1950s side part. He looked like a classic mobster from that era.

"Not bad at all. It's good for the hotel. For us. We won't lose our homes after all." Even though we'd stopped Adele from destroying the hotel, part of me feared that the lack of guests would eventually ruin the hotel's reputation, and we'd all have to look for someplace else to live. Now it looked like we'd be okay for many years to come.

"It'll die down after this," said Jimmy, nodding at a couple of vampires passing by us. "But it'll be better than it was. I gave Basil some ideas for the next theme."

I cocked a brow. "The next theme?"

"Yeah, we're thinking of keeping this as a regular monthly to bimonthly occurrence to keep the guests happy and attract new guests."

"I like it. A different theme every couple of months?" I was curious. "What's your planned next theme?"

"Rock and roll," said a smiling assistant manager. "It'll be awesome. You'll see."

I smiled. "I have no doubt." I studied him for a moment, getting the pricks and tingles of his supernatural shape. "You know, you never did tell me what type of shifter you are."

Jimmy chuckled and adjusted the sleeves of his jacket. "True." He turned around, and when he blinked, his eyes flashed a golden color. He blinked again, and his eyes were back to their normal blue color. "Werefox."

"Is that why Auria's curse turned you into a toy dog? Foxes are canines."

Jimmy let out a long breath. "No idea. Maybe. Or this was just her sick, twisted way of making me suffer. Make me feel useless. Like a fool."

"Never useless. Definitely not a fool either." I stared at his cute face. His sneaking around the hotel, knowing all the nooks and crannies, definitely attributed to his werefox ways. He was sly as a fox. "So, how old are you anyway?"

"What?" Jimmy laughed. "Ninety-eight."

"Well, shit. You're pretty hot for a grandpa."

I broke into a laugh I couldn't hold back, and then Jimmy joined me. Once we started, it was like a switch had turned on. We couldn't stop the fit of giggles until tears streamed down our faces.

"Hey, guys. What's so funny?"

I wiped my eyes and looked over Jimmy's shoulder to find Jade coming to join us. Her blonde hair was dyed pink. She wore a vintage black hat, a floral pink-and-red scarf, a long, black retro blazer, and a floral vest over a white blouse. She finished the look with pink bracelets and brooches.

Looked like she was going for a *Pretty in Pink* movie vibe. I loved it.

"That Jimmy looks younger than us, but the fact is, he's an old geezer."

Jade looked between us. She opened her mouth to say something, seemed to think better of it, and turned her head around. "Basil did good. Didn't he?"

"We noticed," I said. "Is Elsa with you?"

Jade gestured over to the slot machine area. "She's with Catelyn. She's doing really well for a human. I mean, she's only had a few freak-out cries. Two last night and one this morning. That's pretty incredible for a human."

I looked over at the human, now turned giantess. Catelyn's face was tight. She looked like she was the new kid in school—part terrified, part excited—as she was listening attentively to whatever Elsa was telling her. The witch looked positively enthralled that someone was digging her wisdom.

Both women had glasses of wine in their hands, though Catelyn's was empty. I felt for her, and I was glad Elsa had given her the spare room in her apartment for the time being. Elsa was just the sort of soft-tempered, tolerant, and caring, motherly figure Catelyn needed right now. Plus, we needed to keep an eye on her. We weren't sure if she would go insane like the other human subjects I'd encountered. Or worse, die suddenly. So far, she wasn't showing any signs of mania. And she was still alive. Thank the goddess. Maybe giant blood was different. Maybe Adele had figured out the missing link to the transference like she'd said. Maybe, just maybe, Catelyn would survive this.

"You ready?" Jimmy held out his hand to Jade.

My lips parted in surprise as I looked over at Jade, whose face turned a beet color. "You two…"

Jimmy smiled proudly as he took Jade's hand and placed it in the crook of his arm. "Date night."

"Date night," I repeated. My heart swelled as I watched Jimmy and Jade walking away. The two were absolutely perfect for each other. I laughed as Jade looked over her shoulder and gave me a thumbs-up.

I was in such a good mood after that, I had to keep up the good vibes. So, when my eyes found Errol eyeing me with a look of disdain from across the lobby, I knew I had to go say hi.

I leaned over the gleaming stone counter. "Any messages for me?" I had put out the word that I was looking for Bellamy, but so far, nothing had turned up. Earlier this morning, I'd taken a cab out to his fancy apartment on 499 East 34th Street, with a view of the East River, to find it ransacked with no witch scientists. When I checked his bank account, with the help of Jimmy's hacker skills, it had been emptied the day before. Looked like Bellamy was on the run.

Errol looked like he wanted to spit in my face. He reached down, pulled out a message card, and threw it at me.

If I hadn't expected it, it would have hit me in the face. But I knew the little lizard bastard well enough to anticipate what he was about to do. He was conveniently predictable.

I caught the card. "Careful, Errol. Stuff like this will land you in trouble. Buckets-full-of-cockroaches trouble."

Errol glowered at me. "I hate you."

"Right back at you, lizard."

I glanced down at the card.

Stop looking for me. You'll never find me. I'm sorry for what I did to you, but I had no other choice. —Bellamy

"Yeah. I'm not going to stop." I stuffed the message card in my jeans pocket, catching a view of Julian playing cards with our thirteenth-floor twin ten-year-old girls in identical periwinkle-blue, sparkling princess dresses. Tilly and Tracy were the twins' names, though I couldn't tell them apart for the life of me. Julian kept throwing glances at the pretty woman standing over the girls, their mother, Cassandra, I think her name was. But she was completely unmoved by his attention. More like she was ignoring him. That was interesting. Looked like Julian had his lover-boy work cut out for him.

I sighed and gulped the last of my wine. No way would I stop looking for Bellamy. He had to pay for what he did, and I *would* find him. I wouldn't rest until I did.

The Gray Council's officers showed up a few minutes after my friends returned to the warehouse. Again, they packed everything up and hauled it away, not even leaving a single piece of paper. Nothing. But I'd taken enough pictures and stolen some files to keep me busy. I was still building a case against this Darius character.

If Adele was following his orders, he was perhaps even more deranged and dangerous than she had been. I had to find him. The Gray Council was corrupted, and I had to weed out the mess. I'd start with Darius.

"You look nice tonight."

My heart sputtered at the sound of that rough, deep voice. I twisted around to find Valen standing there, all manly, all sexy as hell, all man-beast-like. A brown leather jacket hung over his thick shoulders under a tight, black top and tucked into a pair of snug jeans. A waft of musky cologne and spices filled my nose, sending my skin into tiny ripples. Just his smell turned me on. Yeah, my hormones were still out of whack.

Damn, he looked good. Yet, even if he smelled good enough to eat, he still had shadows under his eyes. He wasn't fully recovered.

"You look pretty good yourself for a man who nearly died a few hours ago. Shouldn't you be resting?"

His dark eyes gleamed intensely. "No." His eyes traveled to Catelyn. "How's she doing?"

I let out a breath. "Better than expected. Really good, actually. She's still in good health too. She knows to tell us if she feels off… more off than when she turns into a giant."

"I talked to Polly, and between us, we'll start Catelyn on a weekly specialized tonic. Like an energy drink. To keep her as healthy as possible."

"That's a great idea."

Valen shrugged. "Who knows. She might outlive us all."

I nodded, knowing giants had inherent healing abilities. Maybe that was the secret ingredient to allow the humans to change into paranormals and stay that way forever without having to worry about their time running out.

My eyes drifted over his broad shoulders and down his chest. Valen caught me staring and gave me a smug smile, the kind that sent my nether regions pounding. His dark eyes pinned me, and I saw a glimmer of desire in them.

He took my hand, and the next thing I knew, the giant was pulling me just off the front desk and into Basil's office.

Valen closed the door behind him. His larger-than-life body pushed me up against the wall.

My pulse throbbed in my throat. "What are you doing? This is Basil's office."

Holy shit. He wanted to take me right here! Not that I was complaining, but I'd always imagined having sex with Valen back at his place, on his comfortable, very private bed. But I could do spontaneity. Spontaneity was my middle name.

His hard body pressed against mine. "You're so fucking sexy tonight. You drive me crazy."

I swallowed hard. "I try."

Valen growled and planted his lips over mine. His tongue darted into my mouth, and I felt my knees go weak. My pulse skittered to high gear as his hands slipped under my shirt and grabbed my breasts. Taking his lead, I slid my hands under his shirt, feeling the warm, hard muscles of his back, which were a stark contrast to his cold skin last night.

His fingers expertly found the back closure and unhooked it, letting the girls fall free. I moaned as he cupped them, my skin erupting in goose bumps at the rough calluses of his hands.

I dragged my nails into his back. He moaned again, or maybe that was me?

I pulled my mouth away. "Are we doing this now? Here?"

Valen's eyes snapped to mine. "We can stop if you want. Is that what you want?"

"Hell no." My lady bits were pounding.

Valen laughed and then dipped his head. His mouth found my neck and sent little kisses, his tongue teasing.

I shivered as my hands found his belt, and I yanked it hard, undoing the top button of his pants. The button fell. I might have yanked a little too hard. Blame it on the raging hormones.

Valen laughed again, and the next thing I knew, he'd scooped me up in his strong arms and hauled me over to Basil's desk. Papers, memorabilia, and mugs all went flying as the giant lowered me onto it.

"Basil's going to kill us," I mumbled through kisses.

"He can try," said the giant, his hands on my breasts again. He pushed himself right between my legs, and I felt how hard he was for me. Yup. We were going to do it in Basil's office!

I was dizzy with lust and emotions. And the fact I hadn't had sex in a long while was making me crazy.

I pulled my mouth away for a second. "It's been a long time for me," I said, knowing he was most probably a destroyer of vaginas from what I'd heard.

"Good," said the giant, going for my belt.

"Could be cobwebs down there," I said.

Valen let out another laugh. But when he looked at me, all I saw in his eyes was desire and a vulnerability that squeezed my heart.

I felt slightly embarrassed at my lower-than-average skill in the bedroom. Martin was more of a wham-bam-thank-you-minute-man kind of lover. Hell, you can't call that a lover. More of a one-way, selfish shag.

"What in the name of the goddess is going on here?"

I looked up from behind Valen's shoulder and saw Basil standing in the doorway. He pushed his glasses up his nose as if that would somehow help him interpret the scene in his office.

Oops. I bit down on my tongue so I wouldn't burst out laughing. Poor Basil. He did look like he was in hell.

But a dark chuckle rolled out of Valen as he slowly slid away from me. "Did you need your desk?"

Basil's face flushed, his eyes moving everywhere but at my disheveled shirt and bra. My eyes found Valen, and I snorted.

"Someone's here to see you," said Basil, staring at

the ceiling. He held an ashtray in his other hand. That was odd. The last I knew, the tiny witch didn't smoke.

"Me?" asked Valen.

"No, Leana," said the hotel manager. "I'll wait outside." And with that, Basil tripped on his own chair, caught himself before he fell, and hurried out of his office.

"I'll join you. Need a minute," said Valen as he adjusted the tented region of his pants.

"Wonder who it is." I hooked my bra and pulled my hair back into a messy ponytail. I felt a little irritated that Basil had interrupted what could have been the best sex of my life, but in a way, I think it was for the best. Best to have that experience elsewhere and in private.

I turned at the door. "See you later."

Valen grinned, desire still in his eyes. "Count on it."

Woo-hoo. It was on later!

I was smiling—feeling like I was in a dream with things finally looking up in the relationship area—as I left Basil's office, closed the door, and joined him near the front desk. At first, I thought Bellamy might have been surrendering himself, as any weasel should. But it wasn't him. And it wasn't anyone I recognized.

Three men stood with Basil. Two wore heavy gray robes and frowns that would scare off little children. The third one sported a black suit made of the finest silk. Their eyes all tracked me as I approached.

I didn't remember meeting these guys before. Maybe they were going to hire me for a job. My heart was still pounding in my chest from Valen's kisses and his touch.

"You looking for me?" I planted myself before them, crossing my arms over my chest. I got a mix of pine cones, sulfur, and vinegar, the scent of both White and Dark witches. Okay, now I was really curious. Why would a Dark witch seek out my services?

The suit-wearing witch frowned at my forwardness, his light eyes assessing me as he took a drag of his cigarette. Basil held out an ashtray, trying to catch the ashes as they fell but missing. That explained the ashtray.

Suit-guy's eyes were too bright, too clever for my liking as they traveled over me, lingering on my neck, where I probably had one hell of a hickey, and I resisted the urge to put my hand there.

Speaking of said hickey, the sound of a door closing twisted my head around, and I saw Valen heading our way, no tented pants. He caught my eye and winked, sending a spike of desire to my core.

I bit down on my smile and turned my attention back to the three male witches.

"Leana Fairchild?" asked the one in the dark suit. The soft yellow light from the hotel lobby gleamed on his dark, slick hair.

"Yes."

"I'm Clive Vespertine, the investigator from the Gray Council," said the witch. His voice grew airy, almost sarcastic, and it triggered something in me.

"Okay. Good to know." Crap. I'd totally forgotten about the investigation with all that had happened. "How can I help you, gentlemen?" I wasn't sure I liked how they were looking at me, like I'd done something wrong.

Clive took a step forward and smiled. "You're under arrest for the murder of Adele Vandenberg."

Well, shit, that was unexpected.

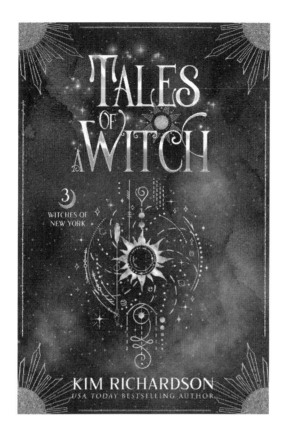

Don't miss the next book in the Witches of New York series. Try it now!

BOOKS BY KIM RICHARDSON

THE WITCHES OF HOLLOW COVE

Shadow Witch

Midnight Spells

Charmed Nights

Magical Mojo

Practical Hexes

Wicked Ways

Witching Whispers

Mystic Madness

Rebel Magic

Cosmic Jinx

Brewing Crazy

WITCHES OF NEW YORK

The Starlight Witch

Game of Witches

Tales of a Witch

THE DARK FILES

Spells & Ashes

Charms & Demons

ABOUT THE AUTHOR

Kim Richardson is a *USA Today* bestselling and award-winning author of urban fantasy, fantasy, and young adult books. She lives in the eastern part of Canada with her husband, two dogs, and a very old cat. Kim's books are available in print editions, and translations are available in over seven languages.

To learn more about the author, please visit:

www.kimrichardsonbooks.com

Printed in Great Britain
by Amazon

21472752R00176